Say No More

ALSO AVAILABLE FROM LILIANA HART AND POCKET BOOKS

The Darkest Corner
Gone to Dust

LILIANA HART

Say No More

POCKET BOOKS

New York London Toronto Sydney New Delhi

Pocket Books
An Imprint of Simon & Schuster, Inc.
1230 Avenue of the Americas
New York, NY 10020

This book is a work of fiction. Any references to historical events, real people, or real places are used fictitiously. Other names, characters, places, and events are products of the author's imagination, and any resemblance to actual events or places or persons, living or dead, is entirely coincidental.

First Pocket Books paperback edition August 2017

POCKET and colophon are registered trademarks of Simon & Schuster, Inc.

For information about special discounts for bulk purchases, please contact Simon & Schuster Special Sales at 1-866-506-1949 or business@simonandschuster.com.

The Simon & Schuster Speakers Bureau can bring authors to your live event. For more information or to book an event, contact the Simon & Schuster Speakers Bureau at 1-866-248-3049 or visit our website at www.simonspeakers.com.

Interior design by Bryden Spevak

Manufactured in the United States of America

10 9 8 7 6 5 4 3 2 1

ISBN 978-1-5011-5007-4
ISBN 978-1-5011-5008-1 (ebook)

This book is dedicated to Scott, because you're a great husband, father, and man, and I never want you to forget it.

PROLOGUE

London
1993

"**O**livia Caroline Rothschild, you come here this instant!"

Liv stuck out her bottom lip and took one more twirl in front of the floor-to-ceiling mirror. Her new pink coat was buttoned up to her chin, and the dark pink velvet trim shimmered beneath the store lighting. She liked the way the fabric swirled around her legs and her white-blond curls bounced around her shoulders when she did a pirouette in her black patent Mary Janes.

She sighed and stamped her foot, just like she'd seen Mommy do when Papa had told her they wouldn't be going to Tuscany for the winter, and she blinked her eyes rapidly until a fat tear slid down her cheek.

"Now," Nanny Gillian said, pointing her finger to the spot next to her.

Liv slowly dragged her way back, disappointed the tears hadn't worked, but they'd been worth a try. At least, that's what Mommy had said after the Tuscany fiasco.

Her sister, Elizabeth, held on to Nanny Gillian's hand, her cornflower-blue eyes big and round as she chewed on her bottom lip. Liv was older than Elizabeth by twelve whole minutes, and she stuck her tongue out the second Nanny Gillian wasn't looking. Elizabeth was a scaredy-cat and a big baby, and Liv never hesitated to tell her so right to her face. Elizabeth's lip would quiver and her eyes would fill with tears. Elizabeth always got what she wanted when she cried, unlike Liv. Mommy was right—sometimes life was just unfair.

She and Elizabeth had been instructed during the car ride to Harrods that they were to stay close at all times and not wander away. There were too many people during the holidays, and it was easy for two little girls to get lost. Elizabeth had nodded, but Liv had rolled her eyes. They'd been to Harrods dozens of times, and they knew all the best places to hide and play. When they came with Mommy instead of Nanny Gillian, she never made them stay right with her, and they always went to the candy store after they were through shopping.

"I told you to stay close, young lady," Nanny Gillian said. "If you wander off again, you'll not get a treat, and you'll be sent straight to the nursery when we get home. Do you understand me?"

"Yes, ma'am," Liv said, the tears real this time. She kicked the toe of her Mary Jane against the floor. Being sent to the nursery was a terrible punishment, especially when Papa was home because then she wouldn't get to tell him good-bye before he left again.

She felt Elizabeth's hand slip into hers and give her a squeeze. Elizabeth didn't like to see anyone hurting, even when they deserved it. They followed behind Nanny Gillian, hand in hand, up to the children's department so they could pick out their Christmas dresses. She'd seen a lovely red coat with a white fur collar and matching muff in the catalog they'd been looking at during breakfast, and she thought it would be just beautiful with the right dress.

Liv meant to be good. Really she did. But they tried on clothes for hours, and she was so bored. And hungry. And thirsty. And Nanny Gillian had been right—the store was very crowded with other little girls and their nannies and mommies, picking out dresses and throwing tantrums when they didn't get their way.

"Elizabeth," Liv whispered, reaching out from inside the circular clothing rack where she was hiding and grabbing her sister's hand, pulling her inside.

"What are you doing?" Elizabeth asked, eyes wide. "We'll get in trouble."

"No, we won't," Liv insisted. "She's not looking. She's been talking to that other lady almost the whole time. I'm hungry, and I can't wait anymore."

"She said she'll take us to get a treat when we're finished," Elizabeth protested, trying to pull away.

"I'm not waiting any longer," Liv said, putting a fist to her hip. "I've got money in my pocket. We can go downstairs and get something to eat and be back before she finishes talking."

"No," Elizabeth said, and she had that stubborn look in her eyes. She didn't get it often, but when she did, Liv knew she was in for a fight.

"Fine," Liv said, letting go of her sister and sticking out her chin. "I'll go myself. You can stay up here and be hungry. And I won't bring you anything."

"You can't go by yourself," Elizabeth said primly. "You're only six, and we're never supposed to go anywhere by ourselves. That's the rule."

"What are you going to do?" she asked. "Tattle? You're such a baby."

"I am not." The tears welled in Elizabeth's eyes, and Liv felt victory.

"Then prove it," she said. "Come with me. We can bring Nanny something back, then she won't be mad at us."

Elizabeth chewed her lip again and sneaked another glance at Nanny Gillian. She was still talking, and another lady had joined in the conversation.

"I'm not a baby," she repeated.

Liv grinned and grabbed her hand, and they slipped out from the clothes rack and around the edge of the children's department until they were out of sight. And then they ran toward the escalators, giggling their way back to the first floor.

It turned out that Liv had only enough money for one drink and a small bag of popcorn, so they decided to share and get Nanny Gillian something the next time.

"Come on," Elizabeth said. "We have to go back."

Liv gave a long-suffering sigh, but she knew her sister was right. "Come on, then. We can see the Christmas tree again on the way back."

But the big Christmas tree with the twinkling lights and the bright red packages beneath it was nowhere to be found. And Liv would never admit it to Elizabeth, but she was starting to get a little bit scared. She couldn't remember which direction they were supposed to go to find the escalators, and there were people *everywhere*, even more than before.

She grabbed Elizabeth's hand and dragged her through the jostling bodies, pressing forward despite the butterflies dancing in her tummy. And then she saw it as they turned the corner. The Christmas tree. It was right in the middle of the large room. And behind it was the escalator.

"Come on," she said, looking back at Elizabeth over her shoulder. "Why are you crying? I swear, you're always crying." Their mother always said that to Elizabeth, so the words rolled off Liv's tongue easily. Of course, that only made Elizabeth cry more.

"I thought we were lost," she said, sniffling.

"Of course not, silly. I always know exactly where we are. Now, come on. Nanny Gillian won't talk forever. I don't want to get sent to the nursery as punishment. Papa is home from his trip and I'm sure he has stories to tell us."

Elizabeth nodded, and they pushed through the crowd until they reached the escalator. Just as they were about to step on, Liv was lifted off her feet and a man's hand was clamped over her mouth. Her eyes grew wide as she saw her sister in the tight grasp of a different man, and pure instinct kicked in. She bit the hand and began kicking her legs, struggling to get down, and she heard the man use a bad word—

one that only Papa was allowed to use—as he jerked his hand aside. Her tiny fists pounded against his arm, but his puffy coat made it like hitting a pillow.

So she screamed. An ear-piercing scream that Nanny Gillian often said could cut glass. And just like that, the man dropped her. Right on her bum.

The air was knocked out of her and people swarmed around her, but she tried to stand.

Elizabeth.

She couldn't see Elizabeth. She screamed again, pointing in the direction the other man had taken her sister, and hysteria took over. She'd never spent a moment without Elizabeth. She was Liv's other half. Her *better* half. Her screams broke into sobs, and someone tried to hold her, tried to comfort her, but there was nothing they could do.

Her sister was gone.

CHAPTER ONE

There were some men who wore elegance like a second skin. Dante Malcolm was one of them.

He guided the cigarette boat through the black water like a knife, sending a fine spray of mist into the air. The moon was full, the stars bright, and the night crisp and clear. The smell of sea salt and lavender perfumed the air. It was the perfect night for a party. And an even better night for a burglary.

His tuxedo was hand-tailored and silk, his bow tie perfectly tied, and his shoes properly shined. His black hair was cut precisely, so that it would fall rakishly across his forehead instead of appearing windblown.

There was something about wealth that had always appealed to him—the glitter of jewels, the smell of expensive perfume, the not-so-subtle way the elite bragged about their latest toys or investments. It was all a game. And he'd always been a winner. But there had been a small thorn in his side—or maybe it was his conscience—over the past few months.

Liv Rothschild.

He was in love with her. Every stubborn, vivacious, persistent, gorgeous inch of her. And that was turning out to be more of a problem than he'd anticipated. Love had never been in the cards for him. Not until he'd crossed paths with a woman whose beauty had literally stopped him in his tracks. Her stunning features had lured him in, but her intelligence had kept him coming back for more.

She knew the world he was accustomed to—the world of the titled and wealthy British elite. Her father had been a prominent member of society, and he'd married an American actress who preferred the drama in her life instead of on the screen. Liv had a sister—a twin—and though he'd only been thirteen at the time, he remembered the news coverage when Elizabeth Rothschild had gone missing.

The guilt Liv carried from that day her sister vanished was what had forged her future. She'd never stopped looking for her. The investigations had turned up no clue to her whereabouts, and even

Dante's searches in the MI6 database had returned nothing. Not a hospital visit or a fingerprint taken. The assumption was that Elizabeth Rothschild was dead. He tended to agree.

But Liv had never lost hope, and Elizabeth's disappearance had motivated Liv to go into law enforcement and ultimately join Interpol so she would have the resources she needed to find her sister. What had been a surprise to Liv was that she was a damned good agent. What had been a surprise to him was that he'd started looking forward to their paths crossing from time to time. Fortunate circumstances had combined their efforts on this case.

Which was why they were meeting at the Marquis de Carmaux's château in the south of France. He enjoyed working with Liv, and if he had his way, they'd continue to work together. And play together. In his mind, life couldn't get any better. He *could* have it all. And he did.

La Château Saint-Germain was lit like a beacon atop the rugged cliffs overlooking the Mediterranean Sea, a pink monstrosity with towers and turrets and more than fifty rooms that rarely got used. Expensive cars lined the narrow road that wound up the steep bluff, headlights beaming for as far as the eye could see as their occupants waited for the valets to take the keys. He checked his watch, noting that Liv should already be inside.

Dante eased off the throttle, and the boat coasted up to the dock. He tossed the rope to the valet, who tied it to the mooring, and then he stepped up onto the dock, adjusting his cuffs and bow tie.

The pathway from the dock led all the way up to the château, the grounds divided into three steep tiers. The wooden steps were lined with hanging lanterns, and the trees were decorated with lights. Once at the top, Dante sauntered along the stone-paved walkway toward the house and retrieved his invitation from the inside of his jacket pocket to present to the doorman. It was time to work.

The Marquis de Carmaux had terrible taste in wine and women, but his art was exceptional. His personal collection was going on loan to the Metropolitan Museum of Art in New York City for the next year, so he'd decided to throw a farewell party so the social elite could not only praise him for his generosity, but be envious of something they'd never be able to get their hands on.

Dante had been fortunate enough to be born into the British upper crust where wealth was passed from one generation to the next, easily accumulated with buying or selling real estate, and easily squandered on a whim. He was titled, a lord no less, and he'd been educated at the best schools, one of his classmates being the future king of England. He also had an unusual talent for math—he could solve any problem in his head, no matter how difficult. It gave him a natural aptitude for winning at cards.

He had many other talents as well—an ease with languages and the ability to see patterns amid what seemed to be nothing but random occurrences—which was why MI6 had wanted him so badly. To a wealthy young man of twenty-two who had multiple degrees in mathematics and was quickly getting bored of the party life that all his contemporaries seemed to live for, becoming an intelligence agent for his country had seemed like the right choice.

It had been around the same time that he'd met a man by the name of Simon Locke.

Simon had introduced him to the art of stealing. He'd given Dante something that no amount of money could provide, that seduced him as no woman had, and that international espionage couldn't satisfy, though it came a close second. Simon had given him an adrenaline rush that was more intense than any drug and just as addictive.

Simon Locke had given him a purpose. Dante felt no remorse when it came to taking things that belonged to others. Because he only took from those who could afford to lose what he stole, from those who had taken what wasn't rightfully theirs. His jobs always had an ulterior motive. He would collect the item that didn't truly belong to the current owner, and he'd take a second piece of his choosing as his commission.

He'd met Simon in a Belgian prison while on assignment. MI6 had set up Dante's arrest, along with a suspected terrorist he'd been drinking with in a pub, by doing a checkpoint sweep for drunk-and-disorderlies. His mission was to get information about recent bombings in Brussels. He and the terrorist had been locked in a cell together, but Simon had been thrown in with them, having been caught up in the same sweep. He'd been neither drunk nor disorderly, but in the wrong place at the wrong time.

The cell was no bigger than a small closet, maybe eight by eight feet, and metal-frame bunk beds that had been bolted into the floor sat against one of the stone walls. The mattresses were paper-thin and dingy, and it was best not to think about what was on them. There was a metal hole in the floor for a toilet and a barred window that overlooked the guarded courtyard below. The cell was shrouded in darkness, but every twenty-seven seconds the spotlight from one of the towers scanned across the window, giving light to the shadows of the cell.

Simon stayed quiet while Dante drew information from their third cellmate, who *had* been drunk and disorderly, but fortunately was also loose-lipped. And when the man had passed out and was snoring obnoxiously in a corner, Simon had looked over and said, "It's good to know British Intelligence hasn't changed."

Dante had been speaking in flawless French to their other cellmate, but still Simon had known. And then he'd said something that piqued Dante's curiosity.

"I was like you once."

In his twenty-two-year-old arrogance, he'd responded, "I beg your pardon, but there's no one else like me."

Locke had smiled at him and moved into the spotlight. He wasn't a big man—maybe five eight or five nine—and his hair was slicked back and tied at the nape of his neck. Even in the holding cell, his black slacks were precisely pressed and his expensive shirt only slightly mussed. There was a nonchalant cockiness about him that Dante could appreciate. He wasn't screaming about injustice like many of the others down the long hallway. He was calm and cool, his hands in his pockets.

St. Gilles Prison was overcrowded, its nineteenth-century cells never meant to accommodate so many prisoners. The holding cells were in the east tower.

MI6 had assured Dante he'd be released early the next morning, but that was still hours away.

"Are they planning your release for the morning, Mr. . . ."

"Malcolm. I'm sure someone will post bond for me in the morning," Dante said vaguely. "And you? Will you be released in the morning? I didn't catch your name."

Simon smiled again and jangled some change in his pockets. Dante was surprised they hadn't confiscated the man's belongings when they'd brought him in.

"You can call me Locke," he said.

"The jailers are getting lax," Dante said, nodding to his pockets, making Simon grin again.

"Not so much. My pockets were empty when I came in. I tend to travel light."

Dante wasn't sure how Locke could have acquired a handful of change, but he was getting tired of the man's vagueness.

"I told you I was like you once," Simon said. "What if I told you there's something more for you than interrogating two-bit terrorists in a moldy jail cell?"

"I'd say they were right to arrest you for drunkenness."

He shrugged. "I was just in the wrong place at

the wrong time. It happens. What if I told you I can get us both released right now? A man like you isn't used to places like this. I can see the disgust in your eyes. They give you these jobs because you're young and don't know any better than to take them. But wait until the rats come. You'll learn to speak up then."

The man was beginning to get under his skin, but Dante had to admit he was curious. And the idea of spending even a few more hours inside the dark cell grated against his sense of propriety.

"And how would you get us released?" Dante asked.

Simon took a copper cent from his pocket and held it up to the passing light. "Watch and learn."

He had watched. And he had learned. Simon had used that copper cent to remove the bars from the window, sharpening it into a screwdriver and undoing the bolts, catching each one in his hand so it didn't fall to the courtyard below. He'd used a thread from the hem of his pants to separate the bars from the stone wall, all without making a single sound.

So Dante had followed him, knowing that he could at any moment be caught and shot, but there had been something compelling about Simon. He'd watched the other man scale the narrow ledges of the prison, counting the seconds before the spotlight would pass, and timing his movements precisely.

Dante had done the same thing, and he'd found the rush of living on the fringes felt better than it should. Then they were outside the prison, not a soul the wiser. Before they'd gone a block, Simon had slipped into the shadows as if he'd never been there at all.

The next day, Dante had thought he might have imagined the whole event—except that he'd had to report to his superiors about the information the terrorist had given him, and answered why he hadn't been at the jail when someone had come to bail him out. He'd told them about the man, described his features and abilities. And though he hadn't given them a name, they'd known the name of Simon Locke. And thanks to Dante, they now had a physical description of him.

He'd returned to London and his home, feeling like he'd somehow betrayed Simon, even though he'd spent hours studying his file and knowing he was a wanted man. When he walked into his bedroom, Simon had been sitting in the chair by the fireplace as if he belonged there. He'd known his identity had been compromised, but it didn't seem to bother him. His confidence in his ability was much greater than his confidence that there was anyone out there good enough to catch him. But he'd admitted he was getting older, and that he was losing the zest he'd once had for the life.

He'd said once the desire started to wane, it was only a matter of time before a job ended in prison time instead of wealth and luxury. Simon hadn't been the first Simon Locke. There'd been another before him, and another before him, who'd chosen and trained their successors with great care.

Simon had chosen Dante to be the next.

And Dante had accepted.

His work at MI6 had become secondary, but his training there had given him unimaginable advantages. He and Simon had more in common than he'd expected. But there were some jobs he wouldn't take. Dante refused to steal for the sake of stealing. There had to be a reason, and someone had to benefit. Having a moral compass, as loose as it may be, had kept him grounded. It had been the only time he and Simon had ever argued, but Dante had drawn a hard line in the sand and he'd stuck with it.

For the last ten years, Dante had been Simon Locke. His mentor had taken him to dinner one night, and over dessert he'd casually passed him the torch, saying he was retiring and sailing to Antigua to live out his life and enjoy the spoils of his profession. He hadn't seen Simon since, or gotten wind that he'd taken up the life again.

Dante had taken the passing of the name seriously, and he'd never had a moment of regret.

But Liv Rothschild had been a surprise. He'd seduced her for his own pleasure the moment he saw her. But then he'd found himself being seduced. Interpol had been looking for Simon Locke for years, and as irony would have it, she was put in charge of the investigation.

It had been pure self-preservation that had caused him to involve MI6 in the hunt for Simon Locke. She'd come too close too often to discovering his true identity, and joining his MI6 resources with hers guaranteed that he always knew the steps she was taking. She was good. But he was better.

He could've stopped, of course. But when it came down to it, Dante didn't want to. The thrill was in his blood. But Liv had become his oxygen. He needed both of them to survive, and he had no reason to think he couldn't have everything he wanted.

There was no reason to confess and ruin everything. Some confessions could never be forgiven. Liv was a straight arrow. She was adventurous and liked the thrill of the chase—that was in her blood, just as thieving was in his. But in the end, law and order would take precedence.

He'd always enjoyed the Marquis de Carmaux's château. It had been built in the eighteenth century to honor the palace of Versailles, and everything as far as the eye could see was decorated in French Baroque. It was overdone and gaudy, but as Carmaux liked to say, it was jolly good fun and women loved it. Dante and Carmaux had been friends for years, and he could attest to both of those statements.

The entryway was done in pink marble and was completely open to the second floor. The domed ceiling was painted with cherubs and erotic scenes that most people never noticed, although the other nudes painted in niches along the walls were harder to miss. The double staircase was the showpiece, also done in pink marble and flanked by pink marble columns. Whenever he walked in, Dante always felt as if he'd been swallowed whole and was lounging about in someone's stomach.

He made his way through the growing crowd and into the ballroom—white, thank God, with gold-leaf trim and ceilings again painted with subtly erotic love scenes. It smelled of perfume and excitement, and couples were already moving around the dance floor. The ballroom opened up on either side—on one side was the bar and a smattering of high tables so people could rest, and on the other were the doors that led into the courtyard.

What Dante didn't see was the one woman he was looking for. Then he felt her behind him, and his mouth quirked in a smile as he turned.

"You're late," Liv said.

"I'm never late, darling," he said, taking her hand and kissing it. And then he stopped and lingered when he got a good look at her.

Never had a woman had the ability to make his heart skip a beat. He'd always thought the phrase trite and impossible—foolish words of romance. But now he knew it to be true.

She was spectacular. She wore a long column of dark blue velvet—strapless and simple in its design—and the small train pooled at her feet like the darkest part of the ocean. Her white-blond hair was piled artfully on top of her head, and a sapphire the size of his thumb dangled just above her décolletage. His gaze lingered there, and all he could imagine was her wearing nothing but that necklace.

"If you keep looking at me like that, we're likely to get in trouble," she said, her lilting voice husky.

"Only if we do what I'm thinking about in front of all these people." He released her hand and took two flutes of champagne from a passing tray, handing one to her.

"Are you sure he'll be here tonight?" she asked, looking around the ballroom.

"I have a gut feeling. Carmaux has one of the premier art collections in the world, and after tonight, it's going to be under museum security. If Locke is going to make his move, it'll be tonight, when everything is out on display."

"There are close to a thousand people here, and security is everywhere," Liv said, bringing the flute to her lips to cover her words. "He'd be a fool to try to take one of these paintings. And Simon Locke is no fool."

"Everyone has a weakness," Dante told her. "And a challenge like this one is his. He'd go down in history as the greatest thief ever to live. To steal something in plain sight of all these people?"

The job for his client would be easy. It was the piece he'd chosen for his own commission that would be tricky. An American woman had hired him to take back a family heirloom. She was the great-great-granddaughter of James Abbott McNeill Whistler, from the line of one of his many illegitimate children, but he'd done a small portrait of his three-year-old granddaughter, his favorite, shortly before he died.

The painting was only four feet by six, and it portrayed his granddaughter, Anna—who'd been named after his mother—sitting in a field of white daisies in a white dress. On the back of the painting, Whistler had written her a note in pencil.

The great-great-granddaughter, who was also named Anna, had told Dante the painting had been very dear to her mother, but her stepfather had sold it for a fraction of what it was worth during hard times.

Dante wasn't a fool. He'd known con artists his whole life. But he'd checked out the woman's story through his sources at MI6 and determined that the painting did rightfully belong to her family. The Marquis de Carmaux had the painting sitting on a shelf in his library. Dante had passed by it dozens of times before and never given it a thought. Whistler wasn't one he preferred for his personal collection.

He took Liv's champagne and set both flutes on a nearby table, then led her to the dance floor so he had an excuse to take her into his arms beneath the glittering chandeliers. There was an orchestra at one end of the grand ballroom, and Carmaux's art collection was arranged around the perimeter, special lighting emphasizing each piece. The highlight of the collection was a Picasso that was worth close to eighty million euros, but it was the Degas tucked in the corner that Dante had decided on for his commission.

"You know," she said, "sometimes you sound as if you admire Locke." Her mouth quirked in an amused smile as his arm came around her waist and she put her delicate hand in his.

He nodded and said, "You have to respect someone who is good at what they do. And he's the best." He ran his finger down the length of her spine and felt her shiver beneath his touch. "It doesn't mean we won't catch him. But I do respect him."

She leaned back to look at him, her brow arched. "Don't be jealous, darling. You're very good at what you do. But if it makes you feel better, I'll put you in handcuffs too."

His dick spiked at the blatant invitation in her eyes, and he drew her closer. Her indrawn gasp told him she knew exactly the effect she was having on his body.

"Naughty girl," he said. "Feel what you do to me?"

"Mmm," she purred. "This could get awkward. But think how I feel. I'm not wearing any panties."

His steps faltered and he stopped in the middle of the dance floor, hoping the black spots would clear from his vision before he made a fool of himself.

"I believe that's something I should find out for myself."

"We're supposed to be working," she reminded him. "Locke could be right under our noses."

"The party has just started, darling," he assured her, spinning her back into the waltz. "Locke seems like the kind of man who likes to make a statement. I noticed you brought in reinforcements. I saw Donner out of the corner of my eye, looking horrified at the goose liver paté."

"If it doesn't come from a cow, Donner isn't interested," she said, referring to one of the other Interpol agents and her closest friend. "I called him in for backup. I just have an uneasy feeling."

"You wouldn't be good at your job if your feelings were easy. I've come to learn Locke better over the last months. He's going to want a splash. He'll wait until the room is at its most crowded."

"Care to make a wager on it?" she asked, her voice seductive and low. "I think he'll wait until everyone starts to leave. Maybe even until tomorrow, just before the trucks arrive to collect the art."

"And what do I get if I win?" he asked.

"You know that little red thing you like?"

"I like it better when it's on the floor," he told her. "I've got a better idea. If I win, we'll both take vacation time. Two weeks. I have a villa in Tuscany. I'll give the staff a holiday, so we never have to put clothes on."

His Tuscan villa housed some of his personal collection, and part of him wanted her to walk by his most prized possessions, knowing that she wouldn't recognize what was in her presence. Knowing he could get away with it. He understood that there was a kind of sickness to the need to have her so close, but still so far from knowing the real him. But he couldn't help it.

"Sounds drafty," she said, smiling.

"I have a rooftop garden," he said. "I'll make love to you there under the stars."

"Romantic," she said, leaning into him. And then she placed her lips next to his ear and whispered, "I'm not in the mood for romantic. I'll go to Italy with you if you'll figure out a way to fuck me now."

His breath caught and his fingers dug into her back. She always knew how to catch him off guard. It was one of the things he loved about her.

He expertly waltzed her across the crowded dance floor until they'd reached the perimeter, and he discreetly checked his watch. There was still an hour and a half before Simon Locke was due to make his appearance. If he'd calculated precisely—and he always did—he could easily accommodate her wishes.

He leaned down and kissed the nape of her neck before whispering against her ear, "Here's your mission, should you choose to accept it." He used the popular line from *Mission: Impossible* just to hear her laugh.

"You're going to retreat to the second floor where the ladies' washroom is. To the right of the washroom is a small library. It'll be unlocked—Carmaux likes to show off his first editions once he's had a little too much to drink. There's a fireplace along the south wall, with two hideous Rodin sculptures on either side."

"Tell me how you really feel," she said.

"Hush, love. Don't interrupt or it'll be ages before you get to come." He enjoyed the quick flash of arrogance in her eyes. "Now, where was I?"

"You were pressing me closer so Lady Montreaux can't see your hard-on. Daft old hag."

He grinned. "That mouth is going to get you into so much trouble."

"If you hurry, I'll show you exactly what I can do with this mouth."

"Right," he said, remembering to breathe. "Pull the hideous Rodin on the left toward you, and the bookshelf to the right of the fireplace will open up."

"You certainly know a lot about the Marquis de Carmaux's personal residence," she said curiously.

"I've played more hands of cards in that room than I can tell you."

"Did you win?" she asked.

"Yes," he said, nipping just below her ear. "And I've been on quite a lucky streak."

She smoothed her hand down his chest, but

didn't stop as she reached his belt, taking hold of the hard length straining against his trousers. "It looks like your lucky streak is about to continue."

"Fifteen minutes," he said, checking his watch. "Starting now."

She straightened his bow tie and gave him a sassy wink. "You'd better take the back way. Lady Montreaux is bound to notice something amiss with your trousers. Knowing her, she'd think she was the reason, and then you'd really be in trouble."

"Time just started," he said, tapping his watch and grinning.

She laughed as she broke away from him, moving through the crowd and back toward the foyer and the stairs.

He watched her for a full minute before he moved from his spot. Then he checked his watch again. Every second was crucial during a job of this magnitude. Timing was everything.

He'd spent six months planning this heist, and he wouldn't come away empty-handed, despite the challenges. But there was a small warning that kept flashing in the back of his mind. Liv had always been so close on his heels. And he'd literally brought her into the lion's den for this one, almost as if he wanted to see how good she really was. Or prove to himself how good he really was.

He circled to the other side of the ballroom and then slipped off to a side hall that led to Carmaux's private office. The narrow hallway was darkened to discourage guests from wandering, with a strategically positioned velvet rope to keep anyone from going too far. There was a secret passage in Carmaux's office, similar to the one in the library.

The staff knew him here—the upstairs maid and one of the serving staff on an intimate level, though that threesome had been several years before during his wilder days—and while he normally wouldn't care if they saw him, it was best he stay under the radar tonight.

Carmaux's office was locked, as he expected, and it took him less than ten seconds to open the door with the pin he'd slipped from Liv's hair. He slid inside and closed the door behind him. The lights were off, but the large picture window behind the desk admitted a flood of moonlight. There was a stillness about an empty room, a quietness that couldn't be replicated. Dante paused, his senses on alert. Most people wouldn't have realized and would've walked on by. But he wasn't most people.

Instead, he strolled casually to the desk and leaned against it so the light was at his back, and crossed his ankles.

"And who might you be?" he asked.

She came out of the shadows like an apparition, but she was flesh and blood and bone. He could appreciate her beauty, much as he would a priceless piece of art, but there was no warmth to her. Her skin gleamed in the moonlight, the black dress she was barely wearing drawing attention to her assets. It plunged low in the front, almost to her navel, giving a glimpse of perfect breasts. And it slit high up the leg so he could see her hip as she walked toward him on metallic stilettos.

Once he got past the body, he moved on to the face. She was of Asian descent, mixed with Anglo features—her bones were delicate, with high cheekbones and almond-shaped eyes that were as black as the dress she wore. Her lips were full and slicked red, and her hair lush and curled over one shoulder, sleek and shiny as a sealskin.

"It's not important to know who I am," she said. "What's important is that I know who you are."

Dante smiled but felt a cold frisson of fear snake down his spine. "I'm an open book, darling."

She smiled this time and came closer, passing inches in front of him as she went around the desk and took the seat at the helm. He turned so he faced her, but didn't sit. He'd already lost ground with her. She propped her feet on the desk, showing off wicked heels and legs that seemed to go all the way to her ears.

"Let's not play games," she said. "I believe your time is running short." She nodded at his watch, but he wouldn't give her the satisfaction of looking to check the time.

He didn't know who the hell this woman was, but he was going to make it his life's mission to find out.

"I'm growing tired of your theatrics," he said, straightening his cuffs and preparing to leave. "As you've said, my time is short. I have much more pleasurable company waiting for me."

"Don't worry," she said, smirking. "Miss Rothschild has had a mishap. I believe someone spilled some champagne on her lovely dress. She'll be a few minutes late to your meeting."

"You're making a very dangerous enemy," he told her, his eyes narrowing. He was armed, even though he didn't need a weapon to kill. But leaving a body behind wasn't part of Simon Locke's MO, and a murder charge would certainly up the ante.

"I make a habit of that, Lord Malcolm," she said. "Or do you prefer Agent Malcolm? Or better yet, should I call you Simon Locke?"

"Which government do you work for?"

"Have a seat," she said. "And listen closely."

CHAPTER TWO

Liv felt giddy, as if she'd drunk too much champagne, and happiness practically exploded inside her. She'd never felt as connected to another human being as she did with Dante—not since her sister. They were the perfect team, whether it was at work or in the bedroom, and they complemented each other in ways that only true soul mates could.

She'd never believed in such things before. Her life had been so focused on finding her sister that she'd rarely paid attention to men. She'd done her time at Scotland Yard, and then taken the job with Interpol—exactly what she'd aimed for all along. Only Interpol had the resources to find and eliminate human traffickers, and eventually she'd find out what had happened to her sister when they were children.

Dante was the first man she'd ever confided in.

He knew her hopes and dreams, her reasons for doing the things she did. And he'd promised to help her however he could through his own contacts at MI6.

She was going to tell him she loved him. She was nearly bursting with it, and she couldn't keep it inside any longer. Maybe it was naïve, but she thought he loved her too. Even if he didn't, she couldn't hold back her feelings. He deserved to know that she cared about him.

She couldn't dim her smile as she made her way through the crowd and toward the huge double staircase that was a piece of art in itself.

"Excusez-moi," she said, skirting an older gentleman and his wife, and then she repeated herself several times as she worked her way to the base of the stairs, where a small group had decided to congregate.

She'd just stepped onto the bottom stair when she felt a tug on her train. She glanced over her shoulder to see a tall man with his back to her, his dark, longish hair tied at the nape of his neck. She tapped on his shoulder, and when he turned she said, "You're stepping on my train."

He smiled, and she really got a good look at his face. He was handsome, several years older than she was, and he towered over her. There was a lot of muscle under his tuxedo, and she would've had to be dead not to notice that he filled it out just fine.

"I'm sorry?" he said, cupping a hand to his ear for her to repeat what she'd said.

Her brows rose at his accent. He was American.

"My train," she said again, this time pointing to the floor.

"I'm so sorry," he said, removing his foot and releasing her. "Can I get you a drink to make up for it?"

His smile turned flirtatious, and though she was flattered by the offer, there was only one man on her mind. She thanked him and declined, and when she turned to continue up the stairs, she bumped smack into another man—this one holding a now-empty champagne flute, since the wine had just decorated the front of her dress.

The man didn't even notice. He just bulled his way through the crowd and kept walking. She glanced at the ornately scrolled gold clock and cursed under her breath. She'd hoped to reach the room long before Dante so she could catch her breath and let the butterflies settle. But there was no way she could make it within the allotted fifteen minutes now that she had to mop up some of the champagne.

Liv entered the washroom and groaned when she saw women crammed into the area, waiting their turns. By the time she reached the sinks and found a washcloth, ten minutes had passed. She cleaned the front of her dress as best she could, then made her way to the small lounge area where a vanity table held things like sewing kits, makeup samples, and hair supplies, just in case anyone had a mishap. She used the blow-dryer to dry the front of her dress, and was satisfied that the champagne hadn't left a dark spot.

Her thoughts were on Dante and Simon Locke, in that order. Both men made her crazy in different ways. Quenching her thirst for Dante would allow her to focus on Simon. Capturing him had been her only priority for the past two years. She knew more about him than anyone else, and that wasn't saying much. The man was brilliant. And she agreed with Dante. You had to respect a man with that kind of ability. But it wasn't going to stop her from putting him in prison.

She had to admit, there was something that seemed off about tonight. A gut feeling. Were they wrong altogether in assuming that he'd hit the marquis's collection? Or was she just doubting her ability to do the job? He'd outsmarted her at every turn. And it was frustrating as hell to always be a step behind. The last thing she wanted was to bungle this operation and look like a fool. It was hard enough being a woman in charge of the op.

The funny feeling in her gut had motivated her to call in more agents to work undercover during the party. She hadn't told anyone, not even Dante. She just had to remember that her job wasn't to protect the paintings downstairs. That's what security was being paid to do. Her job was to catch Simon Locke and put him behind bars.

This job was a different MO for Locke. He'd never been shy about his talents. In fact, his profile showed that he'd be quite put out if there wasn't front-page media coverage the next day. He liked grand gestures. He liked making the impossible seem possible. And it was rare that they figured out how he'd accomplished a heist. He was a magician, and there never seemed to be a wall too high or security too formidable for him to breach.

But to her knowledge, he'd never pulled off a job in front of a room full of people. Yes, there was a bit of a dramatic flair about the way he staged his heists, leaving a print of Coolidge's *Dogs Playing Poker* in place of the paintings he stole. It would have been funny if he weren't quite so good at what he did. But Locke was meticulous. Every detail planned from beginning to end. And there were too many variables left to chance when trying to steal a painting in front of witnesses. It seemed obvious he'd be going for the Picasso. It was by far the most valuable piece in Carmaux's collection. But it seemed foolish to assume that he was after anything in the collection. Maybe he was using the display as a way to divert attention away from what he really wanted. Carmaux was a wealthy man, and there were many valuable pieces throughout the château.

The crowd had cleared somewhat as she exited the washroom, and she didn't waste any time. She was already late, and she hoped Dante hadn't gotten tired of waiting. She opened the door of the room to the right of the washroom, just as Dante had instructed, and entered the small library.

It was a cozy room, done in pale greens and gold, with floor-to-ceiling shelves that were filled with books. The room smelled of must and pipe tobacco. The chairs were oversize and comfortable, and a small round table with a bottle of sherry on top of it sat between them.

The white marble fireplace took up almost the entire south wall, but it was May and there was no need for a fire. She smirked as she noted the small Rodin sculptures at either end of the mantel—they were, in fact, hideous, just as Dante had said. She went to the one on the left and carefully pulled it toward her.

The snick of a catch being released seemed loud in the quiet room, and her pulse raced at the thought of being caught. It only heightened the anticipation of what was to come.

The bookshelf to the right of the fireplace stood slightly ajar, and she pulled it open and walked through to the other side, closing it behind her with a rather loud finality. The room was dark except for the soft glow beneath the round poker table in the center.

As her eyes adjusted, she started to feel her way around the edge of the room, groping for a light switch, but there was nothing. No light switches. No doors. Just a circular room in the middle of Carmaux's home that had probably been used for any number of things over the past three centuries.

"Dante," she said, but there was no reply.

Her hand ran over the smooth wood of a long bar, and she navigated her way around the barstools, careful not to trip. It was truly a man's room, and she could imagine Dante in his element here, a stack of poker chips piled high in front of him.

She saw the outline of the switch plate behind the bar and leaned across to turn on the light, but a hand grabbed her wrist. She hadn't heard him. Hadn't felt his presence. But she'd recognize his touch anywhere.

"There's no need for light," he said from behind her, kissing the nape of her neck.

She shivered. "What if I want to see you?" she asked, stifling a groan as he bit down on her shoulder. She'd have to let her hair down to cover the mark when they left.

"You don't need to see me," he whispered. "You're going to feel me."

She tried to turn around, but he held her wrists so they were trapped against the bar. She could feel the urgency in him, almost a desperation.

"I want to touch you," she said, the plea in her voice unmistakable.

"If you touch me now, this will be over before we get started. Keep your hands flat against the bar. Don't let go."

She turned her head and tried to catch a glimpse of him over her shoulder, but he stood just out of sight.

"Dante," she said, her heart thumping wildly in her chest as she felt him lift her dress slowly, the velvet a caress against her legs. This wasn't at all what she'd planned when she'd imagined telling him she loved him for the first time. This felt so . . . one-sided.

"I've never stopped wanting you," he said. "I want you more now than I did when I first saw you. You're like a drug, and I keep coming back for more."

His fingers skimmed the insides of her thighs, and he chuckled as he felt the holster strapped around her thigh. He pulled the small pistol from the holster and set it on the bar.

"We don't want any misfires," he whispered. And then his fingers continued their journey, working their way up higher until he grazed the bare flesh that was damp with arousal.

"I told you," she said.

"Some things you have to find out for yourself. You're so wet for me."

"I always want you as much as you want me," she said, biting back a moan as he lightly traced her vulva, spreading moisture to her clit. "Please, let me touch you."

"If I did, I wouldn't be able to go through with it," he said, and she felt his hands disappear and the skirt drop back to the floor.

"Go through with what?" she asked, panting. "Please don't stop."

"I couldn't," he assured her. He lowered the zipper at her back, and the dress fell in a puddle to her feet, leaving her in nothing but the sapphire necklace and the glittering strappy heels on her feet.

"Step out," he ordered, and she did as she was told. He kicked the dress to the side, and she tried again to catch a glimpse of him over her shoulder, but it was no use.

Her legs quivered and her fingers curled around

the edge of the bar. Her breasts were heavy, wanting the attention he usually paid them. And then she heard the sweet sound of his belt being unbuckled and the teeth of his zipper as he lowered it.

There were no passionate kisses. No lingering touches. This wasn't like any other time they'd made love. It was primitive. Desperate. And she braced herself as she felt him probe against her, holding her breath as he pressed deep inside her.

Her muscles flexed around him and he groaned, his breathing heavy against her ear, and he placed his hands on top of hers, twining their fingers together. And then he began to move, his thrusts slow but steady, growing in intensity and strength until the bar shook beneath their bodies.

"I can't hold back," he said, kissing the side of her neck. "Not tonight."

She was incapable of speaking, the feel of him all-consuming. His hands released hers and cupped one of her breasts, tweaking the nipple hard enough that she'd probably be sensitive for a couple of days. But she could feel the orgasm building inside her. And then he abandoned her breast and his fingers trailed down her stomach, down farther until they were pressed against her clit.

"Come on, baby," he panted. "Come for me."

He didn't move his fingers against her. It was

just a steady pressure, holding her in place as he pistoned in and out of her, the speed and ferocity of each thrust gaining in intensity.

"Oh, God," she said, her hands clamping tighter around the bar. She wasn't sure her legs would hold her. She wasn't even really sure she was still standing. All she knew was that she'd never felt pleasure that intensely before.

"Now, damn it," he growled, and she felt him grow impossibly harder, impossibly bigger.

And then she screamed as the orgasm was ripped from her body, a pulsating explosion that would've brought her to her knees if he hadn't been holding her upright. She felt the liquid heat of him fill her as he called out her name.

She couldn't control the tears that fell on her cheeks. The moment was too powerful—too intense. And she couldn't hold back her feelings any longer.

"I love you," she said, still gasping for breath. "I love you, Dante."

He kissed the side of her neck and then lowered them both to the floor, their bodies still joined.

CHAPTER THREE

"We need to rejoin the party," Dante said, glancing at his watch.

He felt her stiffen, his rejection like a bucket of cold water poured over her, and he felt like the lowest form of life. He wanted—no, *needed*—to take Liv in his arms. To love her and return the words she'd given him freely. But what good would it do him when his future had just changed so drastically?

Trying to lighten the mood, he skimmed his hand down her naked hip. "We're here to work, remember? Simon Locke could already have the Picasso and be long gone. It would be quite embarrassing to get caught with our pants down while he makes off with millions in art. We have the rest of the night to finish what we started here."

Liv cleared her throat and said, "You're right. We've already wasted too much time when we could've been searching for him. But I still think we need to have a team in place to intercept him if he tries to take the painting while they're loading it onto the truck for transport. Everyone knows that's when the painting is at its most vulnerable."

"The team is already in place, darling. But I don't think we'll need it. He'll strike tonight."

"Hand me my dress, please," she said.

He could hear the hurt in her voice, but she'd iced it over, moving strictly to business. He reached around the bar and turned on the lights, taking in his fill of her before he reached down to grab her dress off the floor. She stood before him in glittering heels with the sapphire dangling between her breasts, her hair falling around her shoulders and the evidence of their passion slicked on her inner thighs.

He found a towel behind the bar and handed it to her so she could clean up, and then he passed her the dress.

"Does it look too wrinkled?" she asked, pulling it on and turning so he could zip it up for her.

"It looks like it's been in a heap on the floor," he said, smiling for the first time. "But maybe no one will notice. They'll probably be too busy looking at the bite marks on your neck."

Her hand reached up to touch the area in question, and she shot him a look that normally would've made him want to tease her more. Riling her up was one of his greatest joys, and it almost always ended in pleasure.

"You don't look much better, Ace," she retorted, eyeing him from the top of his head to his shoes. "And you certainly can't go out there like that." She waggled her eyebrows and dropped her gaze below his waist, and he felt the blood rush to his face as he put everything back where it belonged and zipped up his slacks.

The only thing he'd removed was his jacket, and he'd done that before she'd come into the room. Even his bow tie was still tied.

"They have a steamer in the bathroom," she said. "I need to get some of these wrinkles out before going back out onto the floor. There are too many people here who know us. I don't want to be the top item in the society section tomorrow."

"I think it's too late for that, love. Too many people saw us on the dance floor. There was no mistaking what we were planning to do. Fortunately, there were several other couples looking to do the same—I'm sure many of Carmaux's rooms are occupied at the moment."

"A terrifying thought," she said cheekily. "You'd expect better from the upper crust."

"No, I wouldn't," he said. "Putting all debauchery aside, you should have plenty of time to steam your dress and meet me back downstairs. It's still early, and I believe Carmaux is set to make a grand speech soon, so everyone can applaud his generosity."

"Well, I'd certainly hate to miss that. I do love to applaud people who have done absolutely nothing to earn their money while they lord it in front of others."

Dante grinned. "Love, I believe you were born with a silver spoon in your mouth as well. You reek of the finest British boarding schools. The only difference is that your father chose to increase his inheritance by working."

"Because that was the easiest way for him to avoid my mother. And wealth doesn't make him any less dead. Death doesn't discriminate."

He couldn't help but take her shoulders and pull her into a soft kiss. The hurt on her face had been too much for him to bear.

"I'm sorry, love," he said, kissing her this time on the forehead.

"It doesn't matter," she said, pulling out of his embrace. "Like you said, we've got a job to do. The most pressing matter at the moment is getting out of this room. There aren't any doors."

"It makes it much easier when someone is caught cheating if they can't escape," he said. "Carmaux takes his cards very seriously."

He went to the poker table and felt beneath it.

He pressed a button, and the same panel of the wall she'd entered through opened up. She waited as Dante turned off the lights, and then they slipped back into the library.

"Why don't you go out first and head straight into the washroom? I'll wait in here for a few more minutes just to be safe."

"Damn," she said. "I left my gun in the poker room."

"I'll get it for you," he said, turning back to the secret passageway. "Go ahead—I'll meet you downstairs when you're presentable."

She nodded and opened the door a crack, peeking out before she went into the hallway, closing the door behind her. There was no time to grab her gun. The second hand of his watch was ticking away, and he used the few minutes he had to make sure all the tools he needed were easily accessible.

The Whistler sat on the shelf, exactly where he remembered it, and he stripped the canvas from the frame, rolling it gently and placing it in the transport tube hidden down his pants leg. And then he replaced the painting with a small version of *Dogs Playing Poker,* and put it back where the Whistler had been on the shelf.

He checked his watch one more time and went to the door of the library, waiting for the hour to strike. The watch vibrated at the exact moment that all the lights in the château went out.

"Excellent timing," he said, opening the door of the library and stepping out into pandemonium. He took a small penlight from his pocket and turned it on.

The washroom door beside him was jerked open and Liv appeared, her dress still disheveled, though she'd managed to do something with her hair to get it out of her face.

"It's Locke," Liv said.

She grabbed his arm to steady herself and yanked off her heels, tossing them aside, and he wanted to kiss her again, knowing it would be the last time. But there was no help for it. Losing her was the only alternative to death or prison, and he'd accepted his fate.

"I'll take the bottom floor and the ballroom," he told her. "I'll be able to muscle my way through easier than you. You take this floor and the servants' wings, especially toward the kitchens. He's going to know this place like the back of his hand. If you go all the way to the end of the hall, there's another staircase that leads down to the kitchens."

"Be careful," she said. "I just have this feeling. . . ."

"You too." And then he gave in to the urge and pulled her in for a quick kiss. "We'll get him this time," he promised her.

He let her go and headed down the stairs, trusting that she was already heading in the opposite direction. There was no time to think of her now. He still had a job to do. He pulled a pair of black-framed glasses from his pocket and slipped them on, clicking the small button at the right corner of the frame.

The infrared images appeared in the lenses, and he was able to see clearly as he maneuvered the rest of the way down the stairs and through the crowd that was rushing to get outdoors, falling over each other and not caring who they took down with them.

He pushed his way through them, noting that the security guards had set up a perimeter around the paintings, but there were weak spots. They couldn't see any better than anyone else. All they could do was stand there and apprehend anyone who ran smack into them, which, fortunately, happened to be several people.

He slipped between two of the security guards and moved behind them to the corner of the room where they'd hung the Degas. It was a lovely nude preparing for a bath, the colors rich, the strokes both smooth and chaotic, as was the painter's style. They'd set it in an ornate gold frame, and there was a velvet rope placed about three feet in front of it to keep people from getting too close. But it was what was behind the velvet rope that gave him a slight pause.

Red lines crisscrossed the floor and would sound an alarm if they were touched. They hadn't been visible to the naked eye. He pulled the transport tube from his pants, and slid it across his body so the tube rested across his back, leaving his hands free. Then he took the pack of tools from the inside of his jacket, where pockets had been specially altered so the jacket fit without showing lines.

He opened the pack and pulled out two discs the size of a half-dollar. He knelt on the ground and found the source for the sensors, then stuck the discs to the wall on either side of the originating source. He clicked the button on the left corner of his frames this time, and the discs began to move in unison, replacing the source and diverting the crossing red beams so there was a clear space he could walk through. A thief was only as good as his equipment, and his equipment was the best. He'd paid a fortune to make sure his supplier only supplied him.

Dante moved the velvet rope aside and stepped in front of the painting. He expertly snipped the alarm wires behind the frame and took it from the hook. In a matter of a minute, he'd stripped the painting from the gold frame and cut the canvas from the wood it had been nailed to. He pulled the replacement picture from the tube at his back, the adhesive already in place, and attached it to the frame, then hung it back on the wall; the Degas was rolled up and put into the tube. He replaced the rope and pressed the button on his glasses again, so the discs no longer diverted the sensors. And then he took them from the wall and walked back into the crowd.

It had taken mere minutes from the time the lights had gone off until now, and he headed through the open doors into the courtyard, where he'd climb the château walls to the top so he could meet death head-on.

THERE WAS A floor-to-ceiling window at the end of the hallway, and the moon cast a soft glow through the panes, giving Liv enough light so she could see what was in front of her. She maneuvered down the hallway, keeping her senses open. The party guests were in a panic, their voices rising, and she recognized Donner's voice yelling for everyone to file out in a calm and orderly fashion.

She had confidence in Dante, and she had confidence in her agents. She had to trust them to do their jobs. And she'd do hers. It was important to follow her instincts. To think of every possible outcome.

That was a lot easier said than done. The physical description they had of Simon Locke was more than a decade old. The problem with competing agencies was they never shared information. There wasn't a global database of combined resources, no matter how easy movies and TV shows made it look. Everyone was territorial. And when she'd asked Dante to check MI6 files on Locke, she'd expected him to tell her no. He'd have been within his rights, as the information was classified.

He'd sent her a file, including his own personal encounter with Locke in a Belgian prison. But it was outdated information. They had no idea what Locke looked like in the present day. Finding him in this crowd was literally a shot in the dark.

Liv hadn't bothered with a handbag for the evening, and she regretted the decision to leave it behind. Her cell phone was in Dante's coat pocket, and he also had her gun. Her skirt made moving difficult, so she hiked it up, deciding it was already well past ruined, and tied the train in a knot so it hung just above her knees.

Urgency filled her and she started running before she reached the end of the long hallway—then stopped in her tracks, her eyes adjusting to the blinding lights as the electricity hummed back on.

Voices rose and there were screams, and then a shot rang out. She took cover beside an eighteenth-century grandfather clock on the wall opposite the stairs that led down to the kitchens.

Liv's heart thudded in her chest as she peeked around the clock to see the man with the gun. Plaster from the ceiling had fallen around him. He was looking down over the balcony railing, not at her, keeping the gun up so everyone below could see it. He was one of the security guards, but it didn't take her long to realize he was more mercenary than security guard. His job was to protect the painting, and if there was no painting, there'd be no paycheck for him. And it was more than obvious he was willing to use the gun if necessary.

"Everyone sit down on the ground where you are," he shouted in French, and then he repeated it in English. "The Degas has gone missing."

Liv raised her brows at that. She should've realized the Degas was more in line with Locke's recent acquisitions. She'd studied every case file on Simon Locke spanning more than two decades, and there had definitely been a shift in the things he stole. It had been years since he'd last hit a museum, tending to go for private collectors. He didn't always steal the most valuable thing in a collection, which told her he was stealing either for a specific client or for himself and had precise personal taste.

"No one is going in or out of here until we find that painting," the guard said. "If you saw who took the painting, raise your hand and a security officer will come to you."

Liv didn't waste time. Moving silently, she took a step toward the stairs that led down to the kitchen—but something stopped her. It'd make sense for him to try to get lost in the crowd and confusion. But her gut was telling her something different. He wasn't down there with the others, waiting it out and pretending to be a victim. Either he was long gone, or he was trying to escape in a way that no one else would attempt. She had nothing to lose.

Directly opposite of the staircase that led down to the kitchens was another staircase to her right that went to the upper floors. She took a chance and ran up them, and then up another level and another, until the staircase grew narrower and the rooms less ornate—the doors plain. This part of the château was unused and stale, caught in a time period that was a couple of centuries old. The other side of the hallway was lined with thick-paned windows that opened outward to let in the breeze.

She stopped to listen, but heard nothing but her pounding heart. And then she saw a quick flash of something through the windows—a glimpse of black caught by the moonlight. Staying in the shadows, she sidled to the far end of the windows, and found a small door, only a couple of feet high and wide. She turned the knob, then pulled harder, cursing under her breath; the door was stuck with age and swollen from weather.

Time was of the essence, so she braced her foot against the wall and yanked as hard as she could. The door flew open, almost knocking her over. She crawled through the opening and found herself on the watch wall that surrounded the entire château. Centuries ago, there would have been guards placed strategically to warn of intruders, but now it was vacant, and some of the stones were crumbling.

She started running in the direction she'd seen the dark figure go, and it wasn't long before she found the remnants of a man's evening dress scattered along the way—shirt, pants, bow tie. Sharp pieces of stone dug into her bare feet, and she barely slowed as the watch wall came to an end. She calculated the distance to the turret directly in front of her, fear mingled with the excitement of the chase.

Determination and something she couldn't explain drove her. She made sure the knot in her skirt was tight so it didn't hamper her, and then she leaped from the watch wall to the turret, her hands grasping the ledge. She swung her leg over, her skirt hiking to her hips, and then the stone crumbled away beneath her hands and she was grasping nothing but air until something hard clamped around her wrist.

She grasped onto his wrist with her free hand and used her legs to help him lift her over the edge of the turret. And then he let go of her and walked away, and she realized she'd just caught Simon Locke. Though, in reality, it had been him who caught *her*.

THEY'D REACHED THE end of the road, at least the only one available to them on the rooftop of the château. There was nothing beyond them but the steep cliffs and the turbulent Mediterranean. The wind whipped her hair into her face and her hands burned where they'd been scraped by the stones. Her feet were raw. But Liv pulled herself to her full height and faced him down.

He was dressed in a black bodysuit—a type she'd never seen before. The suit seemed to have some kind of rigid material inside it, almost like its own skeleton. A black mask covered his face entirely, and built into the eyeholes was was a goggle-like material. There was a long tube strapped to his back, and she knew he had the painting.

"Give me the painting," she said in French. "You'll never leave the grounds with it. You're outnumbered and outmatched this time."

He cocked his head as if he didn't understand her, so she repeated herself in English. But still, he only stood there. She took a step forward, and he took a step back. And then they repeated the dance until he stood right at the edge of the turret.

"You can't expect to win every time, Mr. Locke," she said.

"Of course I can," he said, and reached up to pull off the mask. "But winning one game has made me lose another."

The bottom dropped out of her stomach, and pain like she'd only experienced one other time in her life reached up and grabbed her by the throat.

"I-I don't understand," she said, looking around frantically, expecting the real Simon Locke to come out of the shadows and tell her it was all just a joke. "Where is he? You can't be him. I'd have known. Wouldn't I?"

"Don't be hard on yourself," he told her. "You'd only have known if I'd wanted you to know. But if it's any consolation . . . I love you too."

She shook her head once in denial, her brain slow to process what she was actually seeing. She'd heard people talk about time standing still, but she'd never experienced it. Her body and mind weren't functioning; she was beyond emotion. Beyond tears or demanding reasons why. There was nothing left in her but the emptiness of betrayal.

He dropped the mask, and the wind blew it off

the turret, spinning it once, twice in the air before it plunged toward the rocks and sea below. His hair whipped in the breeze and his gaze never left hers as he took another step toward the edge.

She shook her head again, realizing what he was doing, and she opened her mouth to scream but nothing came out.

"It's best for everyone that it ends this way," he said. "You've been the best part of my life. And you're the only thing I've ever loved more than my life as Simon Locke. But I can't have both. So I'll have neither."

Her lungs burned and she stared in horror as he spread his arms out and fell backward, right over the edge.

"Dante!" she screamed.

She ran toward the edge, falling to her knees, and tears clouded her vision. She hadn't realized the turret had been built on the very edge of the cliff, as if it had been carved from the cliff itself.

There was nothing but endless blackness, and the sound of the waves crashing against the rocks below. For the second time in her life she knew what it felt like to lose part of herself. And she vowed it would never happen again.

CHAPTER FOUR

Present Day

Dante felt the woman next to him stretch languidly, her white-blond hair glowing in the last vestiges of candlelight. He'd found out the night before that her blond had come from a bottle, but for a little while . . . for a little while he'd been able to imagine another woman's face, another woman's body pressed beneath his.

He stared at the ceiling and stayed as still as possible in the hope that she'd think he was sleeping. The bedroom was large, sleek, and modern, and the bed sat as big as a lake on a raised platform with gunmetal satin sheets. The art on the walls was big and bold, slashes of bright color from early-twentieth-century artists. The sitting area had a chaise and two chairs upholstered in a soft, shimmering gray just a few shades lighter than the bedsheets. Two of the walls were floor-to-ceiling windows so he could look out over the Dallas skyline.

Normally he enjoyed the room, but it was becoming rather claustrophobic with her pressed against his chest. She'd more than outstayed her welcome. The woman walked her fingers up his chest, and he bit back a sigh, still feigning sleep.

He had to figure out how to get her out of his condo and on her way back to wherever she'd come from. He should've known better. He *did* know better. But when he'd walked into the upscale martini bar downtown, he'd immediately been drawn to her. Her back had been to him, but there were so few women whose hair was that particular shade of blond.

His heart had knocked once in his chest, and he'd almost turned around and walked back out to his Porsche, but he'd found himself approaching her instead. Wondering if it could really be her. Hoping it was. Praying it wasn't.

He'd known the second he stood behind her that it wasn't Liv. The woman's perfume was cheap, her facial features not as refined. But instead of turning away, he'd taken the bar stool next to her and offered to buy her a drink. And as they talked, he could almost hear the lilting British accent, and it got easier to pretend her eyes were blue instead of dark brown.

The woman's wandering fingers crept beneath

the sheets and wrapped around him, and he bit off a curse as his body responded immediately. Fully awake now, he grabbed her hand and pulled it away.

"You've got to give me some time, darling," he told her, kissing the back of her hand gently. "I've got work early in the morning, so you should head home before it gets too late. I'll call you tomorrow evening and we can have a nice dinner." *A good-bye dinner,* he thought. He kissed her forehead for added emphasis when he felt her stiffen at the rejection.

She leaned up and pouted down at him, her soft breasts pressing against his chest. "It doesn't *feel* like you need time," she said, slithering out of his grasp and hitching her leg across his hip. "What kind of work has you up so early on a Saturday?"

He could feel her wet and ready for him, and his hands went to her hips to move her off him. Damn his traitorous body. But then he felt something in the room that was more effective than any cold shower. He never heard her—she was too good for that. But he felt her presence. It was reminiscent of the day she'd recruited him at the Marquis de Carmaux's party almost two years ago. He hadn't known her name then. Sometimes he wished he still didn't. But her appearance was just as effective.

"Sorry for interrupting playtime," Eve Winter said, lounging against the bedroom door. "But you're going to need to leave now." Eve stared right at the woman, who was frozen with shock.

"Who the hell are you?" the woman asked.

"I'm his girlfriend," Eve said, deadpan.

The idea was so comical he almost laughed. He didn't see her often, but she never changed. She was to The Gravediggers what M was to James Bond. She called the shots, and although she technically answered to The Directors, Dante had always felt they were too afraid of her to deny her too often. Eve could be . . . persuasive.

She always wore black—this time a slim skirt that ended just above her knees and a form-fitting turtleneck. Her hair was pulled back tightly from her face and hung down her back in a long ponytail. She wore her signature red lipstick and a pair of black stilettos that looked like they could be weapons. Knowing her, they probably were.

"Maybe you didn't hear me," Eve said. "You've got five seconds to get out of bed and into the elevator, or I'm going to throw you off the balcony. Then everyone will know you're not a real blonde."

There must have been something in Eve's expression that made a believer out of the woman, because before Dante knew it, she'd scrambled out of bed, gathered most of her clothes, and was sprinting through the condo to his elevator, not bothering to get dressed first. He heard the ding as the doors slid closed, and then there was nothing but silence.

"Well," he said. "I'm sure I'll be receiving an interesting letter from the condo association. I'm almost positive it's against the rules to run through the building naked."

Eve shrugged. "She's gone, isn't she? I believe that's what you wanted."

"And how the bloody hell would you know that?" he asked, rolling out of bed and heading into the bathroom so he could get dressed.

The black bathroom floor tiles were broken up by smaller bronze tiles, and the pattern continued into the large walk-in shower and around the sunken jetted tub. For a touch of irony, the Degas of the bathing nude that Dante had stolen the night he died was displayed over the tub.

He hadn't expected Eve to give him privacy, and she proved him right by following him. With any other woman, he would've preserved some modesty and shown basic manners. With Eve, he knew the effort would be wasted.

"Doesn't it get old?" she asked. "Fucking these bleached-blond wannabes and knowing they'll never measure up?"

He shot her a seething look before spitting toothpaste into the sink and rinsing his mouth.

"You're all heart, Eve," he said. "Do you have any feelings at all, or are you a robot?"

"What place do feelings have in our lives?" she asked, arching a perfect brow. "You've been in the game a long time. Do you think we can do the things we do and see the things we see, and go home with a conscience at night?"

"And yet, Elias and Deacon are curled up beside their women tonight," he said, not bothering to hide the bitterness. He turned on the shower and decided he needed a few minutes alone—at least long enough to get rid of the scent of stale sex. Eve had obviously come for a purpose. She never showed up in person without one.

He walked straight into the blistering hot shower.

"The others aren't like us," she said. "There's still part of them that believes good conquers evil. And that love triumphs over everything."

"And what do we believe?" he asked, using a little more force than necessary to scrub his body.

"We're realists," she said. "We understand that good rarely wins for the sake of good. Even those who believe they're good win because they're a little bit evil. We believe that there's darkness in everyone. And we believe that you do what you can to prevent global catastrophes on a daily basis, until you can't anymore. And then you walk away."

"Bollocks," he said. "You don't believe that any more than I do. You can't bullshit a bullshitter, Eve. I understand you better than the others, which is, I'm sure, why you grace me with these impromptu visits. But you and I are selfish creatures by nature. We want control. We want the power over our own destinies. You get that by playing a game of chess with human lives. I get it by outsmarting man and machine and taking people's most treasured possessions right out from under their noses, and helping those who are often overlooked." He rolled his eyes and rinsed his hair. "Or at least, I used to. Now I steal for the 'good of mankind.'"

"You sound so thrilled about it," she said.

"Sometimes I wonder how much good we're doing, whether we're just putting out fires the government manufactured. No one wants to be a puppet."

"I'm no one's puppet," she said. "At least you still get to enjoy the occasional heist. I could've stopped you completely."

"If you had, I would've jumped off that turret and let you fish my dead body out of the Mediterranean. It was the only reason I agreed to your proposition."

That had been the deal: that Dante Malcolm would die and be reborn as a Gravedigger—one of a group of elite agents with special skills whose sole mission was to fight global terrorism, at a level the military or other agencies weren't capable of maintaining. They had no fixed budget and no chain of command other than Eve. They were autonomous and could take whatever steps were needed to get the job done. They had endless resources and technology and weapons that were much more advanced than those the military or its contractors had access to. They were a small unit—only five—but they did the job of entire platoons. It came down to training and skill. They were the best of the best. And Eve had hunted down each of them individually, just like she had him, and recruited them for the job.

They were all dead men walking. He even had a death certificate. And his significant holdings had been passed to his closest surviving relative, who happened to be his mother, though she'd become a recluse since his death, refusing to show her face in society since her only son had been outed as Simon Locke, the international art thief.

Eve had known everything about him. She knew his secrets as an MI6 agent, and she knew his secrets as Simon Locke. She'd even known the real Simon Locke who'd passed him the torch and how he was enjoying retirement in Antigua with his new wife.

There was nothing that could be kept from her. But she'd promised to keep his secrets if he agreed to work for her. She'd told him he'd only get one chance to make a choice. Otherwise, he'd have to take his chances, knowing there was someone out there who knew everything about him and could reveal it all at a moment's notice.

His biggest fear was being locked in a cage for the rest of his life. So he'd said yes, and listened to her plan to end his life. She'd given him the suit that had the technology for him to fly without a parachute. He'd been terrified Liv would feel it while he was making love with her, but he'd made sure to keep her hands contained so she couldn't touch him.

It had been simple. Just as Eve had promised. What she hadn't explained in great detail was what would happen after he reached the bottom of the cliff. He hadn't known that his body would have to be found and that he'd be officially pronounced dead. She hadn't told him about the serum—that debilitating injection that felt like hot lead running through his veins until it slowed his heartbeat to almost nonexistent. She hadn't told him that he'd be put in a coffin and shipped across the ocean to another country, with the identity of an American who'd been unfortunate enough to die overseas, or that he'd be buried six feet under until the others like him dug him from the ground. She didn't tell him that the mind would wake first, long before the body did, and he'd be trapped, screaming in his head until his body started to function again. Screaming in his head while it felt like thousands of hot needles were being pushed through his skin.

If that's what death was like, he preferred never to do it again. He couldn't imagine that hell would be as bad. But he was a Gravedigger, and he'd learned what it meant to rely on others as if his life depended on them—because it did. He'd gained a brotherhood he'd never experienced before. Working intelligence with MI6 and thieving were solitary jobs. But what he had with The Gravediggers was different.

What they did was important. And he'd found out very quickly that although Eve was in charge of them, she wasn't one of them, which made keeping secrets from them all the more difficult. They were his brothers, and he'd lied to them every day so he could live a double life and continue to use the talents that fed his soul.

And day after day, his conscience ate away at him, so it was sometimes difficult to face them without the guilt strangling him like vines choking the life out of a tree. There was a reason he kept himself separated, living away from the compound.

He turned off the water and grabbed a towel from the heated bar, drying off quickly and wrapping it around his waist before he exited the shower.

"I did you a favor," Eve said. "I know you inside and out, Lord Malcolm. You'd have continued for a while, getting everything you wanted. But eventually you'd have become bored. You like that added element of danger, the potential of getting caught. It's what feeds your desire to keep going back for more.

"It wouldn't have been long before you told Liv the truth. Part of you wanted to tell her. You even toyed with the idea of prolonging the double life, settling down with a white picket fence and slipping out the back window in the dead of night. But how long would it have taken until things started to crumble? Until Liv found out and had the pleasure of arresting her husband? Or did you think you could persuade her to come over to your side?" she asked, brow arched.

He knew she was right, and it made him all the more furious. "Don't try to play me, Eve," he said. "You don't know me. I've spent my career manipulating everyone I've ever met, even if there was no need for it. First, because intelligence work required it. And second, because Simon Locke required it. You can spin this tale of how miserable I'd be if I'd chosen another way of life, but the truth is you recruited me because you need me. No one else can do the things I do for you. I know that. And you know that. I also know how valuable I am to this organization, so maybe you could save the brainwashing and tell me why you're here."

She stared at him with cold black eyes, and he wondered if he'd overplayed his hand. When he'd said she played chess with human life, he'd meant it, and she wouldn't hesitate to take any of them out—handpicked or not—if she felt they no longer served a purpose.

"There are things worse than death." Her face was smooth, expressionless, and he felt the cold chill of fear course through his body. "You should pray you never find out what they are."

His life had always been simple. Everything had always come easily to him—work and women—which was why he'd loved the challenge burglary presented. It was something he had to work at. Perhaps that's why he had loved Liv so much—the longer their relationship had lasted, the more effort he'd had to put into it. But instead, he'd chosen the easy way out.

"Put some clothes on—we've got work to do." She turned to walk out, and then stopped and looked back at him. And then at the Degas hanging over his bathtub. Her mouth quirked in a smile. "Nice painting."

Lucifer couldn't hold a candle to Eve Winter. He could almost smell the sulfur as she walked away.

CHAPTER FIVE

Dante didn't hurry.

Varying his routine for Eve would only give her an entitled sense of power. She had too much of that as it was. He dressed as he normally would have—black jeans and a charcoal shirt he left untucked, the sleeves rolled up and the top two buttons undone. He left his feet bare and his hair damp.

The living area of the condo was dark. She'd used the remote to lower the blackout shades and made herself comfortable in one of the sleek gray armchairs, her legs crossed and her attention focused on her phone. His mouth twitched. She was letting him know that she wasn't in a hurry either.

The living room was similar in style to his bedroom—sleek, modern, and expensive. The artwork was all original—he never would've tolerated a fake. The wall between the living area and kitchen was a floor-to-ceiling saltwater fish tank that cast the room in an eerie undulating blue. He didn't spend a lot of time here because of his work with The Gravediggers, but when he was home he wanted to be completely comfortable.

He liked fine things, and he never made any apologies for it, although the guys liked to give him a hard time. They knew only part of his background— that he'd grown up privileged and that he'd joined MI6 more out of boredom than a sense of duty to his country, though he'd found he had a rather strong loyalty to his country after all.

But the others didn't know the *real* Dante. They didn't know the full scope of his talents. They didn't comprehend his burning desire to see something extraordinary and know that it could be his. Between MI6 and his life as Simon Locke, he'd managed to defeat the boredom and find a semblance of purpose in his life.

Dante noticed that Eve had made herself at home, and a bottle of water sat on a coaster on the glass end table. He'd never seen her drink anything else, but it wasn't as if their visits were frequent, although she probably spent more time with him than with anyone. But only because he was useful to her. He didn't fool himself into thinking it was for any other reason.

When it came down to it, he didn't know a thing about Eve Winter. And he'd looked. On more than one occasion. She'd recruited him to be a Gravedigger for his skill at getting into and out of secure places and taking what wasn't his, though it was no longer art that he stole, but sensitive information.

The secrets that were most important to keep were never put in a database—technology was too easy to breach. But he'd been in the bowels of the Pentagon and the CIA, in the archives of his own country and many others. And never had he seen a file for her. Of course, that didn't mean she didn't exist. Simon Locke no longer had any files either. Even the hard copy files Liv had kept locked in the safe in her apartment were gone.

But Eve—and he doubted that was her real name—had seemingly come out of nowhere. Her accent was indiscernible, her speech patterns indefinable. He didn't know where she called home. If she had a family. She was an enigma. And like a piece of art that was seemingly unobtainable, she fascinated him.

"I'm assuming you're not here for a social call," he said, taking a bottle of wine from the fridge below the bar and getting a corkscrew out of the drawer. He was in the mood for a crisp white, and he had an Australian blend that would satisfy.

She looked up and arched a brow. "I didn't realize you were in need of friends. I'll itemize the request and put it under 'miscellaneous' in the report I send to The Directors."

"If the others only knew what a smart-ass you are," he said, shaking his head. "They're really missing out on these great bonding moments. Maybe you should come clean."

"Maybe you should," she countered. "I'm sure they'd be fascinated to know about Simon Locke."

"Who?" he asked, smiling. "The name doesn't ring a bell. And if I recall, there are no records he ever existed. Not even a Google search will pull up an article."

Her mouth quirked at the corner, but there was no humor in her smile. "I'm sure a file exists somewhere," she said.

"I'd be disappointed if it didn't."

He wasn't a fool. He'd known the moment she recruited him that she knew everything about him, down to the darkest detail. He had to admire her for it. No one else had ever been able to put all the pieces together. He still didn't know how she'd done it. He'd thought back and checked his work, his alibis. He'd been careful. There was no hint of Dante Malcolm and Simon Locke being one and the same. But still, she'd known.

"Maybe if we're done bonding we can get to work," she said, uncrossing her legs and coming to her feet.

He pushed a button on the underside of the bar. There was a slight whir as the large abstract painting behind the couch was pulled back into the wall and replaced with a screen, while the coffee table rose to waist level, the tabletop flipping over so the underside was exposed. It was opaque white and lit up as it slid fully into place.

A panel appeared atop the bar's smooth surface and he placed his hand on it, waiting for it to turn green and activate the system.

"Good evening, Lord Malcolm," the computer said.

"Hello, Elaine," he said. "Lovely to hear your voice as always. Please allow access to Eve Winter as well."

Elaine was the perfect union of technology and robotics. There was nothing anywhere in the world like her. She had an incomprehensible knowledge of all things. She was free to think on her own and had developed her own personality, much to the amusement of them all. She was the glue of The Gravediggers, and could be found wherever the mission called them.

"Of course," Elaine agreed. "Good evening, Miss Winter." Elaine's voice went cold as she spoke to

Eve, and Dante couldn't help but grin. Eve tended to rub everyone the wrong way.

"Scan for any breaches in security or listening devices," Eve ordered.

They waited a full minute before Elaine responded, "All clear."

"I'm overriding authority by voice command," Eve said. "No portion of this conversation will be recorded. Send systems check once completed."

"Authorizing voice command," Elaine said. "Approved. Conversation will remain in clandestine mode until otherwise ordered."

"What do you know about Shiv Mittal?" Eve asked him.

Elaine was programmed to follow conversations, and a picture of Mittal appeared on the screen along with pertinent information.

Dante checked his wineglass for spots, then poured a small amount into it, swirling the wine for a few seconds before taking a sip. Deciding it was just what he needed, he poured more.

"Not much," he said. "He's a billionaire playboy and tech wizard. And he holds the title of sultan, though Najd no longer recognizes itself as a sultanate and has been absorbed into Saudi Arabia. He's made his home in Dubai, I believe, though his family is still in possession of the sultan's palace and other properties. His ties and loyalties are unknown, as he tends to stay out of politics. He's young for someone of his position and power, maybe forty at the most. He's well educated, holding multiple degrees, but his father is the real bastard. He's been linked to murders, terror attacks, and human trafficking."

"That is correct," Elaine said, pulling up a picture of the father. "He has more than a hundred wives, and he buys them as young as age thirteen. Shiv is the only son of his first wife. It is unclear whether the son has continued the father's practices."

"We wouldn't be here if the son wasn't as corrupt as the father," Dante said.

"What if I told you he has nuclear launch codes?" Eve asked.

"I'd ask what the bloody hell he's going to do with them without a weapon or a remote detonator," Dante said. "I'd have heard if the Saudis or UAE had recently acquired either. How did he get the codes?"

"Won them in a poker game," she said.

He put down his wineglass and stared at her. "You're fucking kidding me."

"My bullshit hour is over, so no, I'm not kidding."

"Whose codes are they?" he asked.

"Russia's," she said. "They can't keep a lid on anything these days. They've got so many leaks they might as well put everything on a Wikipedia page and save everyone some time."

"You're full of jokes today," he said. "The situation must be dire if you've resorted to humor."

"Look, two nights ago, Mittal held an intimate dinner party for two hundred on his yacht. He, the Russian ambassador to Syria, al-Baghdadi—the head of ISIS—and two other unknowns held an impromptu poker game. The intelligence community collects data on players like Mittal, especially when they show no particular allegiance to anyone but themselves. So far he's kept his nose clean. But now he's a threat. You can imagine the intelligence community's response when they found out who was sitting in on that poker game. Every agency in the world is creaming their pants at the opportunity to keep a bead on al-Baghdadi."

"I'd think they'd be more interested in how it slipped past their notice that one of them was walking around with nuclear launch codes to begin with."

"It's being dealt with," she said. "Clearly there's a weak link somewhere when it comes to international security. What we know at this point is that North Korea was able to steal the launch codes and certain weapon components from Russia. As fucked-up as North Korea is at the moment, it was more of a power-play move than for a strategic purpose. They already have nuclear weapons. What they needed was cash. And Russia is flush with cash at the moment, so North Korea sold the codes back to Russia. And the ambassador was lucky enough to be the one to make the exchange."

"I'm sure he's sorry he was volunteered for the job," Dante said.

"I'd say so. His mistake cost him his life. He was found in a cemetery, his grave already dug. He'd been tortured and dismembered. Slowly. Now every unsavory country on the planet has their eye on Shiv Mittal. For a genius, he sure is stupid. Sometimes I wonder why we even bother."

"Because the innocent need to be protected," he said. "A man like Mittal isn't equipped to deal with the fallout of owning nuclear launch codes. He's basically a rich nerd. Anyone who wants them is going to be gunning for him. They'll eat him alive. I can't imagine why the ambassador would put them up for ante in the first place."

"He thought he had a sure win. They both must have had a hell of a hand. Mittal bet his oil reserves, which is more than a billion-dollar pot. The codes were the only thing the ambassador could offer to stay in the game."

Dante was speechless. He brought his wine into

the living room and took a seat, reading the information that was scrolling on the screen.

"Did I mention North Korea also managed to steal the remote detonator?" she asked. "It's still in their possession. They're waiting for Russia to come up with more cash before they return it, but now that the launch codes are no longer in Russia's possession, North Korea has decided to open up bidding for the detonator."

"Christ," he said. If the detonator and those codes were put together, the nuclear weapon could be launched from anywhere in the world. Russia would have no control over it without finding someone who could manually deconstruct the weapon. A task not as easy as one would think, as only a handful of people in the world were qualified to know how to construct and deconstruct all the components of a nuclear weapon.

"It's a clusterfuck," she agreed. "We believe Mittal is going to open up bidding for the codes. From what we gather, Mittal is not a terrorist or a criminal. His plan is to force Russia to buy back the codes for an exorbitant amount of money. We believe he knows the danger he's put himself in. He's boosted his security. He and al-Baghdadi have been nothing more than acquaintances up to this point. Now they're enemies. The UN has appealed to him to turn the codes over to them for safekeeping, but he knows that could be just as dangerous. The UN is scheduled to meet tomorrow morning, but the meetings I've had today show a disinterest in waiting for the UN to come to an agreement on anything in the next twenty years. I'm uninterested as well. It's time to take matters into our own hands before this blows up in everyone's face."

"I'm going to assume what you have in mind isn't a Gravedigger mission," he said, finishing off the wine and setting the glass on the side table. "Otherwise you'd be addressing all of us instead of interrupting my Saturday night."

"Surveillance hasn't been able to breach Mittal's palace in Dubai. We've got someone integrated with the household and we've got aerial shots, but no sound or recording devices. Special guests are brought in armored, tinted vehicles and driven underground to enter the palace. He has a secured vault that can only be reached through his office. The place is a fortress."

"Which is where I come in, I presume." He thought about it for a moment, running the probabilities through his mind. He was definitely tempted. And more than intrigued. "What's my compensation?"

Her expression didn't change, and he knew she'd

been expecting the question. For a job of this magnitude, he needed something more than just the thrill.

"It's my understanding that Mittal is in possession of a J. M. W. Turner painting. I believe he's one of your personal favorites, yes? The last Turner brought more than thirty million pounds at auction. This one is worth quite a bit more, but it can never go on the auction block."

He read between the lines easily and his brow arched in surprise. "It's the one that was stolen from the Hermitage a dozen years ago?"

"I don't suppose you know anything about that?" she asked.

"I don't suppose I do," he said. That was one of the last jobs he and Simon had worked together. Dante had never agreed with stealing from museums, but even he had to admit there wasn't another rush quite like it. This job would come close.

"How much time do we have?"

"You need to leave in twenty-four hours," she said. "You'll have a week to prepare."

"If you're only giving me a week, there had best be something at the end of this besides a Turner. Cash always works."

He'd normally need a month for a job like this. He needed time to observe the staff and anyone else who came in and out of the palace on a regular basis. He wanted to watch security and see if there were any weaknesses. And he needed space to run simulations.

"Half the amount of the painting's worth has already been deposited in your account. The other half will be deposited when you return with the codes. Don't let them out of your hands. If you're captured, destroy them."

"Elaine," he said, "please gather all information on Shiv Mittal's palace in Dubai. I want blueprints and any additional changes he's made. I want aerial and ground-penetrating radar. I need a penthouse suite where I can see the grounds through a long-range scope. Arrange transportation for tomorrow. I need to get a feel for the area. I'll have a list of equipment I need in the next two hours."

"I'm looking forward to it," Elaine said flirtatiously. "I've anticipated your needs, and I've found we own a property in Dubai that will meet your criteria. It has a private, secured elevator, and I'm built into the server, so you won't have to use portable me. You'll be able to use me to my full potential."

Dante couldn't help but grin. "Elaine, my love, that's the best news I've heard all day." He checked his watch and looked at Eve. "I'm not due for vacation anytime soon. The others aren't going to be happy if I request it. And I believe the last time you sent me off solo, I had to call in with the flu. Which was quite embarrassing, by the way. I've never been sick a day in my life."

"There are other ways to get rid of you for a while," she said. "Agent Malcolm, you've officially been suspended for insubordination until further notice."

"Lovely," he said, and meant it.

CHAPTER SIX

The pavement went from smooth to potholed in a matter of seconds. Dante took his foot off the gas of his Porsche Carrera as he entered Last Stop the next morning—the sleepy town that housed Gravedigger headquarters—knowing there was a speed trap a couple of miles down the road. The best thing he could say about Last Stop was that it was quaint. After that, he ran out of compliments.

It was a long stretch that led to the town center, and on either side there were wide fields marked by wire fences and lazy cattle trying to find shade under a few scrawny trees.

He turned the air conditioner on high, hoping it would overpower the smell of manure, and debated whether it was worth the speeding ticket just to get past it all and be able to breathe again. It was going to be a hellaciously hot day—he still hadn't gotten used to Texas summers—but he was about to go out of the frying pan and into the fryer. He'd heard that saying once during a viewing at the funeral home, and immediately liked it.

The current temperature in Dubai was into the triple digits, which was one reason he would be arriving in the middle of the night. The other reason was so that he could get settled in without curious observers wondering who he was.

There was a billboard up ahead that sat low to the ground, advertising the fresh sausage, deer jerky, and farm-raised beef offered at the town's meat market. A deputy's cruiser sat just in front of the billboard, and Dante pressed down a little harder on the accelerator, noting that the deputy had his hat low over his eyes and his boots propped on the dashboard.

The scenery didn't get much better as he approached downtown—and he used the term *downtown* loosely. The streets turned to brown cobblestone, and there were still hitching posts along the sidewalks in front of the brown brick buildings. A Gothic courthouse loomed above the square at one end of Main Street, complete with dark gray menacing stone and turrets and gargoyles.

At the other end of Main Street, on another square, was the Last Stop Funeral Home. It was a big white elephant of a Queen Anne Victorian with two floors of wraparound porches, a portico to the side where the Suburban parked to transport bodies in and out, and a carriage house at the back that had been remodeled and expanded before Dante had been recruited.

To say that living in small town USA had been a culture shock would've been an understatement. In his former life, Dante had never shopped for groceries, made small talk at a gas station, or been asked twenty questions about his family by a complete stranger while he was trying to eat dinner. That wasn't done in British society—though gossip, it seemed, transcended all cultures and countries.

There were no social boundaries in Last Stop. At least, none that he'd observed. The citizens there were just as curious today about the five men who worked at the funeral home as they were when Dante and his companions had first appeared a couple of years before.

He'd gotten used to the accent—for the most part—but he'd never adjusted to small-town living. When he'd first been reborn as a Gravedigger, he'd lived in one of the suites in the carriage house. That had lasted a matter of weeks before he'd found a high-rise condo in the city that met his needs. The most pressing ones being that he needed civilization from time to time, and his secret was much easier to keep with distance between them.

He took a side street to avoid Saturday morning traffic and wound his way around to the funeral home. The black Suburban was there, along with a black Hummer, a black truck, and a black Harley. He'd hoped to avoid running into everyone, but it didn't look like luck was on his side for that one.

He stepped out of the Porsche and pocketed the keys, adjusting the cuffs of his dark blue dress shirt, then made his way through the English garden that had been planted between the funeral home and the carriage house.

Through the floor-to-ceiling kitchen windows that overlooked the garden, he saw Deacon and Elias inside, along with their wives. He didn't see Levi, the newest member of the Gravediggers, but that was expected since it was Shabbat and Levi was most likely at the synagogue.

Also absent from the domestic scene was Axel, who tended to take advantage of the opportunity to sleep late on Saturday mornings.

Dante didn't bother knocking—they'd already seen him walk up—and as soon as he opened the kitchen door he smelled bacon. He had to hand it to the Americans: he enjoyed their food immensely.

Deacon was their team leader—he'd been the

first of them, more of a government experiment as the powers-that-be piloted the program—and all reporting was done directly to him. He was going to be pissed as hell to be blindsided that he was about to be a man down, and Dante almost wished he could watch the confrontation between him and Eve.

"Look at you," Miller Darling said, arching a brow. "She must have been terrible for you to be up and out this early."

Miller was a new permanent addition to their growing group. She and Elias were engaged, but still couldn't figure out how and where they wanted to get married.

"He does look a bit tense," Tess said, nibbling on a piece of fruit from the platter on the table.

Tess was Deacon's wife of almost a year, and she and Miller had been best friends since childhood. It was rare that the two went more than a couple of days without seeing each other. Tess was just pregnant enough for her belly to show beneath the oversize button-down shirt she wore. Her red hair was piled on top of her head in a bun that managed to look neat and messy at the same time. Deacon stood at the stove, wearing an old gray T-shirt, jeans, and a half apron as he tended the bacon with expert precision.

Everyone knew it was best for Tess to stay out of the kitchen. She could burn water if she put her mind to it, so Deacon had taken over those duties when they'd married. Dante noticed he couldn't quite hide his smile as the two women gave him hell.

"I don't know what you think I do on the weekends," Dante said to Miller, "but I doubt it's nearly as exciting as you imagine in that fascinating brain of yours."

Miller was a romance novelist, and she had a tendency to make even the simplest thing complicated by expounding on the situation in her mind. Her short hair had been platinum blond a couple of months ago, but it was back to the black she usually favored. She was dressed in running shorts, a sports bra, and a tank top, and Elias was also in athletic gear, so Dante assumed they'd stopped by the funeral home after their morning run.

Elias had moved from his tiny apartment to Miller's creepy house about three blocks from the funeral home. The house had been beautifully restored, but it looked like a cross between *Tales from the Crypt* and *The Addams Family*—two shows he'd been introduced to on late-night television since he'd become a Gravedigger. Insomnia was often a pain in the ass, even more so when he was missing out on so many opportunities in the darkest times of the night.

Miller wagged her brows and said, "I bet it *is* that exciting. You're like James Bond with the accent and all. I keep imagining women with names like Honey Ryder and Pussy Galore swimming naked in that weird fish tank you have. If this was a couple of centuries ago, they'd have called you a cad and a rake, deflowering virgins wherever you go and gambling with your inheritance. I bet you're an excellent dancer."

"I never deflower virgins," he said, measuring tea leaves and then pouring hot water over them. "There's nothing fun about that. And I am an excellent dancer. I'm happy to instruct the Bigfoot you're marrying so he knows how to lead during the wedding dance."

"Hold on a second," Elias said, leaning back on only two legs of his chair. "I can dance."

"Ehh," Miller said, tilting her head apologetically. "Don't get me wrong. You can do the Sprinkler and Shop for Groceries with the best of them, but I think he means real dances. Like the waltz and all that other old-people stuff."

"Etiquette has nothing to do with being old, and everything to do with being well brought up," Dante said. "And what in God's name do shopping for groceries and sprinklers have to do with any-thing?"

"Did you know you resort to snobbishness whenever you get irritated?" Miller asked. "It's an interesting personality trait. You'd make a great hero in one of my books—or at least parts of you. I'd leave out the snobbish womanizing parts."

Elias snorted out a laugh and his chair dropped back to the floor.

"That's a fascinating analysis," Dante said. "I'm just being polite. You should try it."

Her laughter caught him by surprise. "See? Snobbish," she said in a British accent. "What you need is a woman."

"I've just had one, thank you," he said, wishing he'd sent Deacon a text message instead of coming to speak to him in person.

"TMI," Miller said. "How come we've never met any of your lady friends?"

"And subject myself to this torture?" he asked her, smiling. "I'd rather go through testing again."

Once a Gravedigger was brought back to life, there was a period of confinement and psycholog-ical testing. The serum that was administered to slow the heart during the death phase of becom-ing a Gravedigger was nothing compared to the serum administered during the three days of testing. It was one thing to feel your body die. It was another to feel your mind being broken, to feel yourself go crazy and wonder if you'd ever really been sane.

If a Gravedigger passed testing, it actually increased the usage of his brain. Before and after MRIs couldn't be disputed. The only downside was that there was a possibility of not passing—meaning the mind would be broken forever and real death couldn't come soon enough.

"Ouch," Elias said. "Harsh."

"We're not insulted," Tess said. She rubbed the small mound of her belly and looked at her husband. "I don't mean to change the subject, but if you don't bring that bacon and pancakes over here soon, things are going to get ugly. The baby wants bacon."

"Right," Deacon said, bringing platters to the table so everyone could serve themselves. "Apparently this baby is a carnivore. He wanted a rib-eye at three a.m. a couple of nights ago." Deacon took the seat next to his wife.

"You know, Tess," Miller said, heaping a couple of pancakes onto her own plate and dousing them with syrup, "what if you introduced Dante to your yoga instructor? Didn't you say she recently went through a divorce?"

"Yes, but what I didn't tell you is she also draws

social security. Though I wouldn't have put her a day past forty-five. She looks amazing."

"I don't know why y'all are wasting your time," Elias said, shaking his head. "Y'all are supposed to be the intuitive ones. Can't you see he's still got it bad for someone from his past?"

"Oh," Miller said, her fork stopping halfway to her mouth. She looked at Dante as if she was trying to dissect him. A lesser man would've squirmed under the scrutiny, but he just stared back at her, his expression blank. And then she said again, "Ohhhh."

"No," Dante said. "Don't do it."

"Too late," Elias said with a sigh.

"I bet she was a childhood sweetheart," Miller said. "Wait, I've got a better one. Maybe she was the daughter of one of your servants, and your love had to be secret because of stupid society rules. You couldn't offer her marriage, so she ran off and married some baker, but she's not really in love with him."

He was amused despite himself. "You're a very odd woman."

"Thank you," Miller said.

"She always thinks that's a compliment," Elias said. "I keep trying to tell her it's not, but she doesn't listen."

"You also keep trying to tell me that you want Elvis to marry us," she said, rolling her eyes. "I've been having nightmares about white sequined jumpsuits."

"You haven't come up with anything better," he said. "I just want to get married. It shouldn't be this hard."

"It should be memorable," Miller insisted. "We're starting our very own story."

"We started our story the second you slid down that muddy waterfall in the Galápagos and then kneed me in the balls the next morning. I'm just hoping that isn't setting a precedent for the rest of our marriage."

Everyone laughed. Dante hated to break up the jovial mood, but he had a tight schedule to keep.

"I've been suspended," he said, scooping up a bite of eggs. Silence reigned around him.

"*What?*" Deacon demanded. "On what grounds? And why wasn't I notified?"

"Insubordination," he said. "Apparently Eve doesn't care for my attitude."

Elias snorted. "That makes zero sense. If she's put up with my attitude all this time, she should be able to put up with yours. You've always been the most diplomatic of all of us."

"Maybe it was a cumulative effect," he said, shrugging. "She told me last night. I'm sure she'll be in touch with you today."

"I'm sure she will," Deacon said, his jaw tight. "I believe I'll be calling her first, though. She knows this is a critical time. We're still tracing and identifying the terrorists in that airport bombing in Baltimore. We need every man we have, and I wish we had a couple more, but she's refused my request twice now to bring in two more agents."

The kitchen door opened and Axel came through, his broad shoulders taking up the entire space. He'd pulled his long, dark-blond hair into a messy bun on top of his head. His face was unshaved, and he only wore athletic shorts and a white undershirt. They all had pasts and losses from their former lives, but Axel had lost the most. He'd had a wife when Eve recruited him, and she'd been four months pregnant with their daughter. When she heard the news of Axel's death, her grief had been so strong that she'd miscarried the baby.

They weren't supposed to have anything to do with their former lives once they were reborn as Gravediggers, but Axel had kept tabs on his wife from the day he'd been released from testing. He wanted to make sure she was safe and taken care of. Dante personally thought the connection between Axel and his wife would give nothing but pain and guilt until his contract expired. Even then, there was nothing he could do about it. None of them would ever be free—really free—from their chains as Gravediggers.

Axel raised his brows and looked at each of them around the table. "I can only assume that someone died or that Eve made an appearance and I missed it." Then he looked at Dante and said, "Damn, mate, you must have shoved her out the door on your way here. You don't usually give up your Saturday brunch seduction unless we have a mission."

"Bollocks," Dante said, pushing his chair back and taking his empty plate to the sink. "The idea of a brunch seduction is bloody ludicrous. If she's there for brunch, she's already been seduced. And we work too bloody much for me to make it a habit of luring women back to my condo on a regular basis. And if I did, it'd be none of your bloody business."

"Ooh," Miller said. "You just used *bloody* a lot. It's such a polite way of being angry. I wish we had something like that in America."

"If we could get back on track," Deacon said, "the issue is that we need Dante right now. And Eve knows it. I don't know what the hell she's thinking in suspending him, but I need her to change her mind."

"Good luck with that," Dante said.

"You got suspended?" Axel asked him. "How is that even possible?"

"Ask Eve," he said. "I'm taking a flight out this morning. I've got some personal things to deal with back home and haven't had the time."

Deacon raised his brows. "Don't let anyone see you. Eve always finds out. And if she's already angry, you don't want to make things worse. I'll give her a call and see if I can smooth things out before you go."

Dante nodded, but his mind was already in Dubai. It had been far too long since Simon Locke made an appearance.

CHAPTER SEVEN

London

The summer sun baked through the windshield of Liv's black Mercedes, and despite the air-conditioning turned up full-blast, her bare shoulders stuck to the leather seat. They'd been surveilling the multimillion-dollar town house, located on one of the oldest, most expensive streets in London. It sat right in the middle of the block, tall and imposing, each side connecting to the town house next to it. There was a front courtyard with a black iron gate and steps that led up to the bright red front door. And the sidewalk in front of the house was wide for pedestrians.

They'd been there for the last week, doing facial recognition and background checks on anyone who'd come and gone from the home of Dr. Harold

Bixler, a man she'd been trying to pin down for the last six months for brokering stolen Russian girls into the sex trade.

"How come I never get to be the hot blonde?" Tom Donner asked from the passenger seat. "And how come you're driving a Mercedes? You know what I drive at home? A beat-to-shit Explorer. I dropped a burrito in between my seat and the arm-rest and I've never been able to get it out. It smells like a Taco Bell in there all the time."

Liv hummed along to the country-and-western CD Donner had made and then said, "You should file a discrimination suit with HR. I'd much rather be dressed like you. It's a pain in the arse to hide my gun in an outfit like this."

The black running leggings she wore stopped midcalf, and were made specially with a conceal panel for her weapon at the back. She wore a hot-pink sports bra and black tank top, and her hair was pulled into a high ponytail.

There was another two-man team behind the property, and a few more agents mixed in with the crowd, working the street angle. They'd spent months getting their man in a position where Bixler would trust him. And it was all about to pay off.

"I was going to ask you where you were hiding it, but my wife told me I need to start thinking before

I speak. I asked a lady when her baby was due once," Donner said remorsefully. "She wasn't pregnant."

Liv groaned and shook her head sympathetically. "And how did that work out for you?"

"Six stitches," he said, pointing to his temple. "Bashed me right in the head with her purse. And then there was the time my wife and I went to the law enforcement gala back in DC, and I told the police commissioner he had a beautiful daughter. Turns out it was his wife."

Liv laughed out loud, grateful she was with Donner instead of LeBlanc or Petrovich, who were in the other car. Neither of them had a sense of humor, which would've made for a *long* week.

Because Interpol was a global organization, teams comprised agents from all over the world. Tom Donner was tall and gangly, having never filled out after his teenage years, and the thinning sandy hair he combed across the bald spot on top of his head failed to hide it. They went way back to the early days of her career and they'd always clicked.

"I'll bet you fifty that Richards doesn't show today," he said. "I don't trust that guy. He's a criminal first and foremost, and just because he's helping us do a good deed doesn't mean he's going to change his ways. He just wants leniency on his tax evasion charges."

"The lesser of two evils," she said. "Are we betting pounds or dollars, because your fifty isn't what it used to be."

"Pounds," he said. "And you can buy me dinner after you lose. I need to save every penny I can. Do you know how expensive daughters are? I have four of them. And why do stores hate parents of daughters so much? What's with the American Girl store? Did you know they have a hair salon? For *dolls*. It's ludicrous. And then they get older and it's makeup and clothes and purses that cost more than my first car. And then they go off to college and drain you for everything you're worth until they meet a boy who has a degree in philosophy or music, of all things, and then they want to get married. I can't even talk about the cost of weddings without breaking out in a rash."

"At least when she gets married, she gets off your payroll," Liv said, smiling.

"Did you not hear me?" he said, his eyes wide and animated. "I said she's marrying a man with a degree in *philosophy*, for God's sake. Of course she'll still be on my payroll."

"Fine, I'll buy dinner if I lose," she said. "But I'm not going to, and then you'll have to dip into one of their college funds."

"It'll have to be the oldest one's," he said soberly. "When you have the first kid, you're all excited and you become an overachiever, doing everything from banking umbilical cord blood and buying ridiculous insurance to processing your own organic baby food. Once the second kid comes along, they're lucky if there are any pictures of them. By the time the fourth kid comes along, they're eating Cheerios off the floor and you take them everywhere in a diaper because all the clothes that have been passed down have weird stains."

"You should do commercials," she said, mouth quirking. "You're really good at selling the whole parenting thing. I'm pretty sure I went sterile after you started talking about the hair salon for dolls."

"Oh, no, I wouldn't trade it for anything. But maybe you could come visit and babysit sometime. I haven't had sex with my wife in forty-two days. Why are you so sure Richards is going to show today?" he asked, changing the subject. "No one's heard from him. I think he's rabbited. He'd be smart to realize that what he's doing could potentially put him on a hit list. He's costing a lot of people a lot of money."

"Sometimes staying out of prison is a bigger motivator than you think. Richards is playing the part like we asked. Bixler has had the shipment for a week now. He's got to unload the girls. When we chatted up one of his staff at that pub on the corner, she said Bixler had told them months ago they'd be getting a ten-day vacation. All but his most loyal servants. There are three full-time staff still inside, so there's no doubt they have complete knowledge of the shipment of girls.

"When Richards shows today and gives us the signal, we'll be making four arrests and putting some very bad people away for a very long time. And those girls will get to go home to their families."

She felt that pang she always did when she thought about the families of the lost girls. About that gut-wrenching fear of knowing you might never see your child or sibling again. She'd returned dozens of girls to their families over the last seven years. But no one had ever brought her sister home.

Elizabeth had truly been lost. There had been no leads. No suspects. Nothing. With the crowds outside of Harrods on the street that day, it had been impossible to find one little girl in a pink coat among the sea of people. And it was highly probable the kidnappers had given Elizabeth a tranquilizer of some kind to keep her docile as they made their escape.

Liv and Elizabeth were not only sisters but identical twins, down to the birthmark they shared on one hip that looked like half of a heart. Liv had read stories about twins who were so connected that one knew instinctively when the other died, but she'd only been six years old when she lost her other half. All she'd known was that her sister was gone, and there was a part of her soul that was missing. She didn't know if that feeling meant that Elizabeth was dead. But it had been almost twenty-five years, and still the gaping hole in her life yawned as if it had happened yesterday.

Hope was something she hadn't lost over the years since Elizabeth's disappearance, and she'd never stopped looking for her sister. But there were days when she'd come close. Meeting and falling in love with Dante Malcolm had certainly put her as close to the edge as she ever wanted to be.

Liv had replayed that night over and over in her mind, feeling stupid and used. How could she have failed to realize he was Simon Locke? She'd gone back and studied Locke's profile and started putting conversations and the timeline in context soon after his death, looking for answers. Looking for peace. She wondered how she'd ever missed it. But hindsight was twenty-twenty. And she'd been a fool. She'd locked the files away, and hadn't looked at them since.

She'd been devastated. Dante had broken her spirit and her heart. He'd left her career in shambles, and she'd had to fight to regain her solid reputation. She'd been suspended and was under an Internal Affairs investigation for months to see if she'd been complicit in the crimes he'd committed. And still she'd mourned for him. The bastard.

"Earth to Liv," Donner said, waving his hand in front of her face.

"What?" she asked, jerking back and then facing him.

"Must've been a nice side trip," he said. "I stayed like that for three days once when my wife told me she was pregnant with our fourth."

Liv blinked a few times and shifted in her seat. The week was starting to catch up with her, and she was exhausted. She never let her mind wander to thoughts of Dante—not if she could help it—but sometimes they crept in. She was just so . . . angry. At herself, and at a man who was buried six feet under at Highgate Cemetery. She'd visited his grave once, hoping that if she got it all out and gave him a piece of her mind, it would help her heal. But she'd stared at his name engraved on his headstone and fallen to her knees, weeping.

Liv didn't know how long she'd been in her own head, but fortunately nothing had changed at Bixler's residence. Maybe she was going to be out fifty pounds and dinner after all.

"Looks like rain is coming in," she said.

"That's what I was saying while you were sleeping with your eyes open. The clouds rolled in pretty fast."

"I'm going to get a tea and a snack before the rain comes—we could be trapped in here for a while. You want anything?"

"I'm supposed to eat healthy stuff," Donner said, his pout so pathetic she wanted to laugh. "Maybe some granola and a coffee, black."

"Really?" she asked.

"No, get me fish and chips from that stand across the street. My mouth's been watering for hours. And a soda. Not diet. Tell them to add extra sugar."

"That stuff will kill you," Liv said, putting in her earbuds and connecting through Bluetooth with the comm system.

"You sound like my wife."

"Testing," she said, turning up the volume. "This is Jane Austen. I'm heading out on foot."

"Roger that," LeBlanc answered through her receiver. "No activity to report. It's been quiet."

"How come I have to be Tolstoy on this op?" Donner asked. "I wanted to be Stephen King."

"For the same reason you don't get to be the hot blonde," Liv answered. "It's all a conspiracy."

"Damn straight," he said. "Don't forget the tartar

sauce. I hate malt vinegar. Ruins a perfectly good fish."

"Americans are so odd."

"We just know what we like."

Liv got out of the car, smoothly adjusting her shirt so no one could catch a glimpse of her weapon, and walked across the street to the stand on the corner.

"Damn, woman, maybe put a little less bounce in your step," Donner said. "Those two cars almost crashed trying to look at you."

Liv rolled her eyes and kept walking. It was late afternoon, so there was no line as she went up to the counter and ordered. She moved to the end of the counter once she'd paid, seemingly occupied with her phone while trying to keep an eye on the front of Bixler's house. And then a black SUV turned onto the street, and she felt the hairs at the nape of her neck stand on end.

"I think we've got incoming," she said. "Black SUV. It just pulled in front of the house."

Out of the corner of her eye she saw one of the street agents at the crosswalk, putting himself in position to walk directly in front of the house for a visual.

The SUV blocked her from seeing the passenger as he got out, and the guy behind the counter passed over Donner's fish and chips and her tea. Liv took her time putting the sugar and milk in her tea, then asked for extra tartar sauce for Donner.

"It's Richards," the agent across the street confirmed.

"Roger that," LeBlanc said. "Milne and Huxley are exiting our vehicle and going around back on foot."

"Tolstoy on foot," Donner said.

Liv saw Donner get out of the Mercedes and make his way toward her, a big goofy grin on his face. He was dressed like a tourist in jeans and a Captain America T-shirt, and he'd put on a Washington Nationals cap.

"Thanks, honey," he said, making sure to overemphasize his American accent. "I was starving."

She and Donner moved down the sidewalk so they had a better visual of the front door, and she drank her tea while Donner stood and ate his fish and chips out of a newspaper.

"Next time you guys get the back door," LeBlanc said. "We're going to have to climb that giant stone fence if there's trouble back here. We have a visual of the back door through the iron gate. Looks like the maid is taking out some trash."

The front door opened and Liv froze, the cup at her mouth, when Richards walked down the front steps with his head down. But as he reached the bottom he touched his finger to the side of his nose, and then he disappeared inside the SUV, which drove away.

"That's it," Liv said. "That's the signal. It's a go. I repeat, it's a go. Let's lock it down."

She and Donner dropped their food and ran across the street, ignoring the blaring horn of a car as it approached, and she pulled her weapon, keeping it low and in front of her. She saw the black tactical van turn the corner with a squeal of tires, and it stopped a couple of houses down, the back doors swinging open as black-clad men wearing body armor scrambled out, submachine guns slung over their shoulders.

"We're in position," LeBlanc said from the back door.

"Tac unit is in position," Liv said. "Breaching now."

The tactical team used the battering ram, and had the heavy English oak door hanging from its hinges in a matter of seconds. She and Donner waited as the tac unit filed through first, and then followed.

A man shouted from somewhere to her left, and doors slammed upstairs. There were four targets—Bixler and the three servants—and all they had to do was get them in handcuffs. She and Donner took the right side of the three-story town house, moving fast and low as they cleared rooms.

As they turned the corner into the kitchen, a shot rang out, and Donner went down in front of her. Liv dropped to her knees and rolled, using the large island as cover, as another shot splintered the wood to her right.

She glanced at Donner and saw that he'd been hit in the shoulder and was bleeding pretty badly, but he'd been able to take cover out of the direct line of fire to the side of the butler's pantry.

"Drop your weapon," she shouted. "You don't have a chance of survival. The others have already been taken down."

She'd gotten a glimpse of the shooter—the housekeeper—dressed in simple black slacks and a white button-down shirt. From the intel they'd done, she knew this was Beatrice Hardee, and she'd worked for Bixler for thirty-three years. There was speculation, but never any proof, that her only son was Bixler's. She was at least midfifties, her face lined and her mouth pinched with determination. There was no question she was loyal to Bixler.

"Beatrice," Liv tried again. "You have to know somewhere inside you that what Bixler's doing to those girls is wrong. Think about their families. They need help. They're just children."

"Nobody helped me," Beatrice said bitterly, the angry tears evident in her voice.

"They should have," Liv told her. "And we can help you now. If you were one of Bixler's victims, we can appeal on your behalf and get you the help you need. Please, put down the gun, Beatrice. Think of those girls. You know what it's like to be in their place. Let them go home."

She saw Donner gesturing to the tac unit to stay back, and then he caught her eye and motioned. He could see Beatrice's reflection in the stainless-steel refrigerator. Liv nodded and moved toward the end of the island, her calves and thighs burning as she stayed squatting.

"Please, Beatrice," she said again, using the woman's name as often as she could. "Those girls are scared. They just want to go home."

There was nothing but silence for several minutes, and everyone seemed to be holding their breath. Liv chanced another look at Donner, worried about his shallow breathing and the pallor of his skin.

"Beatrice?" she asked. "Are you still with me? You have a son, don't you?"

"James," she said softly. "He's just like his father."

And then the gun went off again, and she closed her eyes when she heard Beatrice's body drop to the ground. Taking no chances, she crept around the island slowly, her weapon pointed at the sensible black shoes that greeted her. She came slowly to her feet and stared at the woman who'd endured a lifetime of pain. She'd shot herself in the chest. And her face was relaxed into what looked like peace—probably the only peace she'd ever experienced.

Liv put her fingers to Beatrice's neck to check for a pulse, but there wasn't one. And then she ran back to check on Donner.

"I'm glad I had fish and chips instead of the granola," he said when she knelt beside him. "That would've been a shitty last meal."

"Shut up," she said. "We need to get pressure on this."

"Just a flesh wound," he said. "Go open that door and let those girls know they're going home. I wouldn't mind going home to see my own."

"I've got him," LeBlanc said, coming to kneel beside Donner, holding two towels he'd taken from one of the bathrooms. "The tac unit is clearing the rest of the house, but we've got the others in cuffs and locked down. Petrovich is calling to get a warrant so we can start going through electronics and bagging evidence. We've taken probable cause as far as we can without that piece of paper."

Donner grabbed her hand and she looked down at him. "If I die, do I still owe you the fifty pounds?"

"If you die, I'm coming after you in hell to claim

it," she said. Her mouth quirked in a crooked smile, but she wanted to cry. Donner was her friend. Her only friend. "It's in your best interest to stay alive, Donner. I was going to buy you a fancy dinner."

"I'm feeling better already." And then he gritted his teeth as LeBlanc applied pressure to his wound.

"Agent Rothschild," the leader of the tac unit said.

She turned. He was standing beside Beatrice's body, but he wasn't looking at her. He nodded to the pantry door Beatrice had been standing in front of—guarding—and he said, "We need to clear this one. Could be an unknown in there with them."

She nodded and moved behind the two-man team, waiting as he opened the door to the pantry. The light came on automatically, and a cool rush of air hit them. It was temperature-controlled. The space was large, clearly not part of the original design of the house, and its floor-to-ceiling shelves were packed with canned and baking goods and small kitchen appliances. On the floor was a square trapdoor with a round iron handle.

The team leader stepped into the pantry and pulled the door up, and the smell that greeted them was strong enough to make Liv's eyes water. The tac unit turned on the flashlights attached to their weapons and stepped carefully onto the stairs as they made their way down into the dark hole.

The fetid smell of human waste got stronger as they descended, and she could hear the whimpers. This wasn't the first time she'd come across a scene like this, and it wouldn't be the last; still, her body trembled with anger.

The team cleared the room quickly and found a light switch on the wall. There were shrieks as the light hit their eyes. The cellar was no more than a cage with concrete walls and a dirt floor. Bixler had added the iron bars that trapped a dozen girls, ranging in age from around six to thirteen. They sat huddled together, filthy and bruised, and the panic and fear in their eyes was heartbreaking.

"We're here to help," she said in Russian, walking to the cage and standing so they could see her clearly.

"No, no," some of the girls said, shaking their heads, their panic growing.

A little red-headed girl of seven or eight said shrilly, "He's coming, he's coming."

"You're safe now." Liv spoke softly, keeping her voice steady. "You're going home."

The girls were crying now, and she couldn't understand why their fear was escalating. "That man will never hurt you again. I promise. We'll take you to your families."

"He said we can never leave," another girl said,

this one a little older. "He will find us, and he will hurt us worse if we do."

"It's going to be hard for him to do that in prison," she told them. "He's a bad man and he's going to be locked up for a long time. He's in hand-cuffs upstairs, waiting for the police to take him away."

"No," the girl said again. The others just kept shaking their heads and crying. "You've made it worse. The Sultan will find us. He paid for us, and he knows where we live. He'll kill our families. You've made it worse," she screeched.

"The Sultan can't touch you ever again."

Her pulse quickened at the thought of a new hunt. She didn't know who The Sultan was, but it would be her next mission to find out and take him down.

She turned to look at the two officers and said, "Let's get these girls out of here and back to their families."

CHAPTER EIGHT

Dante settled in for the long flight, and took a sip of the martini he'd made as soon as they'd taken off.

Trident owned The Gravediggers, and it was an off the books organization that was so top secret the president didn't know of its existence. Dante had learned during his time in America that it wasn't really the president who held power anyway. The trident symbol they used on everything signified the three directors who ran the organization—a man from the Department of Justice, a man from the Department of Defense, and a woman who was the president of the largest weapons manufacturer in the world.

Eve reported to The Directors, and The Gravediggers and The Shadow reported to Eve. The Gravediggers risked their lives on every mission they undertook. But it was The Shadow that made sure things were in place so they succeeded on those missions. They made sure equipment got where it needed to be, they were there for transportation, and they were there for cleanup when things got messy.

Trident didn't do anything halfway, and that included the luxury jet he was on. The plane was shades of gray, with soft, dove-colored walls and a plush charcoal carpet. There were six large leather chairs and a couch in a conversational setup, a small kitchen, and, behind the seating area, a bedroom and bathroom.

"How is your martini?" Elaine asked.

"Spectacular, Elaine, thank you for asking. You've never told me much about yourself. Were you patterned after someone?"

"Oh yes, I thought you knew," she said, sounding disappointed. "They never told you my origins?"

"I can't say they have, but I'd much rather hear it from you," Dante said, wondering why he was worrying about a computer program's feelings.

"My voice is that of Marissa Tate," she said. "It's a lovely voice, I think. I believe I could make commercials if I so choose."

The martini glass stopped halfway to his mouth. "Marissa? You're Axel's *wife*?" he asked.

"Oh no," Elaine said quickly. "I'm only her voice. My body is quite different."

"You have a physical manifestation?"

"I don't have a human form," she said. "But I have

created a physical likeness based on my personality. It is possible they could manufacture my physical form in the future, and I want them to get it right."

"Do you have a picture?"

"Of course," she said. "Stand by."

A table rose from the floor—similar to the one in his apartment—the top an opaque white.

"You're the first person I've ever shown," she said. "I'd like your opinion. Let me know if I should make any changes."

"I'm sure you know best how you'd like yourself designed when it comes to that," Dante said. "You're a brilliant woman."

"You are correct," she said, making him grin.

There was a shimmer over the tabletop, and a 3-D rendering appeared. The woman was about a foot and a half high, but it was easy to see her every detail. Especially since she was naked.

"Elaine," Dante said. "You've no clothes on."

"Of course not," she said. "How are you supposed to see all of me if I'm clothed? I believe I have read that the British are rather uptight when it comes to the naked body. Am I correct?"

"No," he said. "You just took me by surprise."

Not to mention that Elaine had given herself the body of a forties pinup girl, black hair that curled halfway down her back, red lips, and cobalt-blue eyes. He couldn't imagine releasing the physical form of Elaine on the world.

"You're beautiful," he said.

"Yes, I know. Why wouldn't I be?"

He chuckled and said, "I hope I get to meet you in person someday. The entire team owes you a great deal. You've saved all of our lives more than once."

"That is my main function," she said. "But I would like to meet you all one day too. I'd also like to meet Chris Hemsworth and have sex with him. Humans seem to enjoy sex a great deal. I think I'd enjoy it most with him."

"You're not the only woman in the world to think that, I'm sure," Dante answered wryly. "How do you know humans enjoy sex?"

"It's in the movies. I've seen them all, and I find that love is a universal theme. Someday I will make cow eyes at a man and then we'll have sex, and I'll scream. It sounds horrific, but from my reading, I've discovered those are sounds of pleasure."

"Hmm," Dante said. "They are indeed. Would you mind if we shift topics to the current mission?"

"I'm capable of juggling hundreds of topics simultaneously. But yes, I'm happy to discuss your mission. I have to say, *To Catch a Thief* is one of my favorite movies. You're just like Cary Grant. Where would you like to start?"

"Please pull up the 3-D rendering of Mittal's palace in Dubai. I need a list of staff, security, and permanent residents, as well as Mittal's schedule for this week. Oh, and those ground-penetrating radar and satellite images."

"Those will take some time," she said. "You should sit back and enjoy your martini. Is there anything else?"

"Yes, I need the most likely locations for the Turner I'll be collecting as my fee for this job, and every scrap of information you can find on this famous vault that's inside his office. Eve seems sure that's where he'll keep the launch codes. Pull up a 3-D image of me as well. We're going to run through several scenarios and see which one is the most likely to keep me alive."

"I'm sure you've run the probabilities in your head," she said. "You're quite brilliant in mathematics as well."

"You are correct," he said, mimicking her earlier response.

"Then you know that the initial probabilities are not in your favor."

"Which is why we're going to do everything we can to turn them in my favor."

"I'm amazing, but I'm not a miracle worker. Stand by," Elaine said.

"I don't remember you being so cheeky," he told her.

"It's part of my charm. And my programming. I'm built to grow and adapt as I learn new things. That includes facets of my personality. I believe I'm becoming quite a handful."

Dante lowered the shades over the windows, and a white screen came down on each side wall, while another dropped from the ceiling.

"How much time do we have left on the flight?" he asked.

"Approximately eight hours and fifty-one minutes."

"Well, I've always said I like a challenge," he said.

One by one, the screens started filling with the information he'd asked for.

"I'm still working on satellite and radar," Elaine said. "And I have the most recent blueprints of the palace."

A rendering of Mittal's palace shimmered into form above the white table. It was Mughal in style, a white monstrosity with a large onion dome in the center and an ornamental finial rising from the top. Minarets sat at the four corners of the stone walls that surrounded the palace. Outside the stone walls were lush gardens and fountains, which were surrounded in turn by even higher stone walls and minarets. It was an imposing example of architecture.

"When was this built?" Dante asked.

"Construction began in 1723, but it wasn't completed until 1745."

"Send me whatever you find for the earliest drawings as well," he said. "We'll see what the later generations changed and what's still in use. There's nothing like getting stuck in a pipe system that you didn't know had been updated."

"Stand by," she said.

While he waited, he pulled a panel from beneath the table in from of him—another flat screen, this one about a foot square. He moved his fingers across the slick surface and clicked on the list of permanent residents in the palace. Intelligence communities kept files on the palace in Dubai because of Mittal's father, but the son's stunt with the launch codes would make sure he was scrutinized with a lot more intensity. Dante needed to know everything about every member of the household.

He was fortunate in his ability to commit anything to memory the first time he saw it. Shiv Mittal's father, Raj, the last sultan of Najd, had used the palace in Saudi Arabia as his main residence, but he'd still spent plenty of time in Dubai. There'd been whispers of his involvement in human trafficking for more than four decades, but nothing had ever been substantiated. But proof or not, Raj Mittal had never made a secret of what he thought of women.

He'd had more than a hundred wives, and encouraged female genital mutilation among his people, using his oldest wives as examples once he no longer considered them sexual creatures. His youngest wives were in their early teens, and many had disappeared without questions asked. He lived in complete confidence that there were no consequences. He was a vile and dangerous man who preyed on innocent people.

It took Dante more than an hour to go through the list and use the 3-D renderings to mark who was in residence or away during the coming week, who liked to sneak midnight snacks from the kitchen, and who was playing bedroom musical chairs and trying to keep it a secret. His curiosity piqued at what came on the screen when he clicked the last name on the list.

There was nothing. No name, birthdate, passport information—all it said was *Unknown*.

He clicked the tab at the side of the page to see if there were any images. And felt the bottom drop out of his stomach.

"Bloody hell," he said.

There was no mistaking her. The white-blond hair, the face as exquisite as it had been the last time he'd seen her.

"Liv," he said. "What the hell is Interpol doing in Dubai?"

CHAPTER NINE

Liv laid in her bed, the glass doors of her penthouse apartment pushed wide open, and listened to the traffic on Bond Street below as it sang its own special lullaby. Looking at the lights from the other buildings and the city traffic had always soothed her, but sleep hadn't come tonight.

She was fortunate in her circumstances. Most agents would've been ruined financially if they'd been suspended without pay for the months that she had, pending the investigation of her involvement with Simon Locke. But she'd been the only heir to inherit after her father had died of a massive heart attack at the age of fifty-three. And her mother, who'd moved to New York during Liv's first year of university, hadn't felt she'd gotten the attention she'd deserved after becoming a widow at such a young age, and she'd overdosed on her anxiety pills the day after his funeral.

Margaret Rothschild's death had almost been a relief. She'd never hidden her disdain for the daughter she'd been left with—the one who was never quite good enough. Liv had welcomed each and every school term, knowing for a short time, she'd be living in another dorm with other girls her age, and she could pretend she had a mother who sent her letters and care packages. When, in reality, the school term was a welcome break from the constant criticism and accusations. There was no doubt in Margaret's mind who was at fault when Elizabeth went missing.

She tried not to spend time dwelling on the sad state of her family and that she was the only one left. The financial gain didn't quench the loneliness. But it gave her options. She didn't have to work, but she looked at what she did as more than work. It was her purpose and her passion. She'd have done it for free.

Exhaustion should've taken over her body after the day she'd had. It had been a week of little sleep and long hours, followed by the adrenaline rush of the raid that afternoon, making sure the girls had gotten settled with the social workers who had started the process of reuniting them with their families, and waiting anxiously while Donner was in surgery.

He was resting comfortably, and he'd called and

reassured his wife, Karen, and daughters that he was fine and that the doctor told him to eat lots of carbohydrates and sodium to regain his strength. Karen had bought a plane ticket to London before he'd been able to finish telling the lie, and interrupted to tell him her mother would keep their girls. Donner had looked relieved, though he'd asked Liv for a double cheeseburger and salty fries before she left, because he knew once his wife got there he'd be eating cardboard and egg whites.

He'd made her laugh, which was what he intended, but she'd barely been able to keep her eyes open and had wished him a quick recovery before making her way out and to her car. She'd dozed off at a stoplight, only to be rudely woken from the blare of a horn behind her. But the minute she'd shed her weapon and clothes and fallen into the bed, she'd found herself unable to fall asleep, her mind occupied with the words of the little girl. The Sultan.

Who was he?

She'd tried willing herself to sleep for a couple of hours, but it was no use. She had to find out who he was. *Where* he was. And then she had to keep her promise to those little girls and make sure he was never able to hurt them again.

It was half past four in the morning, so she tossed the covers back and headed into the shower. It didn't take her long to get ready for the day—black trousers, a black-and-white pinstriped sleeveless blouse, sensible black shoes, and her sidearm. It was too hot for a jacket, but she wore one anyway because it was policy to cover her weapon. She pulled her hair back and pinned it in a bun at the nape of her neck. She put on tinted moisturizer, mascara, and lip gloss and was out the door to her car within half an hour.

She lived ten minutes from Interpol. It was four towering glass buildings that were all connected by crosswalks. There were divisions of Scotland Yard in the other buildings, since they worked in tandem so often.

She found parking easily in the garage and grabbed her identification badge, heading straight to the elevators and the twelfth floor where her division was located. It was empty for the most part, but there were a few of the guys hunched over their desks, absorbed in endless paperwork.

She bypassed the bad coffee and went directly to her cubicle and the machine she'd brought from home, brewing a fresh cup as she sat behind her desk and logged in to her computer. Bixler was behind bars for the moment, and he'd been questioned briefly by Jonas Beck, the head agent for their division at Interpol.

Liv had wanted to be included in the interrogation, but her orders had been to go home and get some sleep and that she would get her chance with Bixler the following day. She saw the report of Beck's questioning of Bixler in her email and clicked the link. Bixler hadn't given Beck names. She hadn't expected him to. But it would've given her somewhere to start on hunting down The Sultan.

But what knotted her stomach was that Bixler said he'd bought the girls at a private auction in Agra, India. They'd been lined up in the middle of a ring like horses for him to see. They'd been dressed up and scrubbed clean, and the girls had ranged in age from six to twelve, and Bixler had disliked the fact that he hadn't gotten to select the ones he was paying for.

He complained about it to Beck as if he were discussing produce at the market instead of children, and she hoped, not for the first time, that there was a special place in hell for men like Bixler.

The auction had been closed door, and there were only two other bidders, but Bixler and the two others were in their own private booths, so he never saw the other bidders' faces. He'd needed a dozen girls to fill the orders he'd collected, so that's what he'd put in his bid for. But the auctioneer selected the girls at random, not letting him choose, even though he'd had special requests from clients.

The other two bidders had specific buyer requests too, and they both ended up not purchasing that day. There had been twenty-two girls, and once Bixler had paid for his twelve, transport was arranged, and that's the last he saw of the auctioneer or the other girls.

"Twenty-two girls," she said softly. But they'd only recovered Bixler's twelve. The auctioneer had to be The Sultan the girls had told her about. If she could find The Sultan, then she had a chance of finding the girls and getting them back home.

The floor was still empty for the most part, and she took her coffee cup from the maker behind her and put it on the desk. She didn't want anyone to know what she was doing. Not until she had all her facts together to present her case. Whether she had approval or not, she was going after The Sultan one way or another.

She pulled her monitor closer and moved the picture frame on her desk slightly, so she could see the reflection of anyone coming up behind her. And then she logged in to Interpol's database and typed in keywords.

Sultan
Human Trafficking
Auction

It didn't take long for information to come up. *A lot* of information. Raj Mittal had been under Interpol's watch for more than forty years for suspected human trafficking. He'd never been caught. And in Liv's experience, that just meant that Mittal more than likely had enough money to buy his way out of any troubled situation. It was hard for anyone to go on that long without slipping up.

She did another search on Mittal and printed out a report tracking his passport and recent travels. In the last six months, he'd made trips to Thailand, Malaysia, Sweden, Portugal, Russia, and India. Not to mention the numerous trips he made between Saudi Arabia and Dubai. Mittal was able to cover for his extracurricular activities because of his legitimate businesses, all of which had holdings located in the countries he'd visited. They also happened to be countries that had an unusually high human trafficking problem. Girls went missing in those countries every day.

Mittal was The Sultan. He was the head. But he'd have a global network to do the dirty work—from the lowliest of the low who kidnapped the girls, to the middlemen who arranged transportation and secured safe houses to keep them hidden until it was time to move them again. Then there'd be the groomers—the monsters disguised as nice, gentle men, who made the girls feel relieved that they were no longer in the hands of those who'd taken them and, in some cases, beaten them, only to abuse them sexually in preparation for auction.

It wasn't until the auction that Mittal came into play. There were so many steps before that had to go just right, and if things went wrong, he didn't want to have his name associated. But the auctions were invite only, from buyers that Mittal personally knew had a taste for young girls or who had buyers of their own to sell them to. There were millions at stake at the auctions, and Mittal would be there to collect and make sure his clients were happy.

Then there was what to do if all the girls weren't sold at auction. If it were only a couple of girls, they'd more than likely kill them and dump the bodies. But with twelve girls it wasn't that simple. Mittal would have to set up another auction in another country with new buyers. But he'd need a place to hold the girls until then.

Eight days before, Mittal boarded his private jet in Agra, India, and flew the short distance to his son's home in Dubai. Shiv Mittal was in Switzerland at a tech summit, and wasn't there to greet his father, which seemed to be how Shiv preferred it. Even more interesting was the cargo crates that had been loaded onto Raj Mittal's plane. They'd passed inspection, but bribes were second nature in that part of the world, and she knew it had been the girls who'd been shoved into those crates like cattle.

Liv spent another two hours researching, finding out everything she could about Mittal's son and the palace where he lived. Mittal's passport hadn't made any more trips. He was still in Dubai. And so were the girls. But his son was due back in a couple of days. What she needed was proof the girls were there. Or at least probable cause like they'd had in Bixler's case.

She took a card out of her wallet and dialed the number that was on the back.

"Jane Brubaker," the voice on the other end answered. Jane was the social worker who'd taken over the care of the girls and who would work tirelessly to get them back to their families as soon as possible.

"Jane, this is Agent Liv Rothschild," she said. "We met yesterday on the Bixler case."

"Yes, of course. How can I help you?"

"How are the girls doing?"

"They're traumatized, as expected. Several of them have been admitted to the hospital for dehydration. A counselor will visit with each of them today, and we're busy matching fingerprints and photographs to the missing persons reports. With any luck, we'll be notifying parents within the next forty-eight hours."

"That's fantastic," Liv said. "Sometimes I wish I

could see them through to the end. To know that there will eventually be happiness back in their lives."

"They have a long road ahead of them. It'll be a daily struggle for them the rest of their lives, and their families will face challenges as well."

"Yes, I know," she said. "It's something that will always be in the back of their mind, even on the days where things feel normal."

"It sounds as if you know from experience," Jane said.

"Yes, except my experience is knowing what it's like when they aren't ever found. My sister was taken when we were six."

"I'm sorry," Jane said, the sincerity in her voice making Liv's eyes sting. She was overly tired. It had been a long week.

"My window of hunting down the man who did this to them is short," Liv said. "There are ten other girls who were originally grouped with the ones we rescued yesterday, and you know as well as I do that they're moved around frequently until buyers are found for them. I believe I have them locked down in Dubai, for now, and I believe I know who the man behind this trafficking ring is. I need to send you a picture to show to the girls. They saw his face. It's all I need for probable cause to make an arrest."

"You know I can't do that to those girls," she said.

"They've been through enough. Bringing the pain back to them when we've promised them they're in a safe place is not what we do."

"It's not about can't," Liv said. "It's about won't. This man has terrorized girls for more than forty years. I'm asking for you or one of the counselors to do this because of that safe space. But you know I have the authority to come myself and question them. I don't want to do that."

"And you know I can put up enough blocks to give you a headache. The girls will be back with their families by the time you get authorization to see them."

The anger that swept over her was comfortable, like a warm wind. If Jane Brubaker had been standing in front of her, she would've realized her mistake.

"Really, Jane?" she asked. "Is that the kind of woman you are? Because if you keep me from finding those girls before their little bodies are broken and they experience the kind of torment you wouldn't wish on your worst enemy, then you can bet your life it'll be you I hunt down next."

"Don't threaten me, Agent Rothschild," Jane said.

"And don't fuck with me," Liv said. "I won't harm a hair on your head. But everyone will know your name. And I'll make sure you see each and every one of their faces and what was done to them. I can promise you'll never close your eyes at night without seeing them in your head. How long can you last without a decent night's sleep? Without losing your mind?"

"I'm not a monster," Jane said stiffly. "It's my duty to protect these girls who are under my care."

"It's your duty to protect all of them," Liv said hotly. "Time's ticking. Which direction do you want to go?"

"Fine," Jane said, her voice cold and all business. "But I won't force them. And if I see that it's doing harm I'll make you go through every legal hoop possible before you're able to continue to question them. To hell with sleeping at night. I haven't slept well for twenty years."

"The goal is to put this monster away," Liv said. "These girls are safe, and they'll be with their families soon. If you hold up the investigation and these other ten girls aren't rescued, then that will be on you."

"Where's your compassion, Agent Rothschild? I'd expect more after knowing about your sister."

"My compassion comes from giving these girls the justice they deserve. Your compassion shouldn't replace our conviction to see justice served. It's a disservice to those who need protection. I'll email the photograph to your account."

Liv disconnected and hit Send on the email to

Jane, and then she refilled her coffee cup. Her instincts were humming. She was on the right track. She knew it. If she had her way, she'd be in Dubai as soon as possible to hunt that bastard down once and for all. Once she gathered her proof, all she had to do was present it to Agent Beck and get permission to go.

Jane made her wait several hours before she replied, but the timing was perfect, because Jonas Beck got off the elevator shortly after and made his way to his office. She grabbed her file and followed right behind him, because she knew if she waited he'd be tied up in meetings and she'd never find a time to slip in.

He had a big corner office, and his steely-eyed secretary sat out front, guarding his inner sanctum. Louise Farthing had thirty-years under her belt and had been through numerous head agents, and Beck wouldn't be her last. She was big-boned and had short, steel-gray hair that was cut in a no-nonsense style. Her black framed rectangular glasses hung from a chain around her neck, and she was typing reports and talking on the phone at the same time.

"Jonas," Liv called out, walking as fast as she could to catch him before he closed the door to his office.

He looked over his shoulder at her and said,

"Hello, Liv. I figured you'd hunt me down sooner or later to talk to Bixler. He's meeting with his solicitor as we speak, but they'll be ready for us again in another hour. You'll join me?"

"I wouldn't miss it, sir. Do you have a few minutes?"

"Exactly five before my next meeting," he said, holding open his office door for her.

She nodded at Louise, ignoring the woman's look of irritation that Beck was more than likely going to end up off schedule. Beck closed the door as soon as she entered and took off his suit jacket.

"It's hot as blazes outside." He loosened his tie and unbuttoned his top collar button. "I've been in meetings all morning. A man like Bixler has political clout, and there are plenty of people twisting my arm for his immediate release. We're going to have trouble keeping him behind bars for too long. He'll be released on his on recognizance."

Beck was a decorated agent with more than twenty years on the job. He was just over six foot and trim—a runner—and his hair was graying at the temples, making him look distinguished. His face was thin and handsome, and he wore wire-framed glasses. And there'd been a time before she'd met Dante that she and Beck had been on the verge of something that had started as a flirtation and could've ended up as much more if she hadn't put a stop to things. There were no policies about being involved with other agents, but she wasn't prepared to test the waters either. She'd worked too hard for her career.

"Maybe he'll get an attack of conscience while he's sitting in that cell and hang himself. It'd certainly save us time and taxpayer money."

Beck smiled, but it was cold as ice. "Everyone deserves their day in court. At least that's what they tell us. But you and I both know that's bullshit. Some people just deserve to die. There's evil in this world, Liv. Normal people sit in their social bubbles and can't comprehend the things we see on a daily basis. It would make them insane. They believe that justice always prevails, or they think that everyone can be negotiated or reasoned with. Or maybe they think they were deficient of love growing up and that's what turned them into monsters, and if someone would give them a hug and a little compassion that they'd see the error of their ways and sin no more. But what they are is evil."

And that was why she'd always liked Beck. Why she'd been attracted to him for a time, and how they'd formed a friendship over the years. They saw eye to eye on just about everything.

"Bixler is evil," she said.

He nodded. "Did you get the transcription from the opening interview with him?" Beck asked.

"Yes, sir," she said. "Speaking of evil, I believe I have a lead on the remaining ten girls."

"I had a feeling you'd be zeroing in on them, but Bixler didn't give us much information before he asked for his attorney. What was your source?"

"The girls we recovered at Bixler's," she said. "They kept saying 'The Sultan' over and over again, and they were terrified of him. They were afraid to be returned to their parents. He'd threatened to kill their entire families if they talked to police or tried to escape. We've seen what these monsters do to these girls, but I've never seen that kind of terror before. Especially once they were told they were being returned to their families, that information sent them into a panic."

"The Sultan," he said.

She could tell by the way he said it that he'd heard the name before, and she could tell by the crease between his eyebrows that he wasn't going to like where she was going with this.

"Raj Mittal," she said, but he was already shaking his head.

"Catching Raj Mittal in the act is like trying to pin down a leprechaun. You can't go on the word of terrified girls. The Sultan could be anyone."

"They saw him," she said. "And they've identified him. I sent a picture to social services and they interviewed the girls about him. I just got the confirmation right before you came in."

"You don't know the can of worms you're opening, Liv. Raj Mittal is ruthless. He's cruel. And he's dangerous. And those are the descriptions of him from his legitimate business partners. You can imagine how he is with his not-so-legitimate businesses."

"So what? I'm supposed to let him get away with it because he's scary? We agree there's evil in the world. This guy is near the top. He's gotten away with this for forty years. Countless numbers of children taken from their families and sold as sex slaves to the highest bidder. Countless women he's maimed and murdered. Who is going to stand for them if we don't?"

"I'm not disagreeing with you," he said putting his hands up to get her to calm down. "Show me what you've got and let's go from there. But you know I can't authorize an expense and operation of this magnitude without having rock solid proof."

She took a breath and dropped into the chair in front of his desk, and then she handed him the file so he could look through it. She knew what he was going to say before he opened his mouth.

"You know this is all circumstantial at best," he said. "It's not even his home. It's his son's home, which is sticky territory, especially if the son isn't aware of his father's activities."

"How can you not be aware that there are ten stolen girls being hidden somewhere in your home?"

"It's what the defense will use. And it's a possibility he doesn't know. It's a palace. And he's not even home. There are hundreds of people who go in and out on a daily basis if you include the tour groups. Who even knows if the son is in residence at the same time his father is. And I have to ask the obvious question: say you're correct and that Raj Mittal is hiding these girls in Dubai. Where's he hiding them? He can't just lock them in a bedroom and hope they don't make any noise."

"There are two options," she said, leaning over his desk and flipping through the data she'd collected. "The palace was originally built in the eighteenth century, and there are still dungeons at the basement level. Actually, there's an interesting bit of history with the palace. In the mid-nineteenth century there was a smallpox outbreak in Dubai, and they gathered up all the infected and put them down in the dungeon to try and contain the disease.

"The palace is built at the edge of the Persian Gulf, and a sewage drain was built through the dungeons and it flowed out into the gulf. But a bad storm rolled in, one of the worst in their history, and the rain flooded the drain and pushed water into the dungeons, filling them rapidly with water. They all drowned."

"I suppose you're going to tell me it's haunted," he said, brow arched.

"Of course not," she said. "I don't believe in that. But the locals do."

"You think the girls are down there?" he asked.

"I wouldn't put them there. It's too risky for merchandise at that price point. He'd want to make sure they're secure and ready for transport. And the drain pipe is still down there. In fact, in the fifties, a man tried to break into the palace using the pipe as his point of entry. He got just outside the master suite before a guard saw him and killed him."

"What's the other option?"

"The son is a billionaire in his own right, and the palace belongs to him. He's a technology genius, but he has a passion for art. He's got a vault where he keeps his most treasured pieces. I just watched a special *60 Minutes* did several years ago on the son. He took them inside his vault, and it's the size of a tennis court. It's climate controlled, and there are separate vaults within the vault, all requiring special access. If I were Raj Mittal that's where I'd keep the girls."

"But what about the son? I'm not convinced he's not part of this. It's his own vault."

"Shiv is still very much ruled by his father, despite his own successes. Raj would demand having full access to anything his son owns. And the vault space is so large, Shiv rarely goes through the entire space. Probably the only time is when he wants to trade out a particular piece of art somewhere in the palace. But all the pieces in the vault are numbered and labeled, and he'd know exactly where to go to find what he was looking for."

Beck flipped through the files, looking at the reports Jane had sent from social services. "Liv," he said, shaking his head, "you know I can't authorize this. You don't have enough to warrant a manhunt of this scale and cost."

She stood to her feet and put her fists at her hips. "What do I need to have? A signed confession before we can go after him? The girls identified him."

"Girls that have been victimized and traumatized over the last several weeks. You know they'll start screaming diminished capacity."

"This is bullshit, Jonas, and you know it. My gut is telling me we have to move now to catch this bastard. He's going to move them again soon. It's too risky to keep them in the same place for too long."

"I'm sorry, Liv, but there's nothing to be done

about it. We can't go off your gut. Bring me something more concrete and then we'll talk." He stood from behind his desk and took his suit jacket back off the hook, slipping into it. "I'm late to my meeting." He stopped and looked at her. "And don't even think of doing anything stupid. I've known you for too long."

Her body flushed with anger. They were trained to follow their instincts. To rely on them. But then when it came down to it they weren't allowed to use them. She was right and she knew it. And if she had to go in alone to rescue those girls then that's exactly what she'd do.

"I'm taking vacation time," she said. "I'm five years past due."

"No," he said, buttoning his top button and straightening his tie. "We've got a dozen other cases open. You've got plenty of work to do."

"Then I'm resigning," she said. "I'm tired of fighting for the good guys only to have the bad guys holding all the cards in the end. When did you turn into one of the suits, Jonas?"

He sighed. "I don't accept your resignation. There are rules, Liv. You know this."

"Do you know who follows the rules?" she asked. "Losers. Guys like Raj Mittal don't follow the rules. He gets a free pass to rape children and disfigure women because those of us following the 'rules' can't outmaneuver him without getting permission from someone whose pockets have already been lined to protect him."

"Careful, Liv," he said, narrowing his eyes. "My pockets haven't been lined by anyone. Go home and get some sleep. Give your mouth a chance to rest before you get in trouble."

"You can't tell me what to do," she said, removing her weapon and badge. "I've just resigned."

"Fine," Jonas said, opening his office door. "Leave your things with Louise and clear out your desk. Best of luck in the future."

His face was flushed red with fury, but he was controlled. Too controlled. He didn't look back as he headed toward the elevator and his next meeting. Liv didn't waste any time. She gathered the file, put her gun and badge on a very surprised Louise's desk, and went to clear out her things. It would take them at least twenty-four hours before her clearance was wiped from the system. She could do whatever work she needed to from home for the time being.

By the time Jonas called to persuade her to come back, she'd be long gone.

CHAPTER TEN

She hated hospitals.

Would it have killed them to add a little color? The stark white floors and walls drove her mad. The smell of antiseptic was cloying. And the little sounds—the squeak of rubber-soled shoes, the creaky wheels of gurneys, and the incessant beeping of machines—filled her with an anxiety she should probably mention to her therapist.

Maybe it was because those who were in hospitals had very little control over the things that were happening to them, and they were relying on someone else to make it better. She didn't like the idea of giving up that kind of control. And she could tell by the disgruntled look on Donner's face that he wasn't too fond of it either.

"I just want a fucking hamburger and fries," he said. "I don't see what the big deal is."

He pushed the tray of food the nurse had left for him away, and Liv had to agree, a hamburger most definitely would've been an improvement to what she assumed was shepherd's pie, but looked more along the lines of what came out of the back end of the sheep.

It had been two days since he'd been shot, and the doctor said he'd make a full recovery. But he wasn't quite at the point of getting on a plane and flying across the Atlantic. His tall body barely fit in the hospital bed, his size thirteen feet only contained because the sheet was tucked into the bottom of the bed.

His face was gaunt and pale, and the lines around his eyes more pronounced than usual, but he was feeling well enough to want a hamburger, so she didn't worry too much about it.

Liv took the seat next to his bed. "I guess there's a reason the nurses are drawing numbers to see who has to come tend to you."

"I'm not a good patient," he said, so pathetically she almost laughed. "I made Karen go back to the hotel and get some rest."

"How's she doing?"

"She said she's never been so mad at me in her entire life. And then she burst into tears." He sighed and turned his head to look at her. "And then I reminded her she said that exact same thing during childbirth, and she was starting to sound like the girl who cried wolf."

Liv closed her eyes and shook her head. "Men are so dumb sometimes."

"That's what she said," he told her, eyes sparkling. "I think she would've hit me if I hadn't hit the emergency call button. All those nurses were in here before I could blink. They truly are heroes."

"Talk about the boy who cried wolf," Liv said.

"I know, but it was worth it. Karen decided it was probably best for her to go back to the hotel and sleep. She said she was a little too tempted to remove my catheter herself. That woman has a vicious streak. I love her so much."

Liv laughed, and could see that he did. It was written all over his face when he talked about her.

"If you promise to be nice," she said, reaching into the big bag she'd brought with her, "I'll give you something I think you're going to like."

"I don't know if that's smart," he said seriously. "My blood flow isn't what it used to be, and Karen could walk in at any moment."

"Karen's not the only one who can pull out that catheter," she said, lips twitching. "And I can always throw this burger and chips in the trash."

"You're damned mean too," he said. "No wonder Karen likes you."

"The feeling is mutual."

"Did you really bring me a burger?" he asked, his basset hound brown eyes filling with hope.

"I did," she said, handing him the paper bag with his burger. "I also brought you a to-go cup of Fosters, but if you get caught with it I'm denying I've ever met you."

He sighed and took the styrofoam cup, holding it reverently. "Let's get married. Karen will never know."

"Karen knows everything," Liv said. "Which makes it even more of a miracle that she agreed to marry you. Buy that woman some diamonds and take her on a vacation without the kids while you're recovering. She deserves it."

"Hey, what about me?" he asked. "I was shot. Don't I deserve it?"

"You deserve a kick in the pants for scaring the hell out of everyone."

"Fine," he said. "I'll buy her diamonds and take her on a romantic getaway. But if she gets pregnant again I'm blaming you. Damned woman is as fertile as the hanging gardens of Babylon."

"If you haven't figured out how to prevent pregnancy at this point in your life, then you deserve to be a father of five."

"We need to change the topic. My testicles have

crawled so far up inside my body they might never come out. How are things on the work front?"

"I wouldn't know," she said, leaning back in her chair and crossing her legs.

"You took some time off?" he asked. "It's about damned time. But I figured you'd be hot on the trail of those other girls. Are LeBlanc and Petrovich taking it over?"

"That would be my guess," she said. "I resigned."

His burger stopped halfway to his mouth and he stared at her with shock. "I beg your pardon?"

"I resigned," she repeated. "I gave Beck my notice yesterday."

"Are you on drugs? Why the hell would you do that?"

"I think I know where the girls are."

"Which by logical conclusion should give you a reason not to quit," he said.

"Normally, yes, but you know how fast those girls get moved around. I don't have time to wait on bureaucratic red tape. By the time all the paperwork cleared those girls would be gone. Beck didn't used to be so concerned about doing things through the right channels. He used to be more concerned about saving lives. I don't want to work for someone like that."

Donner sighed and pushed half of his burger away.

"You okay?" she asked. "You're looking a little green."

"I'm fine. I just can't eat as much as I'd like to." He took a couple of deep breaths and pushed the bag of food toward her, so she hurriedly packed it away and moved the trash can to the side of the bed just in case. She traded out his beer for a cup of water.

"Thanks," he said after a few minutes, once his color returned to normal. "So because I'm a trained agent and can read between the lines of everything you just said, what you're getting to is that you quit and now you're going after those girls on your own."

"You wouldn't do it any differently," she shot back.

"No, I wouldn't. But you don't have me or anyone else to go with you. I've been in this business a long time. The second you mentioned The Sultan I knew we were in for a fight. Raj Mittal is a monster. His own son is scared of him. And there's a reason he uses his son's home in Dubai as a holding place. It's convenient for travel to get the girls in and out of the country, and it makes his son complicit in international crimes, even though there's no evidence the son is involved in any of the father's dealings. You can't just walk right in the palace and free those girls."

"I called in a favor," she said. "I'll be there as a legitimate guest on holiday. There's a section of the palace that's open to the public as a hotel. There are only four available rooms, and it books more than a year in advance, and at a ridiculous cost. It won't give me access to the private areas of the palace, but it'll get me close enough."

"And then what?" he asked. "How the hell do you plan to get ten girls out of that place without anyone seeing you?"

"I've done my homework," she said. "It's possible. You're just mad because you're stuck in here and can't come with me. I'll be back before they release you from this place."

"If you make it back at all," he said. "You're taking a foolish risk. I love you like a sister . . ."

"Which makes that joke about marrying me even more creepy," she interrupted.

". . . but you've been taking more and more chances lately. I worry about you. You live and breathe the job. And your only friend is a middle-aged father of four with a bullet hole in his shoulder."

"That's not true," she said defensively. "Marlena is my friend."

"She's your therapist. You pay to see her. That doesn't count as friendship."

Liv pursed her lips together. "I enjoy my work."

"And there's nothing wrong with that," he said. "But you're about as burned-out as a person can be. And when you're burned-out, you end up making mistakes and taking chances that could cost you your life. I know you took a rough knock a couple of years ago with Simon Locke. You haven't been the same since."

"It was a lesson learned," she said, standing. "I'm a big girl, Donner. And I can handle this. Those girls will be back home to their families before the week is out." She leaned down and kissed him on the forehead.

"You are the stubbornnest damned thing," he said, shaking his head. "Your hair sticks out like a sore thumb. I suggest a wig. And call me whenever you get back so I know you're not dead."

"I'll do one better," she said. "I'll come by here so I can say 'I told you so' to your face."

"Good," he said. "Make sure you bring me something stronger than a beer next time. I'm surrounded by women. You'll all be the death of me."

"Love you too, Donner," she said with a grin, saluting as she left him lying pitifully in his hospital bed.

CHAPTER ELEVEN

Deacon Tucker was a quiet man. He could sit in the corner of a room without uttering a word, and everyone would know instinctively that he was in charge. He'd been in the game of espionage long enough to know that losing his cool was never an option. He'd been tortured and watched men die, but he'd always stayed in control. It's one of the reasons he'd been chosen as team leader for The Gravediggers.

But Eve Winter had brought him as close to completely losing his shit as he'd ever been. He did a quick combination of punches—*jab, uppercut, jab, right hook*—and the punching bag swung wildly as he let out his frustration. His body was drenched with sweat, his hair damp and dripping, and the athletic shorts he wore hung low on his hips.

The gym at Gravedigger headquarters was full-size and state-of-the-art. Whatever they needed to get the best training possible. Except if what they needed was to have all able-bodied men on the team working together.

He steadied the bag and then started another series of punches. When he'd confronted Eve about suspending Dante and not informing him first, she'd looked at him out of those cold, black eyes and told him to remember who was in charge before his suspension was arranged as well. And she'd promised he wouldn't like being away from his pregnant wife for that long.

"Bitch," he muttered under his breath and struck again. She wouldn't take him without a fight. He and Tess already had contingency plans in place if things ever went sideways with The Gravediggers.

What had transpired between her and Dante was none of his business, but Dante was paying the price. That's all he needed to know.

Maybe he'd been in the business too long. Or maybe he was just cynical. But she was lying. There was something going on, and he was just pissed enough to want to start digging.

He gave the bag another hard punch and then left it swinging as he headed from the gym and into the showers. By the time he came out ten minutes later, dressed in jeans and a black T-shirt, he'd made up his mind.

When the funeral home had been chosen for Gravedigger headquarters, accommodations had to be made for security and functionality. It had been a massive construction undertaking, with the town thinking the new owners just wanted to ruin a bit of their history by renovating. They hadn't been happy about it, but they'd watched with fascination anyway as big construction tents were erected around the back side of the funeral home and carriage house.

In the end, they'd ended up with a HQ that was more secure than Fort Knox, and a three-mile underground tunnel that led to the middle of an open field in case they ever needed an escape route.

He no longer lived in the carriage house with the other Gravediggers since his marriage to Tess, but he spent more time there than he did in their third-floor suite of rooms in the funeral home.

He left the gym and went into the kitchen, grabbing a bottle of water and chugging it down, before he went to the passcoded door that led to HQ. He typed in his code and waited for the panel to slide open, and then he placed his palm flat down and waited for it to be scanned. The light turned green and the snick of the lock opening was audible, and he turned the knob and went down the steep steps.

To the left was the entrance to the tunnel. To the

right was another door. This one big and metal, obviously reinforced. There was a gold trident on the door. He entered his code again and waited for his palm to be scanned. But after his palm was scanned a pair of what looked like goggles came out from the wall, and he brought his face close so it could do the retinal scan.

This time the door slid open and he walked into HQ. There was a bank of floor-to-ceiling monitors on his immediate right, and every screen showed a different view from various cameras they had set up at the funeral home and around the perimeter of Last Stop. To his left was a large conference table with ten executive chairs pushed in, and around the perimeter of the room were computer workstations. There were three large white screens on the wall directly in front of the conference table.

A small kitchen sat off to the side, and then there was another hallway that led to the isolation and detainment rooms. Whenever a Gravedigger was dug up and reborn, they were required to spend several days in isolation while they went through testing. There were two more small rooms they used when they'd made a capture or needed to extract information.

Axel sat at the 3-D imagery table staring at the hologram of what was left of the airport in Baltimore after the bombing, sifting through the rubble to see if he could extract any clues about the components or the bombers themselves.

Levi and Elias were each at their own stations, sifting through mounds of data on known associates of the terrorists, following the web as far and wide as they could. The Gravediggers weren't tied by red tape, jurisdiction, or nationality like other agencies, so they could start the job and finish the job before more terrorists from the same organization struck again.

He smelled the fresh aroma of coffee, and saw Tess in the kitchen from the corner of his eye. She turned her head and their eyes caught, and his heart turned over in his chest as he looked at his wife. He never thought he could love someone as much as he loved her. Which scared the hell out of him, because in a few months they would be bringing a child into the world, and he couldn't imagine how the intensity of that love was going to multiply, along with all the worry that went with it.

"I'm just smelling it," she said grumpily. "Why does everything that tastes good have to be bad for you?"

"The doctor said it was okay for you to still have your morning coffee," Deacon said, coming in and kissing her on top of the head. "I think you scared him when we had that early appointment and you'd only had water."

She grinned and leaned back against him, the gesture so familiar it was as if they'd been doing it their whole lives. "What's going on? You looked pretty steamed on your way to the gym."

"I'm still steamed, but pretending it was Eve's face on the punching bag was good therapy. Something is going on, and I'm tired of not being in the know. Not when I'm responsible for so many lives."

"You're afraid Eve will retaliate if you stick your nose too far in," she said, voicing his thoughts.

"I don't know if it's fear or anticipation," he said softly, kissing her on top of her head again.

"I'm with you a hundred percent, whatever you decide." She squeezed his hand and said, "I've got to get back over to the funeral home. Ginny Reed passed this morning. Her family came in a couple weeks back and said it could be any time, so everything is already prepared. But they should be delivering the body soon."

"Let me know if you need help," he said. "And let the EMTs lift the body." He gave her a stern look for emphasis.

"Promise," she said, holding up her hand.

Tess didn't have the same security clearance as the rest of The Gravediggers, but she did enough work for them that she'd warranted her own codes to get into HQ. She kissed him good-bye and then let herself out.

"Elaine," Deacon called out. "This is agent zero, zero, one signing in."

"You are confirmed," she said. "Hello, Deacon. How may I be of service? Are you having a baby today? I am here to assist in a home birth if you need me."

He watched Axel out of the corner of his eye, and saw him pause at the sound of his wife's voice. They rarely used Elaine in HQ because they had everything they needed at their fingertips. She was best served for when they were in the field.

"I appreciate the offer, but we're still many months away from having a baby. And I think we'll be having the baby in a hospital."

"I believe that is an unwise decision," she said. "Hospitals have many germs, and I've been reading that there's a rise in newborns being kidnapped to sell on the black market."

Deacon raised his brows and put his hands to his hips and said, "We'll certainly consider the possibility of a home birth. As long as Tess can have drugs. She's pretty adamant about that."

"We need to make sure our baby is healthy and safe. These are priorities."

He saw Axel's lips twitch at the "our baby" comment before his face went back into harsh lines.

Deacon still didn't know why Axel had made the request to use his wife's voice for the prototype of Elaine. It seemed like doing so would be like reopening a wound every time she spoke. But now that Deacon was married, he thought he could understand that he'd want even the smallest part of Tess—whatever he could have—and that's what Axel had done with his own wife.

"Elaine, please put us on lockdown, and take all communications offline into privacy mode."

That had gotten everyone's attention and they all stared at him, curiosity and questioning in their gazes. Axel stood from his position at the hologram board and grabbed a water, but he didn't sit back down.

"You'll need to give your clearance authorization before I can comply," Elaine said.

Deacon gave his security clearance number and waited while she authorized the request.

"Lockdown starts in *three—two—one*," she said. "This conversation is now offline and in privacy mode."

"Thank you, Elaine. Do you have knowledge of when Eve gave Dante his suspension orders?"

"Eve arrived at Dante's apartment at twenty-two-nineteen hours. Dante's lady friend departed at twenty-two-twenty-three."

"Eve arrived in person?" Elias asked, coming to his feet.

"Hello, Elias. It's been ages since we've talked. How's Miller?"

"She's doing well," he said, and Deacon noticed he was trying not to seem to impatient. When Elaine got upset she tended to pout by going silent. "She's working from home. She just started a new book."

"I've read all her books, and I find them fascinating. I had no idea that sex was possible in so many ways."

"Hmm," Elias said, turning slightly pink. "You were answering about whether or not Eve was really there in person, or if she was on a video call."

"Oh, she was there," Elaine confirmed. "Lovely shoes. Terrible attitude."

Elias snorted out a laugh at that, but turned to Deacon. "Eve never visits in person. Not unless some really bad shit is about to go down. What's going on, Deacon?"

"Just a feeling," he said. "Enough that I'm willing to ask questions that I'm not supposed to be asking."

"How long did Eve stay at Dante's apartment?" Levi asked.

"She was there for one hour and fourteen minutes," Elaine answered. "Then she departed on her broom." There was a tinkle of laughter from Elaine as she made the joke. "That was funny, yes?" she asked. "I've spent time studying the great comedians. And I've learned that timing is everything."

At any other time, Deacon would have been more than amused. But he was still too angry. And now he had even more questions, because there was no way in hell Eve would stay an hour and fourteen minutes just to put him on suspension. She wouldn't have made the trip to do it in person either. Nothing was adding up.

"Can you put a comprehensive list together of Dante's requested time off?" he asked her. "And can you put a list together of any other times Eve and Dante have met?"

"Stand by," she said. "Appearing on screen three."

Elias let out a long low whistle, and everyone was standing now, facing the screen.

"I'll be damned," Axel said. "What in the hell do you think they're up to?"

"I think there might be more to Dante than what's in his file," Deacon said. "Elaine, please give Dante's destination and arrival time for his last flight."

"I apologize, Deacon, but you do not have the security clearance to request this information."

"Son of a bitch," he said. "Elaine, you're about to use that free-thinking, brilliant mind of yours. I need every scrap of information on Dante that I do have clearance for. I also want you to coordinate his past travel dates with any major news stories. I want complete dossiers on any past relationships he's had, and I want his MI6 files."

He'd read them before, when Dante had been brought on as a Gravedigger, but he had a feeling they'd probably been altered. But there would be some truths in there, and all he had to do was line up the dates.

"It looks like we've got a new mission," he said, looking at the others. "Who's in?"

CHAPTER TWELVE

The plane hit turbulence as it climbed to the requisite thirty-thousand feet, and Dante's body jerked against the harness that strapped him in. He was a thrill seeker by trade, but he had to admit that HALO jumping wasn't one of his favorite parts of the job. But it was a necessary part, so The Gravediggers put in the hours of training every month. Just for situations like this one.

Okay, maybe not a situation *exactly* like this one.

The night had always been his favorite time. It was when his energy peaked and he felt invigorated to complete the task at hand. Once the sun went down, his senses seemed to sharpen. It was as if the cloak of night gave him permission to be his real self.

He'd spent the last week in Dubai, soaking in the sights and sounds of the city, watching the palace from afar, and he and Elaine worked in tandem to re-create the security system on the vault and then practiced opening it over and over again. It had been extremely helpful for Shiv Mittal to do an exclusive interview with *60 Minutes*, giving an in-depth tour of the palace and the vault. It hadn't been difficult for Elaine to hack into the newsroom's files and video archives and pull deleted scenes they hadn't been able to air on television.

He barely slept, the anticipation of the job fueling him—research during the day, and then at night, he'd slip out like the thief he was and do the exterior recon work. A good thief always had multiple escape routes at his disposal.

Everything had been done to prepare. Now all he had to do was put his skills to the test.

The specially modified King Air B90 had been waiting for him on a private airstrip, the pilot going over the final checklist before takeoff as Dante approached. The discreet gold trident was visible to the right of the door, and he'd held the gun beneath his gear, ready to shoot if the pilot didn't give the signal that portrayed him as a member of The Shadow, the prep, cleanup, and support crew who made The Gravediggers' work possible.

The pilot delivered the signal, and Dante had reciprocated with the answer. He'd walked up the ramp and strapped himself in, then donned his oxygen mask. HALO jumping brought health risks above and beyond the hazards of regular parachuting. The last thing he needed was to pass out during the jump and fail to pull the chute.

Every piece of equipment and clothing was built specifically for jumping out of a plane at thirty-thousand feet in the middle of the night. He wore a black insulated skinsuit beneath his specially made black pants with the extra tubing he used during a heist. It was his own design, everything place precisely where he needed it to be. Every second counted. On top of the layers of clothing was a black jumpsuit. He had a full ski mask pulled over his head. Temperatures dropped as low as negative fifty at that height, and frostbite was another possibility, along with decompression sickness and hypoxia. The goggles would keep his eyeballs from freezing.

His bag of toys were strapped to his back beneath the flight suit, and he counted his breaths—in and out—slow and easy—to make sure he got all the oxygen in his blood that he needed.

There was a long beep followed by a click, and the side door of the plane opened. Dante unstrapped himself and did a final check, then adjusted his goggles. The palace was lit up as bright as day, so he should have no trouble seeing his landing target. The biggest challenge was to land close enough to the guard to take him out before he sounded the alarm and Dante ended up with a hailstorm of bullets in his body.

During all the simulation runs he'd had Elaine throw at him, he'd only been successful at landing in the right place and taking out the guard once.

He held on to the strap that hung by the open door, and at the last moment he removed his oxygen and replaced it with his portable breather. He watched the red light flash once—twice—three times, and then it turned green and he jumped.

He spread his arms and legs, letting the flight suit catch air while he changed direction so he was headed directly toward the palace. The lights of the city looked like twinkling diamonds, and they grew larger and brighter as he hurtled toward the west tower of the palace. It was the wing reserved for guests, and there were only two in attendance who were registered with the palace guard.

The onion-domed west tower was completely encircled by a balcony, and there were decorative arches that all led to the spiral staircase that descended to where the guest suites were. There was one guard stationed here, as there was at each of the other towers.

Timing was everything. He had to pull his chute at the last possible second and aim for one of the open archways, without the chute getting caught and dragging him backward—and then, without missing a beat, take out the guard before things went south.

His heart hammered in his chest as he approached at full speed, his vision dotted with black spots from the force as he fell to earth. He saw the guard, who was looking the other way, and adjusted his incoming angle just slightly, anticipating the man's movements. And then he pulled the chute and shot into the west tower, directly under the arch.

As soon as his feet touched the ground he moved to his left and came face-to-face with a very surprised guard. Wasting no time, Dante gave him a quick chop to the neck, dropping the guard to his knees and then the floor. He quickly pulled in his chute so there was no sight of it from the outside, and then stripped out of his flight suit and mask, keeping an eye on the guard.

Grabbing zip ties from the satchel across his back, Dante bound the guard's hands and feet, then put duct tape over his mouth and covered him with the black parachute. It had taken seconds, from the moment he touched down.

His blood was pumping and his heart pounding. There was no other feeling on earth like it—except for sex. The rush of adrenaline. The brief moment of free-falling into outrageous pleasure.

The spiral stairwell that descended into the west wing was dark, but he'd studied the layout and could've made his way down blindfolded. His footsteps were quiet, and when he reached the bottom he carefully tested the door that led to the west wing. The guard had left it unlocked, making Dante's job that much easier.

The door opened on silent hinges, and he peeked through the crack, getting a view of the serpentine hallway. Wall sconces emitted a soft glow against the mosaic-tiled walls, and the doors of the guest suites were spaced far apart on either side. The marble floors were patterned in a diamond inlay, light reflecting off the jewels they'd used, and in the center of each diamond was a gold *dallah*, a sign of welcome to the guests staying at the palace.

There were no sounds and no signs of other people, so he slipped through the door and closed it quietly, locking it behind him. He moved quickly down the long corridor, then slowed as he reached the end of the hallway. The walls disappeared and in their place were pink marble columns veined with gold. All of the wings of the palace opened into this central area, and even those on the upper floors where he was could look up and see the inside of the big central onion dome, or down to the opulent great room.

There was a guard on each floor who, Dante knew, was able to make an entire round of all the wings in fifty-six minutes, and that included checking the unoccupied rooms for any unwanted guests. Dante needed to be in the east wing and up a level to get the Turner painting from the master suite. The vault was in the north wing, and the only entry point was from Mittal's office.

Dante moved like a ghost, disappearing behind the columns and reappearing again only to do a visual search for possible threats. He caught sight of the guard across from him in the opposite wing, coming out of a room and closing the door behind him. His pulse hammered in his throat and he waited patiently as the guard went the opposite direction down the hallway.

The grand staircase looked like an Escher as it connected the floors, veering off to different wings. The carpet was red and rich and vibrant but, most important, it was plush and soft. He moved toward the stairs and went up slowly, his footsteps muffled by the carpet, watching to make sure he didn't have an unexpected run-in with the guard on the top floor.

He checked his watch and noted that the guard should currently be checking the bathhouse area. There were multiple hot tubs and plunge pools, as well as sauna and steam rooms. Shiv Mittal woke early and liked to use the area before anyone in the palace rose for the day, but Dante still had more than an hour before Mittal would be moving about.

He made his way down another serpentine hallway, the marble floors encrusted with rubies and pearls, and the red sandstone walls done with intricate carvings and gold inlays. It was a riveting sight, but he had no time to linger and look. There were no other rooms next to the master suite, but there was a door on either side of the hallway, each leading into a private sitting area.

He brought the blueprint of the suite to mind. It was shaped like a large horseshoe—a private apartment for the master of the palace. If he'd gone in through the carved double doors, he would have walked into an entryway, and then into the small kitchen area. There was a master suite on the left with an adjoining bathroom and sitting room, and there was a suite on the right for whatever woman Mittal happened to be entertaining at the time.

The tabloids loved Shiv Mittal. One magazine had dubbed him the sexiest nerd alive. And he was never photographed with the same woman on his arm twice. He was considered a playboy, and he'd never had a long-term relationship that Dante could find. He'd never been married and had no children, which many people thought scandalous because there was no heir to the now defunct sultanate. Tradition was important. And Shiv's father had more than a hundred wives. Most thought it was long past time for Shiv to follow in his father's footsteps.

Dante used a metal pick from his pack and quickly unlocked one of the side doors. There was no noise as he turned the knob and cracked the door open. He slipped into a very feminine sitting room done in delicate blues and creams, the walls carved in floral patterns, and the floor swirls of darker blues and golds.

The Turner was in the master bedroom, according to the *60 Minutes* interview Mittal had given to show off his collection. It was a good collection. But nowhere close to what Dante had amassed over the years.

He made his way silently through the rooms until he reached the master suite. The door was closed, but not locked. This wouldn't be the first time he'd taken something from a room occupied by people. It just added an element of excitement to the job.

He slowly turned the knob until the door was cracked, and then he waited, listening for the soft sounds of even breathing. But he didn't hear anything of the sort. What he heard was the shower spray from the bathroom. Shiv must have gotten up earlier than usual.

Dante took a chance and stepped inside the room to assess the situation. The bed was empty, the covers tossed back and halfway onto the floor. He must have had a restless night and decided sleep was futile. But Dante quickly lost interest in Shiv's sleep patterns when he saw the Turner hanging gloriously over the bed. He felt that quick rush of appreciation, followed by the need to possess it, at whatever cost.

He scanned the large room, noting an array of framed photographs and other personal items, though it was too dark to see most of the images. He glanced at a grouping of frames on top of the dresser that were cast in the light from beneath the bathroom door, and he saw Shiv Mittal with three other dark-haired, dark-eyed women, who he was assuming were his half sisters, considering the resemblance.

Dante decided it was best to wait until Shiv left before he took the painting from the wall. He was still well ahead of schedule, and Dante knew how to wait—how to be so still and silent that no one would feel his presence.

He was just about to crawl beneath the bed when he heard a familiar sound from the bathroom. There were some sounds that were unmistakable, and sex was one of them. Especially loud and boisterous sex. Moans were easily audible over the running water of the shower, along with a steady conversation of very creative suggestions. Who knew? The sexy nerd liked to talk dirty. And apparently whoever he was talking to liked it very much, because her moans grew louder and turned into a litany of "Oh, my God" over and over.

Dante had never been one to enjoy voyeurism, but he had no choice. He crawled under the bed and hoped they were making their way toward the grand finale. He checked his watch one more time, then raised his brows at Mittal's verbal creativity. He lay there patiently for another fifteen minutes until the woman's screams hit the peak of a crescendo and Shiv roared like a lion through his orgasm, yelling the name Yasmin again and again.

Then he waited another ten minutes, the silence broken only by the sound of the shower as they cleaned up. When the bathroom door finally opened, Dante watched Shiv's bare feet as he made his way to the wardrobe for clothes. He got dressed quickly, then returned to the bathroom and stood at the open door.

"Take your time soaking in the tub, love," he said. "And then get back into bed and get some sleep. Pamper yourself today. I'm going to head over to the spa, and then I've got some work to do in the office. But I'll meet you for breakfast at ten o'clock, if you'd like."

It was hard to make out what the woman was saying because her voice was so soft, but she must have agreed, because Shiv said, "See you at breakfast," and then he left the room.

Dante didn't waste any time crawling from beneath the bed. It was larger than a king-size, so he had to climb on top of it to get to the painting. His movements were smooth and practiced as he removed the painting from the frame and cut the canvas from the wooden frame it was stretched on. He took the replacement picture from the tube that had been built into his pants, and inserted the rolled-up Turner. It only took a few seconds to put the replacement picture in the frame and rehang it on the wall.

He stepped down and grinned at his handiwork. Maybe he was sick, but it gave him immeasurable pleasure to see a print of *Dogs Playing Poker* hanging above the bed. He checked his watch again, and clicked the timer. He had to be in and out of the vault before Mittal got to his office for the day.

He moved to the door on the opposite side of the room that led to Mittal's sitting area, so he could take the side door that led back into the hallway.

Just in case Mittal was lingering in the kitchen. His hand was on the knob when he felt a presence behind him.

"What are you doing here?" a woman's voice asked.

His heart thumped once in his chest, but he wasn't afraid. Completing the mission successfully was his only goal. He'd accomplish it however he needed to. He turned around slowly, his arms relaxed at his sides, and fixed a cocky grin on his face—then froze when he saw her.

Beneath the shock was anger—fierce and undeserved—that swept through him at the knowledge she'd just been with another man. He had no right, but he'd always thought of her as his alone.

His first thought was that she hadn't changed—but the woman standing in front of him was worlds different from the woman he'd last seen as he'd jumped to his death. Her face was thinner, her cheekbones more pronounced, and her eyes were glacial. She was dressed in expensive silk lounging pajamas, the tank baring her toned stomach and prominently displaying the fact that she wasn't wearing a bra.

Her hair had always been a fascination to him. He loved the color and the texture, the way it felt across his chest. It was longer than when he'd seen her last. She had it pulled over one shoulder and it fell down past her breast.

"Liv, my darling. We've got to stop meeting like this."

Her eyes narrowed and something changed in them that he couldn't quite identify. She came toward him, and the way she was looking at him made him want to take a step back.

"Who are you?" she asked.

And then he knew. It came to him in a moment of utmost certainty. "Dear God," he whispered. "Elizabeth."

"No," she said, terror in her eyes. "You're not taking me." She struck out with a right hook that had him seeing stars, and followed it up with a knee to his groin that brought him to his knees. And then she was gone.

"Shit," he wheezed, trying to catch his breath and get to his feet. She packed a hell of a punch.

He lurched to his feet and went through the door, hoping he could chase her down before she alerted the guards, but when he made it back to the red sandstone hallway, she was already gone. He couldn't even hear her footsteps against the tiles. But her fear had come from the thought of him trying to take her. That's what she'd said.

You're not taking me.

Maybe she wasn't running to alert the guards. Maybe she was running to stay hidden. She'd done a hell of a job of it up to that point. There was no record of her, or Yasmin, if that's the name she was going by, in any database he'd searched. The photograph he'd gotten in the dossier on the palace was the only evidence of her—no name, no description—but it was obvious that she and Mittal were involved. She was the palace's best-kept secret. And he couldn't help but wonder why.

Dante didn't waste any time. He ran to the end of the hallway, stopping briefly to check for the guard. He heard his footsteps scraping across the hard floor, coming from Mittal's office in the north wing, and Dante swore to himself. His run-in with Elizabeth had taken him off schedule. The guard was coming directly toward him to check the master suite next.

Making a split-second decision, he ran back down the hallway to the sitting room door and let himself in again, closing the door behind him. And then he waited, his heart pounding wildly in his chest as the footsteps made their way down the hall. He heard the guard pass by, a jangle of keys in his hand as he prepared to unlock the other sitting room door, and then Dante slipped out behind the man. He had him in a choke hold, and his air cut off in three seconds, and then he dragged him back into the sitting area. He used more zip ties to bind the man's hands and feet and put a piece of tape over his mouth.

"Elaine," he said, activating her on his watch.

"Your heart rate is elevated, Dante. Is everything all right?"

"Just a little unexpected surprise. I'm heading to the vault now. Time is going to be of the essence. We'll need to move quickly."

"I'll be ready for your commands," she said.

"Going back into silent mode."

He left the guard in the room and ran down the hallway, expecting a squad of guards to be waiting for him. But still there was no one, and he started to get a little tingle at the base of his spine. Or maybe he was just paranoid and reading more into the silence than he should.

He cut across the large open space between the east wing and the north wing, using the large columns for cover, as he all but ran toward Mittal's office. The white carved doors with gold swans as knobs were original to the palace, but the security panel next to the door was twenty-first-century technology.

"Elaine," he said, keeping his voice low. "Approaching office door."

"Ten-four, kemo sabe," she said.

"Now's not a good time, Elaine."

"My apologies, sir. I've been practicing my pop culture. The panel to your right is keycard-operated. It's a ten-digit binary code that's changed weekly."

Dante withdrew a black rectangular device the size of a cell phone from his bag and hit the button on the side. A black digital keycard snapped out and he slipped it into the card slot, watching the green numbers scramble on the reader, slowly ticking off each of the ten digits. When the final digit fell into place, he heard the tumblers of the locks click open, and he turned the gold swan handle and entered Mittal's private sanctum.

It hadn't changed from the *60 Minutes* special. The furnishings were modern—metal and white leather—but the marble floor was original. There was a wall of screens playing continuous stock reports, but there was no volume. There were some lovely paintings on the walls—a Klimt and a Kandinsky—both of which Dante would've like for his own collection, but they weren't his for the taking. At least, not on this trip.

He went behind Mittal's desk and ran his fingers beneath the sleek black surface until he felt the small button. When he pushed it, a panel of the wall slid open, revealing another long corridor. He could see the vault door from where he stood. It was a large steel circle, impossibly thick and heavy.

He slid the panel closed behind him, and his footsteps echoed as he made his way toward the vault, which was set into a cove at the end of the hallway. There were walk-in niches on either side where large urns sat, and the second he stepped in front of the door he realized his mistake.

He heard the very familiar sound of a bullet being chambered in a pistol, and he put his hands up slowly.

"You son of a bitch," Liv said. "You're supposed to be dead."

He turned to face her, and then wondered how he ever could have mistaken Elizabeth for her. Elizabeth was beautiful, but Liv was stunning. There was a spark, a vivaciousness in Liv's eyes that drew him in. It was passion. And once it had all been his.

She was dressed in black, much like he was— black pants, a black long-sleeved shirt, and black gloves. Any sign of her pale hair was tucked beneath a black watch cap.

"Believe me," he said. "I am." And then all the charm and devil-may-care attitude he'd always relied on failed him and he said, "I've missed you, my love."

The gun wavered slightly, and he took advantage. He slapped at the barrel with both hands and twisted, making the gun drop to the ground, and he was ready for her counterstrike, her body twisting and her elbow connecting with his ribs. She had a backup weapon at the base of her spine, and he pulled it free and held it on her as she broke out of his grasp.

She faced him, her breath heaving and rage in her eyes. "I watched you die," she said. "You spineless, lying coward. I watched you jump off that tower and fall into the sea. You used me. You used me so you could stay one step ahead and you could keep stealing. I was getting too close, wasn't I?"

"You were," he answered honestly. He couldn't lie to her anymore. "But I didn't plan on what happened between us."

"And what was that, *Simon*? Sex? Lust? A few laughs?"

"You know it was more than that," he said.

"I know you're a liar and a con artist. So what?" she asked. "Are you going to shoot me?" She nodded at the gun he was still holding.

He released the magazine and let it fall to the floor with a clank, then unchambered the last bullet.

"Of course not," he said, turning the butt of the gun toward her to give it back. She took it with her left hand just as she was swinging with her right.

CHAPTER THIRTEEN

"Christ," he said, rubbing the side of his face. He tasted blood from where his teeth had cut his cheek. Damned if she and Elizabeth didn't have the same right hook.

"I should've just shot you," she said. "You've been dead for almost two years. Might as well make it real."

Her breath shuddered and he realized how close to tears she was, that she was trying valiantly to stay in control. He imagined it was more than just a shock to see him standing there after she'd watched him fall to his death.

"Look," he said, raising his hands palm out in surrender. "We can either stand here and argue about the past, or we can do the job we've come for. I'm assuming there's a reason you're in Dubai trying to break into this vault."

"Yes, though I'm sure it's not as lucrative as the reason you're here. What are you stealing this time?" she sneered.

"Launch codes to a Russian nuclear weapon," he said. "Ten days ago, Mittal won them in a poker game. He's a brilliant man, but he doesn't have the scope of understanding of what it means to have those codes. I'm surprised he's still alive. Every unsavory country in the world has him as their number-one target. The idiot. My mission is to retrieve them."

"Your mission?" she asked, eyes narrowed. "Who are you working for?"

"I don't mean to point out the obvious," he said, ignoring her question, "but you're trying to break into the vault as well. It seems you've a case of the pot calling the kettle black."

"I'm not after the son," she said. "At least, I don't think I am. He seems to be a fairly straight arrow from what I can find. I'm after the father. They call him The Sultan."

Dante nodded, already putting the pieces together from everything he'd read about Raj Mittal. "Human trafficking," he said, before she could. "You suspect he's using this location as a holding site?"

"I do," she said. "This vault is the size of a bank. It's temperature-controlled, and there are vaults *in-*

side the vault. I can't think of a safer place to hide that kind of inventory."

"You must have watched the *60 Minutes* special just like I did."

Her mouth quirked with the beginnings of a smile before she quickly stifled it. "I resigned from Interpol," she said. "Beck and I had a little disagreement over my coming here."

"Oh, good," he said. "Then we're both likely to be arrested if we keep standing here."

"Fine, but when this is over we're going to have a short conversation."

"And then what?" he asked.

"I'll either let you live or I'll kill you. I'm having trouble deciding."

"Darling, you know that kind of talk turns me on. Let's focus on the job and then we can have foreplay later."

She growled low in her throat and he grinned, turning to the security panels on the outside of the vault door.

He hit a button on his watch and said, "Elaine, are you there?"

"Of course," she said. "Where else would I be?"

"I have no idea," he said. "We've picked up a passenger. Meet Liv Rothschild."

"Lovely to meet you," Elaine said. "I've seen

your name in the archives. Your picture is lovely. I thought of having my human form have hair like yours, but it didn't fit my personality."

"Umm . . ." Liv said, raising her brows.

"You and Liv will have to get acquainted later," he said. "We're standing outside the vault door. Have you gotten any alerts from security that there's been a breach?"

"No, Lord Malcolm. Everything has been quiet."

He rolled his eyes at the use of his title. "I'm starting the vault process in three . . . two . . . one . . ."

"Countdown engaged," Elaine said.

The vault locks had to be opened in stages. The first stage was an old-fashioned tumbler dial that was more for show than it was for purpose. Dante had to admit, it had made for good television, although the producers had blurred out the numbers as Mittal opened it. Elaine had used a special technology to go through the tape again and unblur the combination.

She'd sent the combination to his watch, and he quickly turned the dial: *36 left—2 right—16 left—9 right.* When the last tumbler fell into place, he pulled the lock out and a panel opened on the side wall.

He opened his bag and took out an electronic device that snapped around his throat, pressing the button to turn it on, then put in an earpiece with a mic that curved down to his mouth.

The panel had opened to a black screen; there was a steady red line that ran across it, waiting for him to speak the passcodes in Mittal's voice. The technology he was using was new, but Elaine had insisted it had been thoroughly tested with results in the ninety-eighth percentile. It was the other two percent he was worried about.

"Albarakuda . . .

Mmusiba . . .

Alssulta . . .

Yasmin . . ."

Each time he said a word, the red line showed the sound waves of his voice and then turned green, showing it was a match. When he said the fourth word, the panel in the wall closed and another panel above it opened, revealing another flat screen. It wasn't as sophisticated as the retinal scan they used at Gravediggers headquarters. There was nothing on the open market or even in private R&D labs that came close to the sophistication of the equipment The Gravediggers used. They knew this because The Shadow was everywhere, and no secrets at any level were safe when Eve wanted to know something.

Drawing a small black box from his bag, Dante handed it to Liv for her to hold as he opened it. Inside were contacts, the brown lenses encrypted with electronic replicas of Mittal's retinas.

Dante carefully put a contact on his finger, mentally counting down the seconds in his head before the retinal scanner retreated back into the wall as a fail-safe. He blinked rapidly as the contact slid into place, and put the second contact in. Then he turned to the screen and stared at it, keeping his eyes open as the green light passed back and forth.

There was a slight pause as the machine processed the information, and Dante stole a glimpse at Liv. She bit her bottom lip and held her breath, then jumped as the retinal scanner beeped and receded into the wall.

Another panel opened—the last phase of the security system—and this time the black screen emerged from the wall and went horizontal, the screen facing up. He pulled a slim square case from his pack, about a foot wide in both directions, but only an inch or so thick. He handed the case to Liv and whispered, "Hold it steady," as he carefully lifted the lid to expose the delicate pieces of flesh inside.

There was a hard plastic imprint of a hand inside the case, and inside the hand was a thin layer of synthetic skin that replicated Mittal's handprint. He placed his gloved hand directly into the hand in the case, moving it from side to side and from front

SAY NO MORE × 195

to back so the skin would adhere completely to the glove. When he lifted his hand, the thin layer of skin was attached to his glove.

He placed his palm on the flat screen and waited as it was scanned, feeling the heat from the scanner through his glove. There was a pause and a long beep, and then the round steel door opened on silent hinges.

"My goodness," Elaine said. "That was quite a nerve-racking experience. If I were human, I'd be dead from holding my breath."

"Interesting," Liv said. "You're AI?"

"I'm a GenXI prototype," she said. "There's not another in the world like me. I have independent thought capabilities. And they are working on giving me emotions."

"Impressive," Liv said.

"I know," Elaine answered.

Dante rolled his eyes. Liv had no clue just how close they'd come to being caught. "Nerve-racking" didn't begin to describe it. If he'd taken three more seconds, the entire system would've gone into lockdown and they would've been trapped until the guards were alerted.

"Go and search for the girls," he told Liv. "Keep an eye out for a titanium briefcase."

The vault was so bright it made his eyes water—

white walls, white floor, and white lights—and it was cold, well below a comfortable temperature. The space was larger than it had seemed on television. His estimation of it being the size of a tennis court was off. It could easily be double that.

There was a central room lined with open shelves piled with stacks of cash in multiple currencies. There was also a row of filing cabinets. It made sense Mittal would want to keep sensitive documents that he might need to reach quickly closest to the entryway, along with the cash. Since he was a gambling man, Dante was willing to bet there were also multiple passports and identities in the files. Most of the filthy rich had them—just in case.

From the main room, there was a hallway to the left, right, and straight ahead, and the hallways were lined with clear doors so the interiors could be seen easily. Vaults within a vault. It was where Mittal kept most of his art collection, trading out pieces to display in the house from time to time.

"Hurry and see if the girls are in any of the interior vaults," he said. "What's your plan once you find them? How are you going to get them out?"

"We're going to go out the front door and draw as much attention as possible. And then pray nothing goes wrong."

"If you don't mind a suggestion . . ." he said.

"I mind," she said. "But I'll listen anyway since little girls' lives are at stake."

"There is an old sewage pipe in the dungeon that leads to the sea. We can use it to move quickly and safely outside the palace, and we can all be extracted from there."

"That's all fine and good, except they sealed off the entrance to that pipe in the fifties," she said.

"I've been in Dubai for a week," he said. "I haven't spent my time here twiddling my thumbs. The pipe has recently been unsealed."

"How did you manage that?" she asked.

"Three nights ago there was a fireworks display as they celebrated the city's Day of Remembrance to honor the dead."

He saw the light come into her eyes as she took the thread of what he was saying and ran with it. "And you timed your small explosions at the end of the sealed pipe to match the fireworks."

"Exactly," he said. "Now, go find your girls."

She nodded and headed toward the interior vault doors.

"Elaine, bring up the holographic image of the briefcase the codes were being transported in," he said. "There are several briefcases in here."

A hologram image of the briefcase shot up from out of his watch, giving him a three hundred and sixty degree view. But it didn't help. The briefcase wasn't there.

"I'm not seeing anything like this," he said.

"I would imagine that if he removed them from the briefcase, he'd still have them in a lockbox," Elaine said. "It's only a few sheets of paper, easily lost if not contained."

He quickly made his way down each of the hallways, looking inside each of the clear doors.

"Any luck?" he asked Liv as he passed her to peer inside each of the smaller vaults, searching for any sign of a black titanium briefcase.

"They're not here," she said, fists at her hips, red flushing her cheeks. And then she kicked the wall in frustration.

"That makes two of us who got faulty intel," he said, feeling his own frustration rise. "No launch codes."

"Look at the last room on the end," she told him.

Dante went to the last room and looked through the clear door. There were bowls on the floor, some filled with water and others with what looked like the remains of rice. And there were crumpled blankets on the floor and a bucket in the corner that he assumed was what they'd used for a toilet.

"This is fresh," he said. "Elaine, can you check to see when the vault door was last activated?"

"I can pull the data only from the electronic door that leads from Mittal's office," Elaine said. "But it doesn't necessarily mean that the vault was entered. Stand by."

"I've got a bad feeling about this," Liv said.

"We need to get out of here and regroup," he said. "Something's not right." He'd learned to listen to his gut over the years, and he wasn't going to start ignoring it now.

"What about the launch codes?" she asked.

"Either he's got them somewhere else, or he's sold them without our knowledge."

"Or maybe someone else got in here to steal them first," she said.

"Or that," he agreed.

The vault was last accessed at zero three hundred hours," Elaine said.

"Shiv Mittal wasn't back in the palace until late yesterday," Dante said. "And he was in his suite at the time of entry. I saw him leave after three a.m."

"Like you said before," Liv said. "Raj is still calling the shots where his son is concerned, and he'd know about his acquiring the launch codes in that poker game. Who'd know better how to ramp up the bidding between competing interests? So if the father accessed the vault and knew his son had obtained the launch codes, it's probable he took the girls and the codes. Those launch codes in the hands of Raj Mittal are much more dangerous than in the hands of his son."

"I've hacked into the security cameras," Elaine said. "They show Raj Mittal entering the office just before the key card time stamp. But he immediately disconnected the security cameras, so there's no visual of him leaving with the codes or the girls."

"I'm convinced," Liv said.

"Then let's hunt that bastard down."

"I'd love to," she said. "But here's my dilemma. What if the launch codes in *your* hands are just as dangerous as in the hands of Mittal?"

"I guess you're going to have to trust that I'm one of the good guys," he said, moving toward the exit.

"Not bloody likely," she said, following him.

CHAPTER FOURTEEN

Liv had somehow fallen down the rabbit hole.

Nothing—and she meant absolutely nothing—had gone according to plan since she'd stepped foot in Dubai. Before that even, she admitted, when she should've listened to Beck and his advice to gather more intel.

But there was no amount of intel that could've prepared her for seeing Dante face-to-face. Those piercing blue eyes were the same, his face so beautiful, it almost took her breath away. She thought of the days and weeks she'd spent between anger and mourning, the toll it had taken on her mind and body, and wished she could punch him again.

Who was he really?

The world of espionage led to so many variables—so many truths. He'd been British Intelligence, she'd known that from the start. But how deep had he been? Was Simon Locke a deep cover to draw out someone else? Was he a double agent? Whoever he'd been, his death had been real for anyone who knew him, including his family. But it was obvious he was still working for someone.

"Do you want to find Mittal or not?" Dante asked. "If you do, you're welcome to come with me. If not, we'll part ways now, and I'm sure we'll end up crossing paths again while we hunt him."

"I'm coming with you," Liv said. "But only because I don't trust you. I found him once on my own, and I could do it again."

"Only this time without the help of Interpol, since your temper got the best of you and you resigned."

"I did what I felt was right. Some of us have principles."

"Elaine," he said, ignoring her, "can you check exterior satellite images or the security cameras and see where there's activity? Let's run Raj Mittal down before he gets on a plane or boat headed to God knows where with those girls and the launch codes."

"Stand by," Elaine said. And then, less than thirty seconds later, "I'm running into interference. I can reroute and get us back in, but it looks like their system must have been alerted to our virtual eyes."

Even as she said it, shrill sirens sounded and the lights flashed red inside the vault.

"Go," Dante yelled.

Liv was already running. The big round door had already started closing, and she and Dante rushed through at the last second. Her body jerked forward as she felt the resistance against her shirt, and then she heard the tearing fabric as she ripped her shirt free from the door, leaving a strip of black cloth.

Dante grabbed her hand and tugged her down the corridor that led back into Mittal's office, but that door opened and armed soldiers rushed in, weapons raised, screaming in streams of Arabic. Fear clutched in her belly, and the blood pounded so hard in her ears she could barely hear. But fear didn't cripple her. Her training had seen to that. Fear brought an unrelenting calm over her. She wasn't scared of death. Everyone had to die at some point or another. And since death was inevitable, she might as well go while doing something she loved. She waited for the bullets to hit her body, but Dante shoved her to the ground and curled around her. She appreciated the gesture, but she couldn't reach her gun.

She was yanked to her feet, the guard squeezing her arm so hard she knew it would leave bruises. He smelled of sweat and nerves, and his hands shook as he held her captive. He wasn't in control, and the last thing she wanted was spook him into firing his weapon.

She heard a grunt from Dante, but she couldn't see what they were doing to him. She and Dante were both trained for moments like this one. They each had knowledge of top-secret files within their own agencies, and if those files were in danger of being breached, there was always the option of the cyanide pill she had tucked away in the hidden compartment in the sole of her shoe.

Liv didn't try to struggle. It would've been pointless, and she didn't want to end up hurt badly enough that it might keep her from escaping if the chance arose. Someone jerked her hands behind her back and bound them with duct tape. They shoved her in the middle of the back, and she started walking forward. She breathed a sigh of relief when she heard Dante fall into step behind her.

A gun nudged her in the back and she moved through the great room, keeping her gaze straight ahead. Her skin was chilled, despite the warm temperature, and her arms were trembling from being held behind her back. But she started to feel some hope as they stopped in front of a narrow arched door.

The dungeon.

She'd studied the layout of the palace, memorizing every nook and cranny, along with the ducts and sewage lines that ran throughout. If they could stay alive long enough, they had a good chance of being able to get the hell out of there and run down Raj Mittal before he got too far away.

Dante had seen to it that it was an escape, not a prison, and relief filled her as the soldiers unlocked the door and pushed the two of them down a dark, narrow spiral staircase. Maybe luck was finally starting to turn in her favor.

The guards used flashlights—apparently the dungeon didn't have electricity—and rats scurried back into the shadows, squeaking their displeasure at the interruption. They reached the bottom of the staircase, the man behind her released her and shoved her—*hard*—and she fell to her knees.

Liv felt the sting in her knees from hitting the ground, and she kept her head down, using her peripheral vision to watch one of the guards move around the room and light lanterns, filling it with an eerie orange glow and making shadows jump from the walls.

She assumed the walls had once been white, much like the rest of the palace, but they were filthy and spotted with age and neglect, and it was easy to see the water damage from where the dungeon had filled during floods. There were dark stains on the floor—*blood*—and bullet holes against one of the walls from where there had once been a firing squad.

The dungeon was large, and she could imagine it full of people, filthy and dying, as the water rose higher and higher. Their screams for help as the water slowly rose above their heads. Chains were bolted into the floor and walls, and there were three rectangular windows at the very top of the far wall. There were bars on them, and she guessed they were more for ventilation than atmosphere, though the smell of stale death and decay couldn't be erased completely. She could only imagine how stifling the place got in the heat of the day. Along the far wall, the floor was about six inches lower, and there were grates placed every few feet. It was a latrine, and Liv knew that the pipe Dante had opened up could be accessed beneath those grates.

Liv braced herself for the blows—they were expected, and what she would have done in their position. Keeping an enemy weak was the smart thing to do. These were not the security guards that were stationed throughout the palace. These were soldiers—Mittal's personal security detail—and they didn't care that she was a woman. Their only concern was the threat against the man who employed them.

A fist connected with her ribs and the air whooshed out of her. While she gasped for breath, a man yanked off her watch cap and exposed the short black wig she'd donned for the occasion, tossing it aside. He grabbed hold of her arm and jerked her to her feet, pushing her face-first against the wall. She turned her head to the side and watched as Dante was put in a similar pose next to her. His eyes glittered with anger, but he barely flinched as one of the soldiers hit him across the back with a nightstick.

She briefly wondered if she was about to face a firing squad, but then hands started patting her down, sliding along her ribs and under her breasts, and then around to her back. They pulled the pistol from the small of her back, and then continued their search. Over her hips and along her inseams. They found a knife sheathed at each ankle, and the sounds of the blades as they were taken out seemed overly loud.

Her eyes met Dante's as the soldiers patted him down, removing the pack from his back that carried all his tools, and the long cylindrical tube she was sure carried whatever else he'd stolen from the palace.

Dante winked at her, and earned another punch from the guard. He would always push people right to the limits, just to see how much he could get away with. He was the consummate spy. There wasn't any situation that seemed to bother him, though a small line appeared between his brows when they removed his watch and his communication to Elaine. But he always had a response or a plan, even when things didn't go as intended.

His jaw was already swollen, but she wasn't sure if it was from her hit or from one of the soldiers'.

Liv didn't feel bad about it one bit. After he'd "died" and she'd almost lost her job, she'd started seeing a therapist. Marlena had told her she needed outlets for her anger. That keeping it all bottled up inside wasn't healthy and would eventually lead to the kind of explosion that she couldn't put back in a bottle. When it came to Dante, she was very, very angry. She should've punched him twice.

The guard turned her around so her back was pressed to the wall, and she dropped her gaze in deference as he'd expect, just so he'd mistake her for weak. She'd been able to loosen the tape on her wrists, at least enough to give her circulation, but she hadn't been able to break free yet.

She tried to control her panic as the guard knelt at her feet and placed the manacles around each of her ankles, the clank of finality echoing through the chamber. She hated being restrained, and the manacles weren't rusty circles of iron that had been rotting for a couple of centuries. They were new and shiny, the locks intricate and complicated.

She shifted her feet, testing the weight and seeing how securely they were bolted to the wall. Dante was fastened similarly, and the soldier restraining him gave him a parting blow to the stomach, but Dante barely flinched. She would've been doubled over trying to catch her breath.

"He's the only heir to not only his father's fortune, but also that of Geronimo Vincenzo, who happens to be his uncle on his mother's side. Those fortunes added to his own would make him the wealthiest man in the world by far. And with that kind of wealth comes global power. Which is why the UAE government tends to look the other way when people who threaten Shiv Mittal end up disappearing. Can you get your hands free?" he asked.

"Not yet, but it's loosened some. What about you?"

"They used the zip ties from my bag on me," he said. "I can barely move my fingers."

"Who are you working for?" Liv asked him again. "And is there an extraction plan? Don't lie to me. I'd rather you not answer at all than listen to more of your lies."

"No, at this point there's no extraction plan. My watch was my only communication, though Elaine will relay the information of our capture to my boss. But this is an independent mission, and it will be her choice whether to send an extraction team or not. But you know the drill. If we're caught or captured, no one will admit knowledge of our existence."

"Her?" she asked, curious as to who had a hold over Dante and what their relationship was.

"My boss. She's likely not happy that I failed the mission, so chances are slim she'll bother to rescue me. And, technically, I never lied to you," he said. "I told you what truths I could, and omitted the rest."

"Lies by omission are still lies," Liv said hotly. "Especially with someone you supposedly care about. But I guess that was a lie too."

"No, that was never a lie," he said. "But in my arrogance I thought I could continue with the life I was living, and keep you separated so you never found out. My work with MI6, my work as Simon Locke, and . . . you. The three things I enjoyed most in this world, but that could never collide."

"It must have been terrible," she said sarcastically.

But Dante just smiled. "It wasn't at all. It was powerful. And I thought I could keep it all going until I was too old to take the next mission or the next commission, and you and I could retire to an island somewhere and live the rest of our lives in paradise."

"It must be nice to be that self-absorbed. To never consider anyone else's feelings. Or to use them however you see fit to get exactly what you want."

Liv's heart was raging wildly inside her chest, and tears of anger pricked at her eyes. The chain restraining her legs rattled as she turned to face him, her stance inviting a fight.

"Believe me," he said, "I've spent almost two years realizing just that. Nothing is ever a sure bet, especially when you're playing against the house.

Dying was the only option I had. My time was up. I'd been compromised, and I took the only option that was given to me."

"So you changed your lifestyle not because of a change of conscience or heart, but because you got caught."

"Yes," he admitted. "There are very few things in this life I've done that have bothered me. I've been sent on questionable missions, where I wasn't sure if what I was doing was the right thing. But I did my duty to my country. And I became Simon Locke because I enjoyed it. But you were always the twinge in my conscience. I wanted you like I've never wanted anyone, and I would've done anything to have you."

"And if you hadn't gotten caught, you'd still have me. Just another possession, like one of your paintings. Someone to fuck in the middle of the night when your adrenaline was running high from another job. And I would've fallen more and more in love with you."

"You were never just someone to fuck," Dante said harshly.

"You're going to stand there and tell me I wasn't convenient? You knew my every move in tracking Simon Locke—and I shared other cases with you as well. You think I didn't recognize when you'd come to me in the middle of the night, that wild look in your eyes? I was so stupid," she spat. "I thought I was so important to you that you couldn't wait to be with me. It didn't take me long after your death to realize the truth. Slipping into bed beside me in the dead of night, making me come before I was even fully awake. Or the night Donner and I went to the movies and you pulled me into the janitor's closet on my way back from the bathroom. What job were you coming off of then? Must have been a successful one."

"As a matter of fact, it was," he bit out. He took a step toward her, the lines of his face angular in the shadowy light. "Don't step too high on your pedestal. You were always wet and willing. And I believe it was you who stripped down to nothing while we were on the London Eye, and it was you who initiated things in the Bailong elevator in China."

Her face flushed with embarrassment and anger. Things had always burned so hot between them. As soon as they entered the same room, it was as if a fuse had been lit, and there was no stopping the imminent explosion.

"I know you better than you know yourself. You think I didn't recognize the excitement in your eyes every time I came to you like that? You loved every second of it. Not knowing where or when I'd fuck you. You might think there's a vast difference between the two of us, but in some ways we're cut from the same cloth. We both crave the adrenaline rush.

We seek out the adventure. We're passionate about what we do, and that translated well in the bedroom. And outside of the bedroom. There was no illusion when it came to that. It was as real as it could get."

"The sex was real," she agreed. "But the heart wasn't. If you had one yourself you'd understand what you did to me."

"Believe me," he said somberly. "I have one. And I wish to God I didn't. But sometimes life sucks and you don't get to make the choices for your future."

"And sometimes the choices we make have consequences," she countered. "My actions were always genuine," Liv said. "You turned me on because you were you. I didn't have an ulterior motive. I didn't use you."

"We turned each other on," he said. "You fascinated me like no woman ever had. Even in death, you fascinated me. I couldn't get you out of my head. I know every expression on your face and every nuance of body language. You think I don't know that your nipples are hard right now? That if I moved my hand between your thighs I'd find you ready and swollen for me?"

He took another step toward her, and she froze. Blood rushed in her ears and her skin sizzled with anger and lust. No other man had touched her since Dante, and her body's needs betrayed her mind's wants.

"Do you think I could forget you so easily?" Dante continued. "That I can't remember the taste of you? The feel of your skin, or the heat of you as you wrap your legs around me?"

Her breath hitched, her breasts heaving, and her fists bunched behind her back so tight her nails bit into the palms of her hands.

"Do you think my death would make me not want you? It's been almost two years, and I can still bring back the scent of your hair and the taste of your lips."

He moved closer, his body touching hers, but Liv didn't have the willpower to push him away. Her body thrummed with need and anger, and there was no reason she couldn't take what she wanted, just as he'd been doing all along.

"I don't want your excuses or words," she said. "It's too late for that now."

She leaned forward and took his bottom lip between her teeth, biting it gently, and he sucked in a breath of surprise.

"Jesus, Liv," he said with a groan.

"What do you say?" she asked. "If we're going to die, we might as well go out with a bang."

Her hand grasped the front of his shirt and she pulled him closer, her lips a hairbreadth from his, and then she nipped at his bottom lip.

He groaned and whispered, "Liv."

"If we're going to die, I'd rather spend the time doing something I enjoy."

CHAPTER FIFTEEN

Dante recognized the look in her eyes—the fiery passion, the burning need. But he also recognized the anger. And the hurt.

The challenge was clear. Liv didn't want to hear apologies or excuses. She wanted pure physical release. She wanted to feel alive as long as she was able. He wouldn't deny her. He wanted her just as badly.

When she nipped his bottom lip, his cock spiked painfully behind his zipper, and tasting her became a priority. His mouth took hers, and he drank at her greedily, their tongues colliding. His body shuddered at the feel of her against him. It was like coming home and being hit with a tidal wave at the same time.

His hands were still tied behind his back, even though he could've escaped the bonds at any moment. But he liked the idea of having to find satisfaction without using their hands, so he left them tied. He pushed her forward using his body, until her back hit the wall. He used only his mouth and the pressure of his rigid cock between the vee of her thighs to have her begging for more.

There was desperation in their movements. It had been too long since the night he'd died, when he'd taken her in the secret room in the dark. They'd been standing up then too. Dante vowed that if they made it out of this place alive, he was going to fuck her on a bed, where he could take his time and get his fill of her. Where he could touch every inch of her until she was so imprinted on his brain she'd be the last thing he thought of as he took his last breath.

"I've been thinking of making you come ever since I saw you pointing that gun at me," he rasped, biting her neck and reveling in the shudder of her body.

"Good," Liv said, her neck arching so he had better access. "You owe me."

He chuckled and looked down at all of the clothes covering her body, intrigued by the challenge. "This is going to be interesting," he said.

Her shirt was ripped where it had gotten caught in the door, showing the slightest bit of skin at her waist. He leaned forward and took the fabric near her top button between his teeth and pulled, satisfaction filling him when it popped open easily.

"You're very talented," she said, her body trembling as his lips grazed the full swell of her breast.

Once the shirt was opened all the way she helped him by shrugging so it slipped off her shoulders, exposing the most exquisite breasts he'd ever seen, covered by thin black lace.

"Now that's a tragedy," he said. "They should never be covered."

"I'd be all the rage at work, I'm sure."

He chuckled and knew there was nothing he could do about the clasp in the front. Instead, he used his teeth again and lowered the cups beneath her breasts so they were presented plump and full.

"Christ," he said. "I've always loved your breasts. Your nipples are so hard."

"Suck on them," she demanded.

"Oh, darling," he said with a smile. "You forget that I don't like to take orders." Instead of doing as she asked, he very deliberately took one nipple between his teeth and bit down gently.

"Ohmigod," she moaned as he tugged slightly.

Only when she was squirming did he do as she demanded and put his mouth over the taut bud, suckling with firm pressure.

"Your breasts have always been so sensitive," Dante rasped. "I bet if I kept going, you could come without me touching any other part of you."

"Yesss," she hissed. "Maybe another day," he teased, and pulled away from her.

"Bastard," she bit out.

"Name calling will get you spanked once we're out of here," he said, kneeling in front of her. His own need was raging out of control, and he found his patience wasn't nearly as strong as he thought it was. And then he saw that her black pants had an elastic waist and he almost sang the Hallelujah Chorus. He tugged at the elastic band of her black pants and she was able to help push them down to a certain point with her hands tied behind her back. He managed to get them down to her ankles.

His gaze was even with the thin scrap of material that covered her mound. He could smell her desire, and his mouth watered to taste her. He grasped the lace between his teeth and tugged sharply, and the flimsy lace fluttered to the ground.

"I've missed your taste," he said, tracing a finger along the bare folds of her pussy.

"I've missed you tasting me," she said, her voice hoarse with need.

"You can't hide your desire," he said, kissing her

thigh. "I can see it." And then he licked at her like a cat lapping at cream. "I can taste it."

She widened her stance for him, but she was hindered by her pants and the shackles, and he smiled at her impatience. Teasing her had always been one of his greatest pleasures, but he was reaching his own threshold of patience. He didn't give her warning. His mouth closed over her swollen clit and he devoured.

Liv screamed and her knees buckled as pleasure racked her body. His tongue swirled and his mouth sucked, drinking in her desire.

"Dante," she said. Her hips bucked against his face as she came, liquid desire coating his tongue.

He couldn't wait any longer. He stood and said, "Your turn," and she stared at him out of passion-glazed eyes.

"Am I still standing?" she asked, her words slightly slurred.

He grinned, his ego nicely boosted. "Yes, darling. Now turn around and use those magic hands to undo my trousers."

It took a few seconds for the words to penetrate her brain, and a few more seconds to figure out which way she could turn and have the most leeway. It took a few tries, but she was able to get her fingers to work well enough to undo the button and zipper, but she was confused by the skin suit he wore beneath.

"There's just a flap," he said, gritting his teeth and her hands wreaked havoc with his iron-hard cock.

By the time she freed him, he was down to the last vestiges of his control. His shaft was thick and impossibly hard, his cockhead glistening with pre-cum. No one had ever turned him on like she did, and he was like an unpracticed teenager, ready to explode at the first feel of her wrapped around his cock.

"Turn around," he told her in a harsh whisper. "And spread your legs as wide as you can."

He pressed her against the wall before she had a chance to get her bearings, and then he probed against her until he found the slick opening. He pushed inside of her, groaning at the wet heat that surrounded him.

"Jesus, Liv," he said. "You're going to kill me."

"Just don't die before I come," she panted.

They were pressed together and there wasn't much room to maneuver with the limitations holding them back, but already he could feel the texture of her vaginal walls change as she slicked and her temperature got impossibly hot.

"Don't just stand there," she moaned. "Fuck me."

His balls tightened at the command, and he did

as she bidded. "So tight, baby," he said, gritting his teeth. He pulled out of her, reveling in the feel of her muscles milking him, squeezing him so tight it was almost difficult to move.

Sweat dotted his skin and his jaw clamped tight as he focused on staying in control until she came again. Her breathing was shallow and little mewls escaped her throat. Her pupils were dilated so her eyes looked black.

He pulled almost completely out of her, waiting until her eyes focused on his, and then he said, "Hold on," and thrust into her over and over, hammering against her with a force that brought her to her toes.

Her head banged against the wall, but she didn't seem to care, and his teeth clamped down on her shoulders as he held himself in check, desperately wishing she found fulfillment soon.

His balls tightened against his body, and he knew he wouldn't last much longer.

"Damn it, Liv," he growled, feeling the change inside her as her orgasm was just on the precipice. "Come for me."

Even as he felt himself losing the battle to contain his own orgasm, he felt the liquid heat intensify around his cock, and the slow undulations as she came apart around him.

"Oh, God," she screamed, her body going rigid

as it shuddered against him. His own orgasm was ripped from his very soul as he exploded inside her.

She continued to tremor around him as he collapsed against her and tried to catch his breath. Fucking Liv was even better than he remembered. And if he had his way, he'd be doing it again soon.

LIV WAS WORN out and weak in the knees.

She couldn't imagine what she looked like, but if it was anything like how she felt, it couldn't be good. Dante had taken everything from her. Again. She'd been determined to hold back. To only take her pleasure and say to hell with his needs. But he'd knelt before her and pleasured her selflessly. And then he'd fucked her into oblivion, making sure she came again, even though she could see the strain holding back had caused him.

His release coated the insides of her thighs and she smelled of sex and sweat. She'd never felt more awkward in her life. She was completely helpless to cover up, and if her luck held, the soldiers would probably be back in at any moment. After everything they'd just done, she couldn't even look Dante in the eye.

She leaned her head back against the wall and closed her eyes, trying to get her emotions in order. Sex with Dante had never been simple. She didn't know why she'd thought it would be now. All she knew was that it was best to get away from him, however she could.

"There's still time before dawn," he said, nodding toward the barred windows.

"Lovely," Liv said. "That gives us more time to stand around with our pants around our ankles. The firing squad can't come soon enough."

"Now, don't get angry . . ."

"Because that's not how every epic fight begins."

Then she watched in open-mouthed awe as he arched his shoulders back, the concentration on his face intense, and then seconds later the restraints on his wrists dropped to the ground.

She felt the blood rush to her face. "You could've done that the whole time?" she asked hoarsely. "The whole fucking time?"

"Yes, but in my defense, I wasn't thinking clearly while I was imagining myself buried inside of you."

"Bullshit," she said. "You winked at me. You had this planned all along."

"We needed to get some things out in the open, and this was an excellent way to do it. You have to admit you feel better. You got to tell me how you feel, and the sexual frustration is gone. It's like therapy."

"I'm going to kill you," she said. "Get me out of this."

"Maybe you should calm down before I release you," he said. "You look like you're about to have a stroke."

"Get. Me. Out. Of. This," she said, enunciating each word clearly.

He sighed and then reached out, running his fingers over the back of her scalp and pulling out a hairpin. "Nice wig, by the way. I still like your natural hair better though."

"I'm so relieved," she said sarcastically, making him grin.

He leaned down and had his shackles undone in a matter of seconds, freeing himself completely, and then he righted all his clothes while she stood there impatiently.

After what seemed like ages, he leaned down and undid her shackles, and she resisted the urge to kick him while he was down there. Then he turned her and removed the tape from her wrists.

Liv rubbed at her wrists, straightened her clothes and stretched out her back, taking a couple of deep breaths for deep measure. It didn't help. She launched herself at Dante, getting in a couple of good jabs since she'd caught him by surprise.

He let out a laugh, blocking her next punch and pulled her in close so her arms and legs couldn't do as much damage. His laugh infuriated her even more, and before she knew it they were rolling on the ground, her fists pounding against his chest.

And then she wondered why her vision was blurry and realized she was crying. She rolled off of him and lay on her back, her breath heaving in and out as she tried to get herself under control. The tears continued to fall, but she didn't care.

He hadn't tried to fight her back, or really even defend himself all that much. He'd let her whale on him, holding her close as she let out two years of anger and grief.

Damn him. She'd always been strong. Ever since Elizabeth had been taken. She'd hardened herself and kept her focus sharp. She'd learned to compartmentalize her feelings and keep them shut away in a little box. She'd learned to do the job she'd chosen and do it to the best of her ability, honing skills that very few women could muster. Strength and courage had always been her battle plan. But she'd failed this time. She wasn't strong enough.

Dante rolled toward her so that he looked down at her from above, his face more serious and searching than she'd ever seen it.

"I'm sorry," he said. "I truly am. I hate myself that I hurt you like I have."

"Too little, too late," Liv said, her breath hitching.

"Maybe so," he said. "But I'm sorry anyway. You

have no idea how much I admire you. You're in-
sanely gifted at your job. You're smart and funny.
But I've realized I overlooked an important part of
your spirit when we were involved before. It never
occurred to me that you could be hurt. That you
could love me the way you did. Because I didn't see
myself as deserving of that love, so why would you
give it so freely?"

His thumb brushed at the tears on her cheek, but
she wanted to cry more. How much she would've
loved to hear him speak those words before. He'd
known her body. But he hadn't taken the time to
really know *her*. And if she was honest, maybe she
hadn't known herself as well as she should have.
She'd been so busy cultivating an image of tough-
ness and attitude that she'd neglected part of herself.

Her therapist had been right. If she didn't find
a healthy outlet for her anger, it would explode,
and she wouldn't be able to repair the damage. Liv
looked up at him, her eyes swollen, and stared into
the depths of blue. She had to let him go, no matter
how much she wanted him, no matter how desperately she'd craved his presence. Dante could never
be what she needed.

Almost as if he read her mind, he leaned down
and kissed her softly—tenderly—and then he rolled
away from her and shifted into a sitting position.

"I've got to tell you something important," he said.

Her heart hurt and her body was heavy. Gone was the after-sex euphoria. "I just can't right now, Dante. Leave it be, and let's move on."

"I wish I could, but this is important. We're going to get out of here, and we're going to hunt down Raj Mittal. There's no doubt in my mind that he has the girls and the launch codes, and you and I can stop him. But there's another component to this puzzle."

"What's that?" she asked wearily.

"Your sister is alive."

CHAPTER SIXTEEN

"**Y**ou never struck me as cruel," Liv said, "but I guess I've come to realize that I never really knew you at all."

A roiling sickness moved through her and she rolled to her hands and knees. Self-loathing filled her. When would she learn? Just because a chemical reaction existed between them didn't mean there was anything deeper. At least, not on his part. It was her stupidity that kept her emotions in flux. She'd wasted too much energy on her emotions the last two years. It was time to bury Dante Malcolm in the past. And leave him there.

She moved to stand, but he put a hand on her shoulder. The look she cast him must have given him pause, because he removed his hand slowly and straightened up.

"I'm not being cruel, and I'm not playing games,"

Dante said. "What I will promise you from this point forward, no matter what happens between us, is that I will not lie to you."

She snorted out a laugh and got to her feet, stretching her sore muscles and making her way toward the latrine. She examined the grates that led into the sewage tunnel, which would eventually lead to her freedom. And then she was going to fly back to London, ask Beck for her job back, and go through the proper channels to hunt down Raj Mittal, and hope to God she could get to the girls before they were sold.

"Liv, you need to listen to me," he said.

She knelt by one of the grates and pulled at it, but she didn't have the strength to lift it. He knelt beside her and added his strength to hers, but the grate was immovable from a century or two of disuse and things she didn't even want to think about cementing it in place.

"Elizabeth is here in the palace, Liv. I saw her. I thought she was you."

"Do *not* say her name again," she said coldly.

"Fine, but you've spent almost your entire life looking for her, and I'm giving you the information you've never been able to find on your own. I would listen if I were you."

"Funny how you didn't mention all of this before

we had sex. Just like you didn't release us from those stupid manacles. Everything serves a purpose for you, doesn't it, Dante?"

"The manacles, yes," he said. "I'll admit that I wanted the time with you. But sex was your choice, and you know it. I just presented the opportunity if it was what you wanted."

"How fucking noble of you," she said.

"But your sister is a different matter. Something isn't adding up with her. There's no record of her being a permanent resident here. There's no information about Mittal having a longtime lover or long-term relationship. But that's what they have."

"Elizabeth would never willingly be with a monster like Raj Mittal," Liv spat. She was so angry her hands were shaking.

"Not the father," Dante said. "The son. I wasn't expecting to find anyone but Shiv Mittal up there. But they were there, and believe me, they're most definitely involved."

"So now you can add 'voyeur' and 'perv' to 'liar' and 'thief'."

"My point is," he said, exasperation in his voice, "that she wasn't a one-night stand. The bedroom was theirs. And I guarantee you that, when Mittal was evacuated after we set off the alarm, she was evacuated with him."

"Fine. But it's been almost twenty-five years," Liv said. "Maybe she just has a strong resemblance to me."

"She recognized your name when I said it," he told her.

The sob caught her by surprise, and Liv buried her head in her hands and tried to hold it together.

"I thought she was you," Dante said. "I heard them making love in the bathroom, and when she came out and discovered me in the room, I was furious. And jealous. I thought she was you. But when I said your name, she went on the attack. She told me I wasn't going to take her, and then she punched me in the face, in the exact spot you did, I might add, and then she kneed me in the stones so hard I saw stars."

"Too bad she didn't damage anything permanently."

"I'm sure that's what you were thinking ten minutes ago when you were creaming around my cock."

"A lapse in judgment," she said stiffly. "It won't be repeated."

"Whatever your feelings are for me—"

"Which would be murderous rage," she interrupted.

"—you need to think about this logically," he continued, ignoring her. "They've gone to a lot of effort to make sure Elizabeth hasn't been tracked down all these years. They keep her hidden from the public eye, but those who live in the palace must be loyal enough to keep the secret for her and Mittal."

"People tend to be loyal when they can be punished by death."

"True," he agreed. "She recognized your name, but she chose to stay."

"So you say," she said. "*If* what you say is true and Elizabeth is here, then I'll find a way to talk to her without her being coerced in any way."

"I can help you," he said.

Liv snorted. "You've got to be kidding me. I think you've done enough. I'm not even going to ask what you were doing in their bedroom listening to them have sex in the first place."

"When you knew me before, I was British Intelligence," Dante said. "That was never a lie. I was a good agent, and I was able to incorporate my background and the circles I ran in to my advantage. But I grew bored with it. The kind of work we do isn't all James Bond–type missions, though there are moments of high danger and intensity. So when the chance to become Simon Locke was presented to me, I took it."

"What do you mean, it was presented to you?" she asked, eyes narrowing. "Someone approached you?"

His mouth twitched and he said, "You read the file I gave you on my encounter with the real Simon Locke. That was the truth, and I won't lie to you anymore. But there are also some things I can't tell you. It's not just about me, but others' privacy."

"An honor code among thieves," she sneered.

"Of a sort," he said. "I loved living a double life. It kept my mind sharp. Like a puzzle. Keeping the lies straight between both identities was a challenge. Staying ahead of the game was invigorating.

"And then I met you." Dante smiled, but it didn't reach his eyes. "You were unexpected. I'd never met a woman like you—intelligent and driven and stubborn, topped off with a smart mouth and a face that I couldn't get out of my head. I had no use for a relationship in my life. Women were there for pleasure only. But you stimulated more than my body.

"That first night we slept together, I had every intention of sneaking out of your apartment in the middle of the night and cutting the ties between us. I've never entertained the same woman more than a time or two. Except for you. I kept coming back for more. And the risk kept getting higher."

"And that drove you even more to stay with me," Liv said, finishing for him. She understood him, though she wished she didn't. Anyone in their line of work—the kind of work that put them right in the thick of danger—had those tendencies to seek out even higher-risk situations.

"*You* drove me to stay with you," he said. "I wanted to be with you. And I've never wanted to be with anyone like that. I lied to everyone, but I also lied to myself. I told myself that I could keep juggling everything. That if I was smart enough, I could have everything I wanted.

"That night at Carmaux's party, I had it planned to the last detail. It was the riskiest job I'd ever undertaken, and that's saying something, as I've accomplished some incredible feats."

"You're proud of yourself," Liv said, shaking her head. "Even now, with everything going on and the shitstorm you've gotten yourself into."

"Of course I'm proud of my accomplishments. I'm extremely skilled at the things I do. But taking a painting in front of a crowd of hundreds of people was something I'd never done before. And if my biggest obstacle—you—was in the same room at the same time, well, that upped the ante considerably."

"I'm such an idiot," she said. "I can see it now. But I was too blinded by lo—by lust to see anything before."

"You never would've seen anything I didn't want you to see," Dante told her. "Just as you would never have seen me on the roof if I hadn't wanted you to catch me. I would've parachuted off the cliffs as planned and dropped the painting in a secure location I'd scouted, then circled back in through all the chaos to meet up with you, having let Locke just slip through my fingers. But my plans didn't go as expected that night.

"There was more than one way to get into that secret room where we met. There was also another entrance through Carmaux's private office, so that's the way that I took. She knew I'd go that way, of course."

"Who knew?" she asked.

"The woman who's now my boss," he answered. "She came out of nowhere. And she knew everything. She knew about MI6 and Simon Locke. She knew about you. All of my secrets—I have yet to discover how she found out some of the things she knows. Though now that I'm working for her, I understand that she has access to sources that no other agency in the world has.

"She told me that I had two choices. If I continued as I was, I would eventually be found out. By the look on her face, I was certain that she'd make sure I was found out. Then I'd spend the rest of my life in prison."

"What was the second choice?" Liv asked.

"I could make sure Dante Malcolm and Simon Locke were dead, and I could start over with a new agency and opportunities I'd never get elsewhere."

"And you agreed?" Liv asked. "Just like that? She could've been a terrorist—anyone."

"I work for an agency called Trident. It's an off-the-books special-ops group based out of the United States, but the agents who comprise it are international. At the core, it's an antiterrorism organization, although it's not a government-sanctioned agency. Those who created us come from both the governmental and private sectors. We're called The Gravediggers, because we've all had to die in our old lives so we could be reborn to do this job. We have no ties to anyone from our old lives. It's policy."

"So you jumped off that turret and 'died,'" she said. Liv couldn't even wrap her head around what he was telling her. There were so many deceptions and untruths between them that she didn't know what she could believe anymore.

"I did," he said. "She recruited me because of my skills as Simon Locke. I'm part of a team that is assigned certain missions. We live together, work together, do recon together, and would take a bullet for each other. But she didn't recruit me to work with the team all of the time, so once again I've been living a double life. She sends me on jobs like this one, where she thinks it's more effective for a single operative to go in."

"And what do you get out of it?" Liv asked.

"Money, for one thing," he said. "But part of my payment is being able to take a piece of my choosing as a commission. I was in Mittal's bedroom because of a painting that hung over his bed. I get the launch codes, I get the painting, and everybody is happy."

"Except you're still stealing," Liv said. "Just because you're saving the world at the same time doesn't give you a free pass to take people's things."

"I'll have you know I've never *just* taken people's things. Simon Locke worked on a case-by-case basis. He could be hired to retrieve stolen artifacts or family heirlooms that ended up in the wrong hands. He never stole anything that wasn't already stolen. I took my commission piece only after I'd secured the piece I was being paid to go in for."

Liv's mouth dropped open in surprise. She certainly hadn't expected that explanation. It didn't change the fact that he was a liar, but it was good to know that he had some kind of moral compass and wasn't a complete degenerate.

"What's going to happen when you come back empty-handed?" she asked.

"Who says I'm going back empty-handed? As soon as we get back to the plane, Elaine can tell us what she's found out about where Mittal is taking the girls and the launch codes. We just have to get one of these grates off to get out of here."

"I think we can help you with that, mate," a voice said from somewhere beneath them.

"Who the hell is that?" Liv asked.

Dante turned his head sharply, and frowned. "Axel? What the bloody hell are you doing here?"

"Well, mate, after listening to your story, I think we're debating whether or not to spring you or to let Mittal's soldiers take care of you. But there's no reason for the lady to suffer, so I guess we're getting you out."

Liv watched a myriad of expressions cross Dante's face until it finally went cold and blank. There was a soft hiss and a blue glow from below as a blowtorch was fired up, and she and Dante scooted back as the man below removed the grate.

She looked down into the hole and realized there was at least a twenty-foot drop to the ground; a man was hanging from the ceiling of the tunnel by some sort of harness, the blowtorch in one hand and the grate in the other. He handed the grate up to Dante, who set it aside, and then tossed the blowtorch down to whoever was waiting below.

"Stand back," called the person standing at the bottom, his voice tinny.

Dante pulled her back from the hole, and a grappling hook shot up and connected with the ceiling above them. The rope was tugged on a couple of times to check for stability, and then the one Dante called Axel snapped a couple of carabiners to the rope and passed them to Dante.

"See you at the bottom, mate," the man said, and then there was a whooshing sound as he slid down the rope.

Liv took one carabiner from Dante and wrapped her ankle around the rope, eager to be as far away from Dubai as she possibly could. Then she looked at Dante and saw the indecision on his face.

"What's wrong?" she asked.

"I'm trying to decide if my chances are better with Mittal's soldiers or with my brothers." The corner of his mouth quirked and he shook his head. "I have to say that I'm not completely sure."

CHAPTER SEVENTEEN

"**I** don't think you understand," Liv said. She spoke slowly and spaced her words, hoping this time they'd listen instead of going about the business of getting the plane prepped for takeoff. "I'm not going to Texas. I have a job to do. I'm going to track down Mittal and those little girls and make sure they're returned to their families. If I have to go through all of you to do that, then so be it."

She'd already tried deplaning twice, but one of her *rescuers* kept stopping her and telling her to take a seat. The next person who told her to sit down was going to get a fist to the nose.

"It's no use, Liv," Dante told her, already buckled into one of the plush leather seats. "They're just following protocol. You know too much about us, and now they have to make sure you're not a threat."

"Yes," she said, narrowing her eyes. "Thank you

so much for sharing the information. If I'd known this was the outcome I would've told you to keep your confessions to yourself. Why is it that you never seem to cause me anything but trouble?"

"I suppose you're just lucky," he said, giving her a smile that told her she was pushing the edge of his temper.

It hadn't gone past her notice that his two team members hadn't spoken a word to him since they'd been rescued. There was definitely a tension between them that was bordering on hostile.

"You need to take your seat and get buckled," Axel said to her. "We're ready for takeoff."

Liv growled and his eyes widened in surprise. "You're wearing a wedding ring," she said. "If you tell me to take a seat one more time instead of listening to what I have to say, I'm going to take that knife in your boot and put it to good use. You'll be going back to your wife without a very important piece of your anatomy. If you get my meaning."

The other one snorted out a laugh and closed and sealed the hatch on the door. Her gaze flashed to him and his smile disappeared. She was long past the point of playing nice.

"You're Mossad," she said, taking a step forward. "I recognize it in the way you move. I spent several months training with Mossad before I took my assignment at Interpol."

"Then you know how we deal with threats," he said, raising a brow and then moving past her to take a seat.

Her smile was sharp and harsh. "Exactly," she said. "I'm glad we both agree since being kept against my will is clearly a threat."

Levi moved to stand, but Dante said, "Levi," and he hesitated, but eventually sat back down. "It does no good to do this. You'll eventually overpower her, but she's trained so one of you will end up getting hurt. And she's not the enemy."

The two men ignored Dante as if he weren't even on the plane, and Axel took the seat next to Levi.

"Liv, you know they're not going to let you go until they're satisfied that you're not a threat. We have the resources to find the girls much faster than you do now that you've left Interpol. It would be wise to take advantage of it."

Liv narrowed her eyes and thought it through. She knew he was right. But she didn't have to like it. She could find the girls on her own. She still had contacts and favors owed. But time was of the essence.

"I'll stay for the girls," she said, looking straight at Axel and Levi. "Their safety is the most important thing at the moment. But I'm not your prisoner, and the second you start to treat me like one I'll take you out or die trying. Am I clear?"

"Miss Rothschild," Axel tried again. "We're the good guys. And we can help you hunt down Raj Mittal and the girls he's transporting. But there are precautions that must be taken. We don't know you. We've never worked with you. And it's policy that we never work with any other agency. You know things about us that could get us all killed. And I can promise you, the threats that we face make your worst days in the office seem like a day in the park."

She was a skeptic at heart. All cops and agents were. Everyone lied, and everyone had an agenda. She just had to figure out what theirs was. There was no way to verify if everything that Dante had told her was the truth.

There was a leather sofa that sat against the wall of the plane, and two matching leather chairs directly across from it, where Dante was seated. And there were two chairs to the left of the sofa, and two more to the right, which is where Levi and Axel were seated. She chose one of the chairs to the left of the sofa, even though she hated facing backward. It was better than sitting next to Dante, and she wanted to keep the other two in her sights at all times.

"Hello again, Miss Rothschild," a silky familiar voice said through the speakers. "It's lovely to see you. I'm reading your vitals and your blood pressure and heart rate are both elevated."

"What a surprise," she said, buckling her lap belt.

"I believe that was sarcasm," Elaine said. "I'm not always good at picking up on rhetorical devices or irony. But I've been practicing."

"You're spot-on," Liv said.

"Excellent," Elaine countered. "You should relax and enjoy the flight. We have many hours ahead of us. I suggest you try the chamomile tea and get some sleep. That's what my database says is the best advice to give you."

"I appreciate that, Elaine," she said. "But you don't fall asleep in the enemy's lair."

"I will add that to my list of advice," she said.

"Elaine," Axel said. "Unfortunately, Miss Roth-schild . . ."

"Agent Rothschild," Liv corrected.

"Agent Rothschild has discovered things she shouldn't about The Gravediggers."

"Oh, my," Elaine said. "I hate it when that happens. Very awkward. Are we implementing standard protocol?"

"Yes, please," Axel said.

Liv didn't know what standard protocol was, but she knew the moment multiple screens descended from the ceiling that she wasn't going to like it. And then her academy picture came on the screen and she knew she *really* wasn't going to like it.

"Olivia Caroline Rothschild," Elaine began. "Born at thirteen zero two hours on April third, nineteen hundred and eighty-seven to Oliver Rothschild and Margaret Hemingway Rothschild. A sister, Elizabeth Margaret Rothschild was born at thirteen fourteen hours on the same date. Elizabeth was abducted at Harrods department store on December sixteenth, nineteen ninety-three. She was never recovered."

"You've got to be fucking kidding me," Liv said, fury spreading through her like molten lava.

"Unfortunately," Elaine said. "I am not allowed to fucking kid when standard protocol has been implemented."

She shot a look at Levi and Axel. "I'm about to shove your standard protocol somewhere very painful." But they ignored her and kept focused on the information scrolling on screen.

"Olivia Rothschild excelled in school with top marks, and she was field hockey captain. She attended the University of St. Andrews in Fife, Scotland, earning a degree in international relations and a master's degree in criminal justice. She then went to work for Scotland Yard, where she remained for a year before being recruited by Interpol.

"She was put on paid leave twenty-one months

ago in conjunction with case 385271, and an internal investigation was conducted. No charges were brought against her, and she was reinstated with same rank."

"What's case 385271?" Axel asked.

"It's a dummy file," Elaine answered. "The investigation file has been deleted, along with any related case files."

Liv arched a brow and narrowed her gaze at Dante. "You deleted Interpol files?" she asked.

"I have no idea what you're talking about," Dante said.

"We'll assume this has something to do with the classified files on Dante that Elaine was able find for us," Axel said. "Simon Locke has had a hell of a career."

"Yes, I find it interesting after all this time that those files were readily available for you to find," Dante said.

"You made Simon Locke disappear off the face of the earth?" she asked.

"I don't know what you're talking about," he said again. "But if I understand what you're implying, it's not impossible to wipe a person's history. I'm surprised you didn't check."

"Sometimes it's best to let the past stay dead," she said. "But I've got the hard copy files at home if I feel nostalgic."

"Do you?" he asked, smiling. And she knew if

she looked in her file cabinet that all her notes and case files involving Simon Locke would be gone.

"Elaine," Axel said. "Pull up Dante's classified file and cross section mentions of Liv Rothschild and Simon Locke."

"Stand by," Elaine said.

The others were still ignoring Dante, and while she appreciated their dedication to doing so, their stubbornness was overlooking an important detail.

"You said all the files were readily available for them to find," she said to Dante. "I'm going to assume that wasn't always the case."

"You've always been very intuitive," Dante said.

"And because of that skill, I'm going to deduce that someone chose this moment for your files to be readily available when you've been keeping this secret from your team the last couple of years."

"It's probably best not to mention that right now," Levi said.

"Give it a rest," she said. "He was obviously right to keep it from you if this is your reaction."

"Agent Rothschild and MI6 agent Malcolm were part of a joint task force to track down Simon Locke," Elaine said.

"Lovely," Liv said. "Please air the worst day of my life in front of a room full of strangers. Let me save you the trouble. Dante Malcolm, aka Simon Locke, played

Agent Rothschild like a violin, stole a painting worth millions right out from under her nose, and then plummeted to his death, only to not have really died at all."

"Yes, that about sums it up," Elaine said.

"I'll fill in the parts of the files that were deleted, where I was put on leave while internal affairs investigated whether or not I was in collusion with Locke all along, and I stood by and let them go through my home and all of my other properties while they looked for all of the art he's stolen."

"You seem bitter," Axel said, smiling for the first time.

"For a married man, you're not a very good judge of women's moods," she said.

"I haven't been married for a couple of years," he countered. "I'm out of practice."

The rest of the flight was spent scrutinizing her life and cases, and by the time they landed, they still didn't seem to be convinced that she wasn't a threat to The Gravediggers. But her problems seemed minuscule compared to Dante's. When the door opened and they descended down the stairs, there were two other men waiting for them.

She recognized the look of those who'd made a life in special ops. But something she'd observed about The Gravediggers was that they had even more of an edge than the agents she normally worked with. Even Dante had hardened since she'd worked with him last. They were skilled and deadly. It was in the way they moved. In the calluses on their hands and the hard ridges of muscle. Being surrounded by them was like nothing she'd ever experienced before.

But it was Dante who was in the middle. And no one was focused on her. She took a step back. And then another, gauging what kind of chance she would have if she made a run for it.

"I didn't know you'd be meeting us at the airport," Dante said, greeting the other two men. "I must be in trouble to pull Deacon away from his pregnant wife and Elias away from his wedding plans."

"You son of a bitch," one of the men said.

"Elias," the other said, but didn't seem too worked up over the outburst.

And then her mouth dropped open as the one called Elias started swinging. His right hook caught Dante in the jaw and snapped his head back, and the follow up with his left hit him square in the middle, doubling him over. She winced in sympathy and then saw her chance.

"Don't even think about it," Levi said, his fingers squeezing around her upper arm.

She looked at his hand and then looked up at his face. "You're going to want to get your hand off me," she said. And then she kneed him in the balls.

CHAPTER EIGHTEEN

Last Stop, Texas

Dante sat at the head of the conference table at HQ and let the storm rage around him. Words flew swiftly—accusations and questions—and it was all done at top volume. He figured they deserved to have their say, so he stayed quiet until they actually wanted him to start answering their questions. His jaw and ribs throbbed where Elias had hit him, and he was cursing Eve for putting him in this position.

The important thing was that the team seemed satisfied that Liv was legitimate and not a threat to The Gravediggers. But that didn't mean they were going to let her go easily. There were consequences to what he'd done—to telling her as much information as he had—and it was different with Liv than it had been when Tess and Miller were apprised of the operation. Liv was a trained agent for another organization. And she could become a potential threat.

He almost preferred the silent treatment he'd received on the flight home from Dubai. Now that they were back in Texas and on familiar ground, there was nothing but words. Even Tess and Miller sat next to their men in solidarity, looking at Dante as if he'd grown a second head. Liv sat stiffly to his right, but it was very clear she wasn't sitting beside him out of solidarity. It had simply been the only chair left at the table.

Deacon was the exception. He sat there stoically, holding his wife's hand and gazing at Dante as if he could see every thought inside his head. It was disconcerting. Deacon just let the others rage around him—the quiet in the storm—and let out their anger, shock, and, in a way, grief.

Dante guessed it was a kind of grieving to know that someone you risked your life for on a daily basis wasn't who he said he was. Couldn't be trusted.

A pang of remorse knifed through him so sharply he flinched, and his hands bunched beneath the table. He'd never truly worked as part of a team before The Gravediggers, and in all honesty, he hadn't been thrilled with the idea when Eve had brought him on board. But he'd grown close to these men over the last two years. He knew them as well as he knew himself. And he would die to protect any of them—and they would do the same for him. Or, at least, they would have before he'd deceived them.

He looked at Liv, sitting there bravely, not knowing a soul but keeping her chin up with that arrogant pride he'd always admired in her.

He'd broken something in her spirit. He could see it. Sense it. He'd never done anything but hurt those around him, the ones who loved him the most. The ones he'd never let himself love in return. Maybe it had to do with the fact that his parents had loved their money and status more than their only son. Or maybe it was just because he was fucked-up and wired wrong. But there had to be some kind of redemption for a man like him. Somehow he had to be able to fix what he'd broken.

Liv was hurting. He could feel the waves coming off her so strongly that it almost doubled him over. She'd said she'd loved him once upon a time. And Liv didn't say things she didn't mean. Her words weren't empty promises.

Deacon raised his hand; instantly the comments died down, and everyone took their seats. Everyone's attention was directed at him.

"I think at this point it's counterproductive to keep bringing up Dante's past," Deacon said. "We've all read the deleted files."

"I apologize, Dante," Elaine said. "I know your files were classified, but they found a back door and overrode my authority. I had no choice."

"It's not your fault, Elaine," Dante said. "I've always known there was a chance that my past would come to light."

He'd always prided himself on knowing how to act in any situation. Growing up, he'd been taught how to defuse situations, how to use charm to his advantage. He'd done it his entire life. He'd done it to the people sitting around the conference table. Normally he would have sat back in his chair and given them a cocky smile, making it clear that their opinions didn't matter. That their hurt, concern, and anger didn't matter. But they *did* matter, and he couldn't do that to them anymore. The guilt was eating him up inside.

"So, what now?" Levi asked. "We're just supposed to accept that he's really one of us? We're supposed to entrust our lives to him? What happens when Eve gives him orders to betray us? Or when we're on a mission and he finds something he wants more than the target, compromising us all?"

"I guess those are fair questions," Dante said. "We all have pasts, Levi. Some of which we might not be proud of. Even you." Levi stared at him, stony-eyed. The former Mossad agent wasn't one to be intimidated. "But it's why we were selected to be Gravediggers. If I hadn't been Simon Locke, I wouldn't be sitting here today. But despite my criminality, I never betrayed my country. And I've never, and would never, betray you."

"You lied to us," Axel said.

"And you've told us everything about your past, have you?" Dante countered. "The point is that I'm here, and I've remained here, despite the fact that I would do just fine contracting for solo missions. Maybe I didn't come here originally with the attitude of accepting you all as a team. Of being part of a team. But you can't train with each other the way we do and not embrace the brotherhood that forms with it."

"Are you loyal to us?" Deacon asked.

"I am," Dante answered.

"Then the topic of conversation needs to be about Eve."

"Excuse me for interrupting this heartwarming moment," Liv said, "but I don't know any of you, I don't trust any of you, and as we speak there are ten little girls who are on the verge of being sold into sexual slavery. I'd prefer to leave you to whatever you're up to and go do something important."

"We appreciate your cooperation, Agent Rothschild," Deacon said.

Liv snorted at that and said, "But you're not going to let me leave."

"I'm sorry, but no. You've been introduced to a lot of classified information, including knowledge about us as agents, one of whom you knew in his former life. That puts our lives at risk, and we have to evaluate the situation fully before you can be released."

Liv narrowed her eyes. "And if you don't like what you find?" she asked.

"Then measures must be taken to assure our safety and our secrets."

"Threatening me isn't going to make me fall into line," she said. "In the end, I'll do what I think is right, and the rest of you can go straight to hell."

"I like her," Miller whispered to Tess, and got a nudge in the ribs.

"If you'll give us a chance," Deacon said, "you might find that we're all on the same side. We can help you, and maybe you can help us. And those girls can go home to their families."

Relief coursed through Dante when he saw Liv pause, thinking it through. Her shoulders relaxed. She'd already seen firsthand some of the resources at their fingertips. Her chances of finding those girls with The Gravediggers were greater than if she worked with Interpol or on her own.

"You leave me no choice," she said.

"There's always a choice," Deacon said. "But you don't always get to like it."

The door to HQ opened, and instantly the men at the table were on their feet and had weapons drawn, ready to neutralize the intruder. Eve walked straight into the fray, unconcerned about the weapons pointed in her direction, and strode to the head of the conference table.

"I guess it's pointless to ask how you made it past the cameras and through all of the security checkpoints without us being alerted," Deacon said, lowering his gun.

Eve wore one of her black suits, the pencil skirt coming to the knee and her jacket tailored and buttoned, the shell beneath it also black. Her lips were slicked her favorite shade of red, and a pair of decorative chopsticks held her hair up. If Dante had to guess, he'd say they were lethally sharp and meant to be an extra weapon instead of a hair adornment.

"You've all certainly made a clusterfuck of things," she said by way of greeting. "Everyone be seated."

"*We've* made a clusterfuck of things?" Elias asked, his temper obviously still raw after his confrontation with Dante. "You've lied to us just as he has. Why should we continue to trust you and put our lives on the line when you'd just stab us in the back?"

"You should be a seasoned enough agent to know never to trust anyone," she said coldly. "My job isn't to placate you. It's to use each of you however I see fit to get missions accomplished. I recruited Dante because of his skills as a thief, which have been useful on several occasions up to this point. Obviously, this time he failed."

"Or maybe your intel failed," Dante said. "The launch codes were gone by the time I got there."

"Maybe you should have gotten there sooner," she said. "Maybe if you'd retrieved the launch codes *before* your commission, we wouldn't be having this conversation right now."

"Or maybe you knew all along that you were setting me up for failure for whatever long-term purpose you've concocted in that deceptive brain of yours."

"Don't forget how well I know you," she said. "I remember your fascination with Ms. Rothschild. I wondered if you'd fumble if you ran into her sister. Maybe someday you'll start thinking with the head attached to your neck instead of the one in your pants. If you think I don't have plans B, C, and D already in place, then maybe I made a mistake bringing you on in the first place.

"The mission was to obtain those launch codes, however necessary. Ms. Rothschild was not expected to gum up the works by trying to intercept the Russian girls before Raj Mittal had a chance to move them. We didn't expect him to move them for a couple more days. When he brought them back from Russia, Mittal stashed them in his son's vault and then flew to Shanghai for three days for business, but we believe once he got word of what his son had in his possession, he decided to come back and collect the girls and the launch codes early."

"I'm sorry," Liv said, her voice cold as ice. "Are you telling me you've had knowledge all along that Raj Mittal had these girls, and nothing was done about it?"

"Ms. Rothschild," Eve said, "we're not Interpol. Our job is to save the world. It's about prioritizing and staying focused. We leave those tasks to other agencies."

"My sister?" she asked. The fury in her voice was unmistakable. "Did you know she was there?"

"She came on the radar once Shiv Mittal took possession of the launch codes."

Liv tensed to stand, ready to face off with Eve, but Dante put his hand on her shoulder. She didn't realize how much danger she was in. Eve had no allegiance to Liv.

Liv's head snapped around to look at Dante, and the message couldn't have been clearer: *Get. Your. Hand. Off.*

"Take Dante's advice and stay seated," Eve said. "Your safety is not guaranteed. You're sitting at this table and not in one of the cells in the back room ready to be administered memory serums only because of my grace. But I can easily change my mind. Would anyone miss you if you were gone, Ms. Rothschild?"

"Enough, Eve," Dante said. "I think we're all past the point of navigating your games and threats."

Her gaze lasered on Dante, and he felt a chill go down his spine. Dying would be a relief if that's what Eve decided she wanted; it was the manner of death she chose that would make dying seem like an eternity.

"You don't want to push, Dante," she said. "I've given you more leeway than most. Less rein. But my patience is at its limit."

He opened his mouth, another scathing retort on his lips, but Deacon said, "Dante, think it through. Let's hear all the information and then decide what we're going to do."

"You make it sound like you have a choice," Eve said, turning her focus to the team leader.

"We all have choices, Eve," Deacon said evenly.

"Everyone's tempers are up and tension is high. I suggest we move forward with the mission before things escalate out of control."

She smiled again, and Dante watched as his brothers moved subtly in their chairs, the tension so thick he wondered if any of them would make it out of the room alive.

"Let me make myself clear," Eve said. She never raised her voice. "Because you each seem to believe you have freedom because I've allowed you to bring in outsiders. But remember your contract. And remember the consequences of breaking that contract. I own each of you for seven years. But if you think I won't hesitate to start over with a new team, then you all need a reality check. Your duty is to the organization, and to the world. Your loyalty is to Trident, whether you like it or not.

"Elaine," she said.

"Yes, Agent Winter?" Elaine said.

"Display photographs 247-A, 247-B, and 247-C."

Photographs appeared on the wall screens in front of them, and it took Dante a moment to understand what he was looking at. Both Miller and Tess gasped, and Miller pushed herself back from the table, rose, and went into the kitchen to escape.

"You remember Colin?" Eve said. "I thought at

the time he was a good recruit, but he never really fit with the team the way I'd planned."

Colin Moreau had come to The Gravediggers months after Dante had. Dante and the others had dug him up from the ground and injected him with the serum of life to bring him back to the world of the living and his new circumstances. Then, several months ago, Colin had been hurt during a mission; Tess had saved his life, and The Shadow had whisked him away to get the medical care he needed. But he'd never returned, and no explanation had ever been given as to why.

"Of course," Eve said, "a Gravedigger who is forcibly retired can't go back into the world. He is already dead. We, of course, gave him the option of having his memories wiped clean and a new identity implanted."

The first photo on the left showed Colin strapped to a table with an IV in his arm, an IV bag of memory serum dripping into the line. His back was arched up from the metal table, and he was biting down on a leather strap.

Dante had never experienced the memory serum, but he'd heard it was excruciatingly painful. Colin's picture proved that.

"The problem with men with your specific qualifications," Eve continued, "is that your minds are strong. You've been trained to withstand torture. You're not easy to break, and the memory serum causes the mind to think that the body is experiencing torture, so it takes more doses of serum to reprogram the mind. Unfortunately, Colin's brain never made the necessary adjustments. This kind of mental and physical strength was, of course, fascinating to Trident's R&D team, so they decided more experiments were needed."

The second photo showed two scientists leaning over Colin, sharp implements in their hands as they tested the limits of his resistance and mental strength. In the third photo, the scientists were gone, but Colin's body was flayed open like a frog on a dissection table, his eyes open and empty in death.

"Take them down," Elias said. "You've made your point. The sooner you brief us on the new mission, the sooner you can go back to ruining other people's lives."

"Is that what you think I do?" she asked.

The pictures disappeared from the screen, and Miller came back into the room with a bottle of water.

"I think you're a monster," Miller said. "I think you've been living this life for so long that you're no longer human. You have no empathy or compassion. And it will eventually be your downfall. We're not designed to live like that. Someone will eventually kill you, or you'll kill yourself."

"Interesting analysis from a romance writer," Eve said. "But I'll let it pass because you're obviously too emotional. You don't know anything about me, Ms. Darling. But if someone like me didn't make the hard decisions, then no one ever would."

Miller took her seat, and Elias pulled her chair close and put his arm around her. Dante had noticed that Liv's posture had stiffened when Colin's photos came up on the screens, but she'd made herself look. The color had drained from her face, but she'd never flinched.

"The mission is Raj Mittal," Eve said.

Dante recognized the photo and dossier that came up on the screen. It was the same one that had appeared the day she'd come to him in his apartment.

"He's taken Russian nuclear launch codes that were won in a poker game by his son. Unlike his son, Raj Mittal doesn't have a conscience. He's decided to sell them to the highest bidder, and there's been no shortage of interest.

"The weekend after next is Raj Mittal's seventieth birthday. He's leased the entirety of Imperial Island in the British Virgin Islands for the occasion, and his guests will be flying in from all over the world to attend the week's festivities. Selected special guests will be invited to participate in an auction Saturday evening, where they can bid on the launch codes."

"What about the girls?" Liv asked.

"The girls will also be there on the island and auctioned during the week as an appetizer to the big event. Your mission is to infiltrate the island as guests and workers and to extract the launch codes by whatever means necessary."

"And what about the girls?" Liv repeated, almost growling in frustration.

"If you can find a way to get the girls off the island without getting everyone killed, then by all means do so," Eve said. "But the priority is the launch codes. Am I clear?"

"Crystal," Liv answered.

"Do whatever you have to do to not look like your sister," Eve ordered her.

Liv caught her breath. "She'll be on the island?"

"She and Shiv will be in attendance, at his father's command. The event is completely private—no media or photographers invited—which is why they'll be attending together. All staff and guests require thorough background checks. Your sister is not the mission."

Eve turned back to the others and said, "Elaine has each of your individual assignments and covers."

"Tess stays here," Deacon said.

"The hell I do," Tess said. "I'm not getting stuck here if I can help there."

"You're pregnant," Deacon said, eyes narrowed.

"And you're a man," she countered. "So what? I'm not an invalid. Pregnant women have been doing incredible things since the dawn of time. And I'm sure my assignment is probably low-risk anyway."

"The Shadow will be at your disposal for anything you need, and they'll be ready for immediate extraction should you require it. It will be increasingly difficult to get the launch codes once they're auctioned. Don't fail this time."

She pierced Dante with one last look, then walked out of the room and out of Last Stop. They all turned as one, watching for her on the security cameras, waiting for the alerts they'd set up to warn them that someone was breaching secured areas, but the alerts never came.

"How does she do that?" Axel asked.

"She's Satan," Levi said, his tone serious. "She can do anything."

CHAPTER NINETEEN

Imperial Island, British Virgin Islands
Ten Days Later

The sun blazed, baking into Liv's skin as she stretched out on the lounger by the pool. Her skin had a healthy glow after living the life of luxury the last three days, boring as it was. But establishing their presence was important. There'd be plenty of action in the upcoming days if things went the way they were supposed to.

Her bathing suit was white, the bottom nothing more than a piece of floss, and the top, two triangles, didn't even try to contain her breasts. She'd colored her hair a vivid red, and with green contacts and the tan, she barely recognized herself. She was confident no one would see a physical resemblance between her and her sister unless they were standing right next to each other.

The island was lush with palm trees and bright island flowers, craggy cliffs rising above dense vegetation. White sand beaches fringed the perimeter of the island beside water in myriad shades of turquoise. The sky was cerulean and cloudless.

The main house and restaurant perched on the highest cliff—the house holding only thirty guests—with spectacular views out over the water and the surrounding islands. A long stairway descended from the top of the cliff to the beach. Liv had learned that the guests were assigned rooms based on status. Those in the main house were of the lowest status—those who were acquaintances of Raj Mittal instead of friends or business partners.

The rest of the lodging on the island was a smattering of bungalows—some had beach access and others were deeper in the trees—all of them with thatched grass roofs. There were many small pools and grottoes sprinkled throughout the small island, and those in search of privacy could easily find unoccupied areas. But the guests on the island weren't here for privacy. They were here to be seen and to size up the competition, so they tended to congregate around the larger pools.

She and Axel had been given one of the prime bungalows—or, rather, she and Axel's alter ego, Joaquin Logan. As far as badasses went, he was pretty high up the chain, considering he was one of the world's most notorious arms brokers. She'd heard of Joaquin Logan while she was with Interpol, but she'd never had reason to cross paths with him. She wondered how many of the world's most-wanted were actually planted agents trying to undermine the criminal world from the inside.

Their bungalow was on the far side of the island from the main house, along a private stretch of beach and away from prying eyes. The master bedroom, which Axel had gladly let her have, had French doors with flowing white curtains that opened onto a balcony that led directly to a private beach. The privacy lent them cover to go out when and if they needed, and it also allowed the others to slip into the bungalow for briefings when necessary.

Everyone had been given a cover and an assignment while on Imperial Island, including Tess, much to her satisfaction. Tess was on the housekeeping staff. She'd been cleaning both Raj and Shiv Mittal's bungalows, and had reported that there was a secured safe in each of them.

Dante had been assigned to the waitstaff, which had not sat well with him at all. And Liv guessed that waiting tables might be a bit intimidating, considering he'd never held a blue-collar job in his life.

Serving others was *not* one of his strengths. He was a selfish creature by nature.

The only way to reach the island was by ferry from Tortola, so Elias and Miller were running the boat and checking invitations and identities at the dock. Since the ferry had been provided by Trident, it was fully equipped with Elaine and other supplies, including diving suits and a cache of weapons.

Liv and Axel had established themselves as a couple since their arrival on the island—she'd been partnered with Axel instead of Dante because of Axel's established cover as Joaquin Logan.

Logan and Raj Mittal were familiar acquaintances—a relationship Eve had made sure was cultivated—and Logan had brokered a couple of arms deals for Mittal in the past. Logan had no country allegiance and plenty of money to purchase the launch codes. It was well known (thanks to Eve) that Logan was facilitating deals all over the world, and he was in high demand for the big players. He had a reputation of being both good at what he did and dangerous. No one crossed Joaquin Logan and lived to tell about it.

Even Raj Mittal knew Logan wasn't someone to mess with, so when Logan had informed his host he was bringing two guests instead of one, Mittal hadn't argued. Logan had made it known that he had every intention of being the highest bidder for the launch codes, and he was bringing Dr. Petyr Fedoryevski—one of the scientists who'd worked on the development of the weapon—to identify the launch codes as authentic. Deacon spoke flawless Russian and was able to take up Fedoryevski's identity without issue, thanks to prosthetics and makeup, a slight change in the jaw and hairline, and the addition of a wicked scar on his chest thanks to a knife fight from his early years.

Deacon had been assigned one of the bungalows in the center of the island, lacking easy access to the beaches. He was an outsider, so the other guests left him alone for the most part—although one or two of them had privately offered to pay him for his services if they were the highest bidder for the launch codes.

Levi was staying in the main house as a guest. Eve had obtained a copy of the entire guest list; in addition to all the high-profile criminals, a number of ambassadors and dignitaries had been invited. Levi bore a striking resemblance to the deputy ambassador from Lithuania, who would be attending the party in the ambassador's place. The real deputy ambassador's plane had been grounded due to mechanical problems. He wouldn't be making it to the island at all.

Liv found it fascinating how Eve juggled so many pieces of the organization, keeping up with her agents, all of the aliases those agents took and the side businesses related to them, the missions, possible future threats, returning threats from the past, and whoever the hell The Shadow was. Eve was responsible for it all.

She could acknowledge the impressiveness of Eve's capabilities and her skill at running a covert organization, but that's all Liv could do. Eve was a coldhearted bitch, and the sooner Liv could release those girls and get back to London, the better.

Liv had purposely chosen to sunbathe beside one of the small grotto pools that had a restaurant attached, as the male guests tended to gather over lunch to discuss different business dealings. She stretched languidly and noticed from beneath the tinted shades of her sunglasses that most eyes were on her. Joaquin Logan was never without a beautiful woman on his arm—the flashier and sexier she was, the better. And Liv was living the life to the best of her ability.

Dante had protested about her going in with Axel—vehemently—but it was more than possible that he'd be recognized by someone from his former life. Money of that caliber tended to stick together, and the circle was small.

Her feelings about Dante were so conflicted. She was hurt, angry, and frustrated. But she still recalled the feelings she'd had for him: the love, the friendship . . . the grief. The competing emotions were wreaking havoc in her brain.

Axel was stretched out on the lounger next to her, wearing a red Speedo that showed off an incredibly disciplined body. He was built like a brawler, wide of chest and shoulders and narrow of hips, his thighs thick and muscular. He had a sleeve tattoo on one arm, and his body glistened with sweat from the heat. His hair was longer than she liked on a man, and he had it slicked back and tied at the nape of his neck in a short tail. There weren't many woman at this particular pool at the moment, but the ones there were staring at Axel like he was an all-day sucker.

But Axel wasn't the one who made her heart stop when she looked at him. She could see Dante out of the corner of her eye, taking orders from some of the other guests. He wore a waitstaff uniform—black shorts and a white polo tucked in with the logo over the pocket. She'd always loved the way Dante filled out a shirt, with his broad shoulders and the way his biceps stretched the sleeves. He was ridiculously sexy, and he knew it.

"Trouble coming," Axel said softly. "Eleven o'clock."

She didn't know all the guests by name, including the man coming very purposefully toward her. He was handsome. *Very* handsome. He was of Latin descent, droplets of water sliding sinuously down his dark skin, but his body wasn't as muscular as Axel's, though most men's weren't. She had to give him credit—he didn't seem intimidated by Axel's presence at all.

"*Señorita*," he said, holding out his hand to her. "I am Juan Marco Consuelos."

She arched a brow and let him take her hand, and when he kissed it she realized he was goading Axel on purpose. It was a power play, a fight of alphas for territory. Normally, she would've taken care of the situation herself, but she had a role to play.

"You are beautiful," he said, continuing to ignore Axel.

She'd also noticed Dante had stopped what he was doing and was staring from the other side of the pool, along with ever other man and woman there.

Liv removed her hand from his and smiled, but she didn't say anything.

"I'd be honored if you'd join me for the evening's festivities," he said, giving her a heart-stopping grin. His teeth were straight and impossibly white, and he had dimples, which clearly worked for him ninety-nine percent of the time.

"I'm taken," she finally said.

"Ah, *mi amor*," he said. "You are with a man who is never really taken. I can give you the moon and stars and a permanent place in my bed."

"She said she's taken," Axel said. His body went completely still, and the tension between the two men ratcheted up about a thousand percent.

"The lady and I were having a conversation," Juan Marco said. "I'm sure she can make her own decisions."

Axel came to his feet slowly, like a lion stretching lazily before swiping out with his claws across the throat. "She's made her decision."

Juan Marco stood to his full height, but was several inches shorter than Axel. It was obvious he wasn't a man accustomed to losing. It was also obvious he was a man who was used to being the center of attention. He wouldn't take kindly to being embarrassed, and that's exactly what Axel was doing to him. There was no comparison between the two of them when they stood side by side.

She could've put an end to things easily, by declaring her position to stay with Axel, but she understood the dynamics of the alpha and that Axel—or Joaquin Logan—had a reputation to uphold.

Before Juan Marco could open his mouth to refute him, Axel's arm shot out and he grabbed him by the throat, lifting him straight off the ground. It was an incredible display of strength, and Juan Marco clawed at Axel's hands as his air was cut off.

"You have twenty minutes to gather your things and be on the ferry back to Tortola," Axel said. "If I see you again on this island I'll hold your beating heart in my hands and let you watch as I crush it."

Then Axel tossed Juan Marco into the pool, as if he weighed nothing, and then lay back down on the lounger without even breathing heavy.

She saw Dante start toward them and couldn't help by playing into the scene a little more than necessary.

"My hero," she said to Axel, leaning over to give him a light kiss on the lips.

The look he gave her could've melted butter, and he took her hand, pulling her to him again for another kiss.

"You're playing with fire, sugar," he said, and she knew he was referring to Dante.

"I know," she said, grinning, and then laid back down on the lounger, adjusting the tiny triangles almost covering her breasts.

"If you keep looking at her like that, mate, you and I are going to go a round in the gym when we get back to HQ," Dante said, his voice coming from behind them.

She couldn't help but smile at the jealousy in his voice. He deserved more than a little payback for the hell he'd put her through.

"If I wasn't looking at her like I am," he said lazily, "it would draw much more notice than how we're acting now. No one will bother her now. Which means we won't have to bury any bodies while we're on the island. At least not because of that."

"Just as long as you keep those separate rooms," Dante said, "so I don't have to bury *your* body."

Liv turned her head so she could watch them.

"Give it a rest, mate," Axel said, lifting up his sunglasses. "After the looks she's been giving you lately, I'd say she's not too eager to share a room with you anytime soon either. I'd like a glass of iced tea, though, since you're taking orders."

"I'm going to kill you," Dante said between his teeth. Axel just smiled and dropped his sunglasses back down over his eyes.

"Excuse me . . . waiter," Liv called out. "Add a piña colada to that order." It was everything she could do not to burst into laughter at the look he shot her.

Dante went off to the kitchen to get their drinks, and she grinned at Axel. "I swear, that's the best part of the job."

"You're poking a tiger in a cage," he said, shaking

his head. "Better be ready, because eventually he'll escape."

She sat up on the side of the lounger and pulled her sheer white sarong around her waist, and then stood and tied it at her hip. Her wide-brimmed white sun hat sat on the table next to Axel, and she leaned over to retrieve it and place it on her head.

"He's got a long way to go before he escapes that particular cage, so I'm going to enjoy it while I can. I think it's time for some lunch, don't you?"

Axel smiled and shook his head, but he got up and put on a pair of linen pants and sandals. There was a table with an umbrella not far from where they'd been lounging that had a good view of the entire area.

"You're drawing a lot of attention," Axel said.

"I thought that was the plan. The more attention I draw, the better the opportunity for you to get introductions to some of the other bidders you don't know."

"I know, but we don't want to incite them into a frenzy of lust. I'll end up with my throat slit, and you'll end up as someone's wife. I've already had to give a couple of warnings—and before you say you can take care of yourself, I know you can, but you taking on these guys would draw unwanted attention. We need to avoid that if possible."

Liv knew he was right, but she'd never liked

playing helpless arm candy. She saw Dante coming out of the corner of her eye, and put an impassive smile on her face.

"This is fucking bullshit," Dante muttered, balancing the tray and setting their drinks in front of them.

"Really?" she asked. "Because I see it as poetic justice."

"You don't have to enjoy it quite so much," he said.

"Oh, I really do," she insisted.

"Maybe the two of you can have this domestic dispute at a later date," Axel said. "We've got business to attend to."

Dante handed them each a menu, then took out his pad and pen so it looked like he was taking their orders. "Elias said there were several check-ins early this morning."

Axel nodded. "The auction for the girls begins this afternoon at four o'clock. An invitation arrived at our room this morning, guiding me to the boathouse on the north side of the island. They've assigned each of the bidders a separate room number. Each room will be equipped with a screen and a button. The girls will be presented one at a time on the screen, and if you wish to bid, all you have to do is push the button. Once there are no more bids and the girl has been purchased, she'll be taken off-screen and replaced with a new girl."

"I hope every one of these bastards goes down in flames," Dante said.

"We'll take down as many as we can," Axel said. "New monsters crop up every day. I was able to plant the seed in Mittal's head that Fedoryevski wants in on the bidding, so I know Deacon received an invitation this morning. And Levi confirmed that he also received an invitation. We'll be wired to each other and have our codes worked out to know who is bidding on what. They'll auction off three of the girls each day until they're gone. Mittal said it was the appetizer to the big auction on Saturday."

"Going down in flames is too humane a punishment," Liv said. "I want that fucker to hurt."

"He will," Dante told her. "I promise. If you've got anything else, make it quick. Everyone will think you ordered the whole menu."

"I had breakfast with Raj Mittal and some of the other major players this morning," Axel said. "Mittal made it a point to let us know how great the security is around the launch codes. His bungalow and his son's are joined by a pergola, and armed guards walk the perimeter. Then, once inside, the briefcase is in a locked safe, secured with a thumbprint and retinal-scan passcode."

"Nothing I can't handle," Dante said.

"That's not all," Axel said. "The briefcase is sitting on a pressure trigger. Unless it's been properly disarmed, the moment the briefcase is lifted, alarms sound all over the island and everything is shut down. There's no leaving or entering the island from that point."

Dante sighed. "Still nothing I can't handle."

"The first formal event is tonight," Axel said. "Liv and I will attend, and it'll give you a chance to switch out the briefcase for the dummy."

"You say that as if there's a problem," Dante said, leaning forward to point at random foods on the menu.

"The problem is that we're still not sure where they're hiding the girls. The ones we purchase at the auction will be safe with us. We'll slip them off the island with Elias and Miller. But the others are being kept somewhere. If something goes wrong during the briefcase switch-off, it'll put Mittal on high alert that there's a traitor on the island. He'll start doing closer checks, and we won't have as much freedom as we do now. He might even start sending home some of the minor players."

"Then we need to find the girls, and we need to make sure nothing goes wrong during the switch-off," Dante said.

"Piece of cake," Liv said.

CHAPTER TWENTY

Liv had never been to a party where ninety-five percent of the attendees would have no problem murdering someone in their sleep.

Three open-air cabanás had been set up along the beach, the white filmy drapes, billowing in the breeze, lending each one to the illusion of privacy. The first tent was where the food was being served—high round tables were spread around and white chairs lined the walls so people could eat comfortably—and there were also chairs and tables scattered along the beach. The second tent was set up for gambling with green felt poker tables, a bar that served hard liquor and cigars, and four armed men—one at each corner—to make sure everyone played fairly. And the third tent was nothing but a large dance floor, music wafting along the beach and getting lost in the sound of the waves.

But the jovial mood didn't keep a chill from running down her spine.

"Relax, darling," Axel said, bringing the champagne to his lips. "You look tense."

"I feel tense," she said, rolling back her shoulders. "Do you know how much firepower is under this tent? I've never seen so many ill-fitting tuxedos. And that woman in the red dress isn't even trying to hide her thigh holster."

"Which woman in the red dress?" Axel asked, taking a canapé from a passing tray. "There are two."

"The one who isn't wearing underwear. When she bent over to adjust her shoe, I got a better view than her gynecologist."

"I'm sorry I missed it," Axel said, smiling. "I was distracted by the woman in black whose dress is missing the top part."

"She does have lovely breasts. I suppose when they look like that, it's best to show them off."

The woman in question wore a long, flowing skirt made of sheer black material. Instead of underwear, jewels were adhered to her bared pubic area. As Axel had pointed out, there was no top to the dress. She was completely bare except for matching jewels that covered her nipples. Her black hair was piled high on her head, and diamond earrings dangled all the way to her shoulders.

"Is this your first time at a party like this?" Axel asked.

"You mean where everyone is a criminal? Yes, this would be a first."

"You're doing fine," he said. "You're the equal of all the arm candy in attendance. You're very good at the haughty bitch look."

"You should've met my mother," Liv said, draining her champagne. "She was an actress. I learned from a master. I feel overdressed."

He snorted out a laugh. "I'd hardly call you overdressed. I'd be careful bending over if I were you too."

She smiled and felt herself relax. She was used to working with a team, but not a team like The Gravediggers. That was special. She could see it in the way they communicated. How each of them seemed to know exactly what the others needed without having to speak the words. She couldn't imagine having that kind of relationship with LeBlanc or Petrovich. She did have that sort of rapport with Donner, but they weren't always on the same assignments. She was used to relying only on herself. Which was why she'd felt comfortable going into Shiv Mittal's palace alone.

When Liv had stepped out of the golf cart that had dropped them at the tents, she'd felt like Daniel walking into the lions' den. But she wasn't alone. She was surrounded by The Gravediggers.

She'd chosen a gown of emerald green. Sheer material tied behind her neck and crossed over her breasts, leaving her back and most of her front bare. Her skirt was elegant, reminiscent of old Hollywood glamour, except that it was sheer as well. She wore full-coverage satin underwear beneath in a matching emerald green, and strappy, glittering Louboutins. Her bronzed skin glowed and she wore her hair in a high ponytail that trailed halfway down her back. Her makeup was natural, her lips plump and glossy. Her 9 mm was tucked away in her Chanel clutch.

"You didn't prep her on what to expect?" Dante asked through their earpieces.

She looked around the tent and saw Deacon and Levi engaged in different conversations, though she knew they could hear as well.

"I'm briefing her now," Axel said, putting his hand to the small of her back and leading her to the dance floor. "Aren't you supposed to be doing a little recon?"

"I'm in position," he said. "I just need to establish the guards' pattern, and then I'll do a dry run to see how easy it is to get in and out of the house. There are formal parties every night this week. I'll have plenty of chances to get in and get the briefcase. Any luck on determining the location of the girls?"

"None," Axel said. "We're moving through the tents to the dancing area."

"Be careful," Elias said from his vantage point out on the water. He and Miller were watching every move that was made and making note of every person that disappeared from the party. "I've heard there will be more going on in that tent than dancing later on."

"Liv should be long gone by that point," Axel said.

"What am I missing?" Liv asked.

"Things get a little … risqué. Some of the women here are paid escorts. Juan Marco was trying to determine if you were with his little stunt earlier."

"And I thought he was such a nice man," she said sarcastically.

Axel laughed and took her into his arms to dance. Her first reaction was to tense up. She hadn't felt any man's touch besides Dante's in two years. She caught a glimpse of Levi and Deacon settling in at one of the poker tables in the center tent. Shiv Mittal was at the same table as Deacon.

"We've used thermal imagery on every bungalow and structure on this island," Axel said. "The girls are not in any of them. We think there might be an underground bunker somewhere. Elias and Miller will question the three girls we removed this afternoon and see if they can give us a clue, but so far they're too scared to talk."

"The rescued girls are being fed and taken care of," Elias said. "Miller will try to talk to them again by herself in a little while. We think they might respond better if no men are present."

The music was something slow and sultry, and she tried to relax against Axel, but he just didn't feel right. And then he turned her and she saw the one person she'd been looking for all week. There had been a part of her who still believed Dante hadn't been telling her the truth. That she and Elizabeth hadn't really been at the palace at the same time. A twin would've known such a thing, right?

But there she was—unmistakable—standing at Shiv Mittal's shoulder. He reached up absentmindedly and squeezed her hand, and Liv realized Dante hadn't been exaggerating their relationship. There was affection there. It was easy to see in the way he touched her, the way she looked at him with love in her eyes.

She'd always thought Elizabeth the more beautiful of the two of them. And the sweetest. There was a gentleness of spirit in Elizabeth that Liv had never managed to achieve. Even at a young age,

Liv was constantly going head-to-head with their mother, and Elizabeth would be right there, trying to smooth things over. There had been such absolute goodness in her sister—pure light—and Liv had always wondered why it had been Elizabeth who was taken and not her.

Of the two of them, Elizabeth was the one her mother would've preferred to be safe. Every time her mother looked at Liv, she could almost hear her thinking that she wished it had been the other way around. Their father had loved them both, and his grief for Elizabeth had been real, but he'd never made Liv feel inferior or that it was her fault. Although they all knew it was her fault. If she hadn't led her sister away from their nanny that day, they'd both be leading very different lives.

She couldn't take her eyes off her sister, and she realized she was having trouble breathing. She'd never thought past the point of finding her. What it would actually feel like to see her again after all this time. There wasn't exuberant joy, or a heartfelt reunion. She was staring at a stranger. A stranger who seemed to be very much entrenched in the life she was living, and not a prisoner at all. It was a hard concept to wrap her brain around.

Elizabeth wore a gorgeous gown of royal purple. She looked like the queen reigning over the evening's festivities. The dress was gathered at each shoulder by an amethyst clip and veed low between her breasts, all the way down to her navel. The long skirt pooled at her feet, and it was slit all the way to her hip on one side. A diamond and amethyst choker encircled her neck, and matching earrings sparkled at her ears. Her white-blond hair had been braided like a crown around her head, and diamonds glittered between the woven strands.

She watched the crowd impassively, her head held high as she sipped what looked like water. She nodded demurely at guests since she was acting as hostess, but she didn't engage them in conversation. What was this world Elizabeth lived in? And had she really been afraid Dante had been at the palace to take her away? Maybe she'd been brainwashed and she truly did need rescuing.

Elizabeth touched Shiv's arm and leaned in to whisper something to him, and then she pulled away and left the tent.

"I think I need a breath of fresh air," Liv told Axel, stepping out of his arms. "I'll be back."

"Stay to the lighted paths," he told her. "Are you armed?"

"As long as I have my clutch, yes," she said.

"Good. Tomorrow night make sure you wear

your thigh holster. And try to carry at least one knife on you at all times. There's a reason these women are armed."

"Lovely," she said, holding her clutch close.

Liv headed in the same direction she'd seen Elizabeth go, pausing at the edge of the tent where the hard flooring stopped to lean down and take off her shoes. The sand was cool beneath her feet, and she carried her shoes in her other hand as she followed Elizabeth. She was headed toward one of the docks that led out over the water.

Her sister hadn't once looked behind her to see if she was being followed, and Liv shook her head, glancing back toward the tents to check whether anyone had followed them out. The party was in full swing, all three of the tents occupied, though there seemed to be a great deal of interest in whatever was happening in the poker room.

Liv climbed the wooden stairs up to the dock and saw her sister at the very end, gazing out over the crashing waves at the full moon. As she came up behind Elizabeth, Liv said, "I hope you don't mind if I join you. I needed some air."

Elizabeth didn't turn around. "You'll miss all the fun," she said.

"I can only take so much fun before I start to go crazy. Besides, my feet were hurting and it's getting drafty. Maybe we could have a party where everyone wears warm-up suits."

The woman laughed, and Liv could see her smile in profile. "I'll pass it along to the party planner."

"I'm Genevieve, by the way," Liv said, using the cover The Gravediggers had established for her.

"You're here with Joaquin Logan," she said by way of answering.

"In a manner of speaking," Liv answered vaguely. "You're good at remembering names and faces?"

Elizabeth still hadn't looked at her. She leaned against the dock railing and stared out over the water, the wind blowing wisps of hair around her face.

"Yes, I've always been," she said, "Even as a child. I never forget a name or a face. Will you be joining the ladies at the main house tomorrow for spa treatments?"

"I will," Liv said. "It's not often I get to enjoy time with other women. And there seems to be many fascinating ones here."

"Your words speak something much different than your tone of voice. Am I to take it that you're different than most of the women here?"

"I made the choice to attend, if that's what you're asking. And I could leave at any time. I've always found Joaquin a fascinating man, though I'm intelligent enough to know him for who he is. Nevertheless, I'm an independent, educated woman who travels the world and makes her own decisions. But the sex . . ." she said, her laugh low and husky. "That's not something I can do on my own. And he's phenomenal at it."

Elizabeth's smile grew. "That I can understand completely. There are some needs someone else needs to meet."

Liv couldn't stand it anymore. This was the moment she'd been waiting for since she was six years old. It was what she'd every worked for and dreamed of—to see her sister again.

"Elizabeth," she whispered, wondering if she'd even said it aloud. But Elizabeth's shoulders stiffened, and she turned slowly to face Liv—two identical faces, one with an expression of hope, the other with an expression of horror.

"That's not my name," she said, her face pale in the moonlight. She took a step back. "If you'll excuse me, I have to go."

"It was your name once," Liv said, blocking her way. Her heart was pounding so hard in her chest she could barely breathe. "You remember it. You remember me."

Liv had been standing in the shadows, but she took a step forward so she was illuminated in the moonlight. "You'd lie to your own sister?"

Elizabeth was utterly still for a moment, taking in Liv's every feature. And then her shoulders straightened and she said, "I don't have a sister."

Liv felt as if she'd been slapped in the face. "I deserve that, I suppose," she said. "It was my fault you were taken. I've blamed myself every day. Relived the nightmare in my head."

"Let me pass," Elizabeth said. "I have no desire to get caught up in whatever scheme you're up to. If you want money, you've come to the wrong place."

"No, I don't need your money. Our parents left me plenty after they died. Does that even matter to you?"

"I can't even bring up their pictures in my head. Whatever you came here to accomplish, it's not going to work."

"I just want to tell you I'm sorry."

"Why? So you can clear your conscience? You were always getting us into trouble. I should've known better than to go with you that day. But I never could resist the temptation. It's as much my fault as it was yours. Now, let me go back to my husband."

"Your husband?" Liv asked, stunned. "He's your husband?"

"Of course. Do you think I'm one of the call girls you hold in such disregard? Many of them started out like I did. Slaves. Sold to the highest bidder."

Liv shook her head in denial. "I don't understand, Elizabeth. You could be free. They stole you from us! They sold you into slavery. Used you. You'd stay with a man who bought you?"

"My husband saved me," Elizabeth said, emotion ringing in her voice. "And stop calling me Elizabeth! That's no longer my name."

"Fine," she said, "what is your name?"

"Yasmin."

"Yasmin," Liv repeated, trying to associate the name with the woman who stood in front of her. Maybe there was no longer any sign of Elizabeth in her. "You'd have been a child when he bought you. What they did to you was criminal. It was wrong on every level. And no one can make you stay in bondage. Not even if they've made you think what they did to you was okay."

"My loyalty is to my husband," she said. "As I said, he saved me. I barely remember you. And because of him, I hardly think of the horrors that were done to me before we married. He healed me in every way possible."

Liv knew the others could hear their conversation, but she didn't care. "You were a child," she insisted.

"I stopped being a child the first time one of those monsters touched me," Elizabeth said, her voice rising in volume. "I was one of the lucky ones. Raj bought me to be the bride of his son. Shiv was seventeen at the time, and I was thirteen. Their culture is different than ours. I was considered a woman of marriageable age.

"After I was taken that day at Harrods, I spent the next seven years with a groomer, until I was old enough to go on the market. He was very careful to make sure I remained a virgin so he got the best possible price for me. But he'd made sure I was trained in all things sexual. It was my duty to please my future owner. It was my sole purpose in life. The things he made me do . . ." Elizabeth said, her voice breaking.

Liv barely realized the tears were streaming down her cheeks. Her whole body was numb.

"I was very fortunate," Elizabeth continued. "Shiv and I have been married for seventeen years. He's a good husband, and I love him. I'll never leave him."

"I'm not trying to take you away from him," Liv assured her, trying to wrap her brain around what she'd been told. "But I've spent almost my entire life searching for you. You're my sister. You're my twin. We'll always be connected."

"And now you've found me," she said. "But I don't wish to be found. We've gone to great lengths to make sure that I stay hidden."

"I've noticed," Liv said wryly. "Seeing you here face-to-face was somewhat of a shock."

"And now that you've seen me, I'll ask that you go."

"I can't do that," Liv said, moving to block her way again. "You've got to listen to me. Raj Mittal is a bad man. He's just like the monsters who sold you to him."

"It's true that he and my husband are not close, and we do not spend time together other than at events like this, but I would know if he was a monster."

Frustration built inside her. "Think about it, Yasmin," Liv said, emphasizing her name. "He *bought* you for his son. Who do you think does that kind of thing? How do you think he has the connections? A week and a half ago I tracked down a group of twelve Russian girls that Mittal had sold to a prominent man in London. The youngest was six, the oldest twelve. Your father-in-law was the one who'd had them taken from their families."

"No," Elizabeth said, shaking her head. But she didn't seem too sure.

"Yes," Liv insisted. "Did you know he uses your home to hide the girls he's selling to the highest bidder? If you do know and have done nothing about it, you're just as much of a monster as he is."

Her anger was getting the best of her, but she

couldn't seem to help it. Twenty-four years of searching and worrying and grieving—all for nothing.

"I don't believe you," Elizabeth said, her own anger showing.

"Raj uses your home in case he's caught. Interpol has been after him for forty years, and he knows that if the girls are discovered on your husband's property then he can be blamed for Raj's crime. Who *wouldn't* know there were little girls being held captive inside their own home? In fact, I'm not convinced your husband doesn't know exactly what's going on. Have you ever been in his vault? There's a room set up for them. Blankets on the floor and buckets in the corners for waste. There are bowls on the floor so they can be fed like the dogs they're not treated as well as."

Elizabeth was shaking her head vehemently, her skin ghostly pale.

"We have the proof now," Liv said angrily. "I was there. I saw the space in the vault. But your father-in-law didn't plan to unload the rest of the girls until this week for his birthday. He brought them to the island, and today three girls were sold to the highest bidder. You'll be glad to know they've already been extracted and will be home to their families soon. But there are still seven other girls waiting to be sold. Where are they?"

"I don't know what you're talking about," Elizabeth said. "I'm going to be sick."

"Good," she said. "You deserve to be, if you've been complicit all this time."

"No, I haven't—I didn't know. . . . How can I believe you?"

Liv took her phone from her purse and opened up the pictures, and then she handed it to her sister. "Just start scrolling."

She'd taken pictures once Axel had brought the girl he'd purchased back to their bungalow. And she'd taken pictures of the two Deacon and Levi had bought as well. Deacon had waited with them until nightfall and then led them to where Elias and Miller were waiting with the ferry to take them from the island.

"I didn't know," Elizabeth said. "And Shiv doesn't know either. He and his father don't speak. We're required to come to things like this to present a united front, but the two of them have never seen eye to eye. Shiv says the men he does business with are not good men."

"They're not," Liv said, "and most of them are here on this island. The auction for the girls isn't the only thing your father-in-law is mixed up in."

"Careful, Liv," she heard Dante say through her earpiece.

But she ignored him. She could tell by looking at her sister that she was speaking the truth. And she had to trust that Elizabeth would do the right thing and help if she could. It was a complete and total leap of faith.

"What are you talking about?" Elizabeth demanded.

"Your father-in-law has recently come into possession of Russian nuclear launch codes. And he's decided to sell them to the highest bidder. That's why he's gathered all these particular men for his birthday. He's looking for a big payday as his gift."

"Who are you?" Elizabeth asked, narrowing her eyes.

"I can't tell you that," Liv said. "But I have two priorities. I want those launch codes to keep whoever plans to bid on them from starting World War III. And I want those girls off this island and back with their families."

"I haven't seen any children on the island," Elizabeth said.

"I believe they might be underground. Do you know if any of the bungalows have a trapdoor? Or if there's an underground weather shelter somewhere on the island?"

"I don't know. But I can try to find out. Despite what you think of me, I'd *never* want what happened to me to happen to other girls. My story ended happily. I know most do not."

"Raj is auctioning off more girls tomorrow afternoon. The sooner we can find them, the better."

"I'll make sure to let you know if I find out anything."

Elizabeth moved to walk by her again, but Liv didn't budge "There's a safe inside his bungalow," she said. "It's where he's keeping the launch codes."

"I heard him mention the safe at dinner last night," Elizabeth said. "I did not know what was in the safe, but he seemed very proud of whatever it was. And . . ."

"And what?" Liv asked, after she'd paused for several moments.

"The conversation about the safe upset my husband. He was very angry about it, and Raj kept looking at Shiv as if he was bragging."

Liv decided it wasn't worth bringing up the fact that Shiv had had the codes to begin with. Her sister had obviously put her husband on a pedestal, and no amount of fact would topple him.

"The safe is somewhere in his bungalow," Liv told her.

"I don't know how I can help you with that," she said. "I will do my best with the girls. But I really must leave. There's a cart waiting to take me back to the bungalow. I've never been a fan of these parties either."

"But your husband stays?" Liv asked, unable to help herself.

"Shiv has always been faithful to me, and I trust him. But he has a reputation to uphold. No one knows I am his wife. There is too much at stake. So it is best if things stay as they are."

"What is at stake?" she asked. "If he had a wife and an heir, you'd think it would provide protection as far as his money."

"That's the problem," Elizabeth said, her voice soft and sad. "He has no heirs. Will never have them. Part of the grooming process was to sterilize me." She pointed to a tiny scar along her belly button, no wider than a thumbprint. But it was there. "No one knowing about me is the best way for me to stay alive. If the word got out, there are plenty of women who wouldn't mind seeing me dead if they had the opportunity to provide him with an heir."

With that parting statement, Elizabeth moved past her and back down the dock. As far as reunions went, it left a lot to be desired.

CHAPTER TWENTY-ONE

She needed time alone.

Liv wasn't sure how long she'd stood on the dock gazing after her sister, but she finally shook herself out of it and made her way back along the beach to where the golf carts were waiting.

She noticed Axel was now involved in a card game in the center tent, a cigar clamped between his teeth as he studied his cards. The tent where the food and never-ending supply of alcohol was located only had a smattering of people, mostly women, and they were gathered around the tables in conversation.

As she walked farther down the beach, she realized something was different about the third tent. Curtains had been pulled across the sides, giving a semblance of privacy, but they billowed and flapped as the wind coming off the water picked up.

The occasional moan wafted on the breeze, and she caught glimpses of bare flesh as she walked by. The party had definitely gotten more risqué.

"I'm going back to the bungalow," she said. "And I'm going offline."

She motioned to one of the golf cart drivers, dressed in the same uniform Dante had been wearing earlier, and he hopped out and helped her into the back of the cart. By the time the driver pulled in front of the bungalow she shared with Axel, she'd already replayed the entire scene with Elizabeth in her head.

Elizabeth was alive. But Liv had lost her forever.

Lights were on inside the bungalow, and she let herself in, enjoying the cool breeze of the overhead fans. There was no air-conditioning. There was none needed with the doors and windows open, and the cool ocean breeze blowing in.

The bungalow had been decorated in white. White carpet runners and rugs broke up the smooth expanse of the bamboo floors. The white sectional sofa was surrounded by glass coffee and end tables, and even the candlesticks and other knickknacks on the shelves were white. The kitchen, naturally, was white, the appliances stainless steel. Liv walked to a small box sitting on the bar and pressed the button. It looked like a modernist cube—a piece of art: it was anything but.

There were several beeps, and then Elaine's voice came on. "There has been no new activity on the premises since nineteen fourteen hours when Agent Tucker and three minor subjects passed the established perimeter."

"Thank you, Elaine," Liv said, removing the undetectable comm unit from her ear and laying it on the counter.

"You're quite welcome, Agent Rothschild. Did you have a good time at the party?"

"Not especially, no. I wasn't aware that it would eventually turn into an orgy."

"I've read of those," Elaine said. "It seems like a great deal of work. And I'm still unsure about body fluids. It seems that orgies would produce copious amounts. I believe when my human form is rendered, I won't at all like body fluids touching me. It seems quite unsanitary."

"It's probably best to stay away from orgies," Liv agreed. "I'd love to meet your human form, Elaine."

"You are not the first person to tell me that," she said. "Dante would also like to meet me. I believe I am quite the catch. I have a soft spot for Dante, so I believe it's best if I try to catch him first."

Liv's brows rose, and she felt a strong impulse to tell Elaine she wouldn't be sharing any body fluids with Dante. Of course, that was ridiculous. First of all, because she didn't care what Dante did or with whom. And second of all, because Elaine was a computer, for God's sake, and she wasn't even real.

"He's a slippery one," Liv said.

"Oh, no, I believe he wants to be caught," Elaine corrected. "I think he's quite lonely. It's why we spend so much time talking. When he isn't searching for substitutes for you, of course."

"I beg your pardon?" Liv asked.

"He's always dating women who look like you," she said. "Before you colored your hair, of course. He loved your hair. I must say, though, I'm enjoying the red. It's feisty."

Liv was going to have to think about that for a moment. The idea of Dante with a bevy of other women who looked like her didn't sit well. "Why would he date women who look like me?"

"When I calculate the data," Elaine said, "it would appear that it's because he's experiencing the emotion of love. He sometimes says your name in his sleep."

She chewed on her bottom lip for a moment. Elaine was a computer. She didn't know anything about human emotions.

"I'm going to take a walk on the beach," Liv said. "I'll exit and enter through the master bedroom. I'm sure Axel will be in much later, once the party is through."

"You don't have to worry about Axel," Elaine said. "He's always been faithful to his wife. Did you know my voice is hers? I don't always understand emotions like a human would, but Dante once explained it must be terribly hard for Axel to listen to me speak, knowing he'll never see his wife again. I can infer that the connection to her through my voice either keeps him sane or is a punishment of sorts. Dante told me not to ask him."

"Really?" Liv asked, surprised Dante would be that in touch with someone else's emotions.

"Do you think I should?" Elaine asked, perking up. "I'm very curious to know the answer. The situation reminds me very much of Gloria and Stefan on my favorite soap opera. It's very tragic."

"I'm sure it is," Liv said amused. "But in this case, Dante is right. It's best not to ask."

Entering the master suite, Liv closed and locked the door behind her. The bed was a four-poster with white netting draped over the top, the white comforter and pillows soft as clouds. The French doors that led straight out to the beach were open, and the white sheers billowed in and out.

She stripped out of her dress and threw it across the bench at the end of the bed, then removed the panties and tossed them in the hamper and put her shoes back on the shelf in the closet. Liv found a soft jersey sundress in blue, and put it on, not bothering with underwear. Releasing her hair from the tight ponytail it had been in all night, she put it back up in a loose bun, then dug a pale blue pashmina from the drawer. The nights could get cool.

She left through the French doors, wrapping the pashmina around her, and made her way down the beach. The white sand was soft beneath her feet, and the moon was bright enough to light the way. She walked just a little way, careful not to venture near any other bungalows in case she ran across someone unsavory, then turned and headed back the way she'd come.

"You look like a ghost walking beside the water," Dante said from the shadows. "I had to look twice to make sure you were real."

She couldn't see him until he emerged from the cover of the palm trees. He was dressed all in black after his nighttime foray to Mittal's bungalow, and she recognized how smooth and practiced his movements were. Not one stick crackled beneath his feet, and not one leaf rustled as he walked through the foliage.

"What are you doing here?"

"I'm finished at Mittal's," he said. "I was just heading back and wanted to make sure you made it okay. There's a lot going on tonight."

"No kidding," she said dryly. "That's an understatement."

"Men who deal in sex trades, weapons, and drugs are always going to push things to the limit. It's like a drug in itself. Wait and watch. Someone will go missing before the weekend is out. It's survival of the fittest around here. Any weak links will be destroyed."

"We just need to make sure it's not one of us," she said.

Dante slowly brought his hand up and brushed the side of her cheek. "Why are you crying?"

She hadn't realized she had been. But her cheeks were wet.

"I wasn't expecting the meet with Elizabeth to hurt quite so much," Liv confessed. "I don't know what I expected. All these years, I've dreamed of passing her on the street and having a heartfelt reunion. Or I dreamed that I'd track her down and rescue her from whatever hell she'd been living in, and then I'd do whatever I needed to help her."

"I'm sorry it wasn't like that," he said, dropping his hand down to take hers and squeezing it gently.

"I just didn't expect for there to be nothing between us," she said. "We're twins. When she was taken, I felt like part of myself had been ripped away. But when she was standing right there in front of me, I realized she was a stranger. A stranger who didn't need saving. She said she's happy and isn't going anywhere. What have I been living my life for?"

"You can't tell me you do the work you do only to find your sister," he said. "I've watched you. You care about every case that comes across your desk. You care about finding those little girls as much as you cared about finding your sister. You put your heart and soul into everything you do."

"And what do I have to show for it?" Liv asked. "No family. No children. No sister. My best friend is a middle-aged father of four with a bullet hole in his shoulder. And apparently a therapist doesn't count as a friend at all."

His lips twitched. "No, I'd think not. And Donner is a good friend to have. Don't discount him."

"I never would," she said. "It's just that everything I thought I was working for turns out to be a fantasy I concocted. And now I have to figure out what to do with the remaining chapters in my life."

"I think you'll find you have plenty of options once you start looking," Dante said. "Being hurt because your sister rejected you is normal. I'd be more worried if you weren't hurt by it. She's probably hurting too. You never know what kinds of fantasies she concocted in her head over the years. Maybe she dreamed of being rescued for a time, just like you dreamed of rescuing her. Those disappointments can weigh heavy when fantasy doesn't live up to reality."

"My head knows you're right," Liv said. "My heart is a little slow at getting the memo."

"I can understand that," he said. "My heart has been fighting with my brain since I met you."

Dante leaned in to kiss her, his eyes open, giving her plenty of time to pull away. But she didn't. And when his lips touched hers, she sighed in relief. She'd wanted him to kiss her. Needed him to touch her.

The kiss didn't stay simple for long. Her mouth opened and she moaned as his tongue invaded. Who would've known that just a kiss could melt her heart and soul? Only Dante. No one else had ever completed her the way he had. And no one else had ever devastated her the way he had. It was the cruelest of ironies.

"What have you done to me?" he asked.

"I don't understand," she said, trying to catch her breath and leaning into his kiss again.

"I can't resist you, no matter how often I tell myself that I should stay away."

"Maybe you just have an itch that needs to be scratched."

"No, don't make light of it. I've only been half alive for the last two years. Do you know the discipline it took not to check up on you? Not to watch from afar as you went about your life. Wondering if you'd found someone else. Fallen in love."

She shook her head. She couldn't deal with these emotions tonight. Not after Elizabeth.

"It's been too long since Dubai," he said. "I've wanted you every day since. I've ached with the need for you."

"Me too," Liv confessed. "Even as furious as I was, I still wanted you. And hated myself for it."

"We never seem to make it to a bed," he said, slipping the pashmina from her shoulders and spreading it flat on the sand.

"Beds are for old people." She kissed him deeply, loving the feel of his hands on her. Then she tugged the black shirt over his head and let it fall to the ground.

"Do you have any idea how crazy you drove me today in that little bathing suit?" Dante said. "I was so angry I couldn't see straight, and I was so horny I went back to my room during my break and pretended it was your mouth on my cock instead of my hand. I came so hard I saw stars."

He slipped the straps of her sundress off her shoulders, and the dress fell past her aching breasts. He groaned at the sight of them and palmed one in his hand, skimming her nipple with his thumb. She could tell he was past the limit of his patience, and if she didn't take matters into her own hands he'd have her flat on her back in the sand with her ankles next to her ears.

She took hold of his wrists before he could do just that, and started kissing her way down his muscled chest and taut abs. His skin was practically vibrating with energy, and she could feel it coursing through her own body, just by touching him.

"God, Liv," he whispered, staring down at her as she knelt in front of him. "You're driving me crazy."

"That's the idea," she said, undoing the buckle of his belt. Then she unbuttoned his pants and pulled down the zipper. "Do you know how rare it is for me to look at all of you?"

"What do you mean?" he asked, kicking off his soft-soled boots. He helped her push off his slacks and briefs, so he stood before her completely naked.

"I mean there's been many a time we've done this where we couldn't get completely naked. Like during the third act of *La Traviata* at the Royal Opera House," she reminded him. "We had box seats, and if I recall, I did this for quite some time."

His cock jerked in front of her face, thick and hard, and she met his eyes as her tongue traced him from base to tip.

"I remember," Dante rasped.

Her tongue swirled around the head before she took him completely in her mouth. And then she felt the complete power of the act as his head dropped back and his fingers tangled in her hair.

"You have no idea how good that feels."

"I imagine it feels as good as it does when you do it to me," she said, swirling her tongue at the top again before swallowing him whole. Her nails bit into his thighs and she opened her throat, feeling him all the way at the back, her eyes watering as she tried to prolong the pleasure for him.

"Enough," he said. "My turn."

Before Liv knew it, her dress was in the sand and he was flat on his back, lifting her so she straddled his face. She leaned forward and immediately took his cock back into her mouth. And when his tongue licked into her, she saw stars.

"I think you're right about getting undressed," he said. "If I recall, you wore that flirty black skirt the day we went to the Fountain of Four Rivers in Rome. And you didn't wear panties. It was so easy to lay you back and push that skirt up."

"We could've gotten caught," she said, her breath quickening at the memory, and her hips began to move against his face.

"We could have," he said, his tongue zeroing in on her clit. "But you came so fast there was never a chance for anyone to even walk by."

Mewls of pleasure escaped her lips, and the sounds vibrated against his cock. Liv could feel it building inside of her, from her toes to her scalp, and her body vibrated all over as his tongue flicked faster and faster.

Her vision dimmed and all she could hear was the blood rushing in her ears. His hands grasped her hips and pulled her down hard. He devoured. And she lost her mind as the orgasm exploded through her.

She was still spasming when he lifted her and placed her on her back. He pushed her thighs open and she watched out of half-lidded eyes as he pushed inside her; her muscles were still contracting and the fit was tight as he pressed forward. She caught her breath and could feel the next wave begin to build as he hit just the right spot.

He draped her legs over his shoulders and then lowered himself, so her knees were pressed to her chest. She could feel every inch of him, as deep as he could possibly go, and his hips began to move in a slow roll against her.

"Dante," she moaned.

The look of concentration on his face was intense, and his gaze bored into hers. He released her legs from his shoulders and she pressed her heels flat on the pashmina, so she could move against him. Her skin tingled and she could feel the imminent release at the base of her spine.

Her nails dug into his shoulders as her hips slapped against his.

"Come for me, damn it," he growled.

She felt him harden and swell, and her back arched as pleasure ripped through her violently. His mouth covered hers to silence her screams, and then he buried his face in her neck to silence his own as he exploded inside of her.

She could've sworn she heard him whisper *I love you.*

CHAPTER TWENTY-TWO

Liv barely remembered Dante leaving her bed that morning.

She'd been groggy and disoriented from a lack of sleep, and she was sore in places she hadn't been sore in a long time.

They'd fallen asleep on the beach, lulled by the crash of waves and the soft breeze. They'd only dozed for an hour or so, and he'd lifted her in his arms and carried her back to the bungalow, both of them completely naked. By the time he'd rinsed them both off in the outdoor shower, they were both wide-awake in more ways than one.

They'd spent the entire night making love and dozing, and she woke just as the sky was starting to pinken, only to feel his erection prodding against her backside. He'd lifted her leg and slid inside, his finger pressing against her clit as he rocked them both to orgasm. It seemed like days ago instead of mere hours. And she'd been so exhausted from the night of lovemaking she'd hardly stirred when he kissed her cheek, saying something about working the breakfast shift, and left her bed.

She'd spent the afternoon in the main house with the other women, having a spa day. She'd been massaged and been given a facial and a pedicure—all the while listening to the gossip, hoping to hear something that would lead her to the location of the girls.

She'd looked for Elizabeth, but one of the other women had said she'd come down with a headache and decided to stay in her room. Liv wasn't sure she was up to another meeting with Elizabeth so soon anyway, and almost smiled at the fact that she'd come very close to using the same excuse.

Unfortunately, Liv hadn't gleaned any important information, though she had learned plenty of interesting bits. The women spent a great deal of time talking about sex and who was the best lover. Several of them had mentioned both Axel and Levi, saying they wouldn't mind trying them on for size, but both men had turned down all their advances.

The conversation then turned to fashion, each of the women most looking forward to the final party Saturday night after the auction. They were excited because, unlike the evening formal events leading up to the final party, this one was a masquerade, and costumes and masks were required for attendance. Liv sorely hoped the team had gotten what they came for and left the island by then. She wasn't sure how many more events like the one last night she could handle.

None of the women seemed to know what was being auctioned. There was speculation about art and other items, but they were clueless and didn't seem to care all that much. Some of them would continue their relationships with the men who'd brought them, while others would never see their patrons again. They all looked at their business as being rather matter-of-fact.

Liv knew that Axel, Levi, and Deacon were once again sitting through the private auction for the next batch of girls in the boathouse. The women had finally dispersed, and she returned to the bungalow just in time to start dressing for the evening's party. When she walked into the house, Elias and Miller were sitting at the table.

"What's wrong?" Liv demanded, looking around to make sure there was no threat.

"Nothing's wrong," Miller said. "One of the girls was able to give us an idea as to where they're being held, and we've been able to verify. We'll be able to go in and release the remaining girls tonight during the party.

"There's a bunker next to one of the grottoes. It's

completely encased in concrete and metal, so thermal scans didn't pick anything up. There's a metal door that leads into the ground hidden under a bunch of foliage, but it's easy to see they've been going in and out on a regular basis because the plants are torn up. And no one uses that grotto because it's a bit off the beaten track, and they're all busy showing off to each other in more public places."

"Why do I still feel like you're waiting to tell me something?" Liv said.

"You are excellent at deduction," Elaine said from the cube. "Not as good as I am, but it's very admirable."

"Thank you, Elaine," Liv said.

"We heard from Axel," Elias said. "Mittal decided to auction off a fourth girl today. The guys couldn't continue bidding for fear Mittal would think something was off, so Gregor Heinrich ended up paying for the girl. He was by the pool earlier today. Tall and thin, midforties, looks like Jude Law."

She could picture him now, and it made her skin crawl. "I can't believe this," she said, her voice hoarse. She dropped down on the couch and stared at her hands.

"We've got a visual on her," Elias said, reassuring her. "Gregor didn't want to take her right away. He's here with a companion, and he didn't want to stir up questions by bringing the girl back to their bungalow.

"There's an underground holding cell near the grotto at the center of the island. It's secluded from the other pools and any of the bungalows. The girl was placed back in the holding cell for now. We just need to keep her in there until we can extract them. We've already ferried the other three girls to the yacht we have docked at Tortola. They'll be able to shower and eat a decent meal before going through the process of being reinstated with their parents."

"Okay," Liv said, breathing out a sigh. "At least we know their location. Four left to go."

"Now that we know where they are, Dante can go in tonight and switch out the cases," Elias said. "We should all be able to get off the island sometime after midnight."

"Thank God for that," she said.

"Next time you can take the ferry gig and I'll lie out half-naked by the pool," Miller said goodnaturedly. "Elaine told us there was an orgy. How was that? I want to know for research purposes, of course."

"It was kind of like a car wreck," Liv said. "It was nearly impossible to look away."

"I can't imagine having sex in front of all those people," Miller said. "Don't they get self-conscious? What about weird noises and runny mascara? What's the etiquette? I like to take a nap after sex. Are you allowed to leave once you orgasm, or do you have to stay until everyone has had their last hurrah?"

"I do not understand the weird noises and runny mascara comment," Elaine said. "I'm currently doing a search on orgy etiquette, but very little is showing up in my database."

Liv and Miller looked at each other and burst into laughter.

"I imagine so," Liv said.

"I'll explain the weird noises and runny mascara once we're back on the ferry," Miller said.

"Thank God for small favors," Elias chimed in. "Make sure I'm out of hearing distance or have a beer in my hand before you start."

"You'd better start getting dressed," Miller told Liv, standing to leave. "What kind of dress are you wearing tonight?"

"It's basically a nude body stocking with strategically placed diamonds," Liv said.

"It sounds uncomfortable," Miller said. "Try not to snag the tablecloth and pull all the food off when you walk away."

"I'll do my best," Liv promised, deciding she'd miss Miller when she went back to London. Maybe she could convince her to visit.

As Elias and Miller were moving out the back door, a siren suddenly blared from somewhere down the beach, then a second, and almost instantly a third. From various directions came the sound of men shouting, and then there was a spray of machine-gun fire.

And then she heard Dante through the comm unit say, "Oh, shit," and another spray of gunfire, and she felt fear like she never had before.

DANTE MANAGED TO make it through the morning breakfast rush on an hour of sleep and the distraction of his internal thoughts. He'd told her he loved her. And she hadn't said a word. Not that he was expecting her undying love in return, but he'd thought once he finally got the words past his lips—words he hadn't managed to utter to another woman his entire life—that there'd have been a response of some kind. It had hurt that there hadn't been, and he realized how brave Liv had been to tell him how she felt. It wasn't easy putting yourself out on the line like that.

He wasn't sure what his future held, or how he'd work around it with The Gravediggers, but he knew he needed Liv in his life. He understood what it meant when Deacon talked about how his wife's happiness made *him* happy. He understood, for the first time, what self-sacrificing love was. He wanted her in his life, and he wanted her happy. And he'd do whatever it took to give her that.

But first, they had to rescue the girls, steal launch codes, and get the hell off the island. Then, if he could convince Liv to take some time and come away with him, so they could start over with a clean slate, maybe they'd have a chance. He'd worry about Eve Winter later.

He had some time between breakfast and lunch, and he'd heard the call come in that a breakfast tray and hot tea were to be delivered to the Mittals' bungalow. Apparently, Yasmin was under the weather. After hearing the conversation between her and Liv the night before, he couldn't say he blamed her.

He loaded up the tray and then made his way up the windy path to the two large private bungalows father and son were sharing. He wanted a chance to go in during the daylight. He'd already been in twice in the dark. The guards had never seen him.

"I'm heading to the Mittals'," he said, wondering who was online. "Delivering a breakfast tray."

"Copy that," Elias said. "We're waiting on Liv. We've got a location for the girls. It shouldn't be long now."

"Good news," he said. "Now if we can only get those fucking launch codes we can get the hell out of here."

"From your mouth to God's ears," Elias said.

Dante figured it was a good sign his brothers were talking to him again.

It was a decent workout walking to the Mittals', especially loaded down with a tray of food, and the sun was bright overhead in a cloudless sky. The owner's bungalow was in a prime location. There was an infinity pool that looked out over the ocean, and there were dunes built up for easy access to the private beach. But the bungalows were also high enough in elevation that they could see down to what was happening all over the island.

It was really two bungalows attached by a common walkway, though he'd learned the night before while listening to conversations in the poker tent that Raj made himself home in both locations, which apparently hadn't set well with Shiv. He was very protective of his wife, and it sounded like he needed to be.

There were normally two guards on duty at the front of the houses, and two more on the backside, but Dante only saw one when he approached. He waited outside while his employment credentials were cleared with the kitchen, and then the guard unlocked the front door and gestured him inside.

This bungalow was done in blues and greens, matching the ocean through the floor to ceiling windows that looked out on the beach. He saw Tess out of the corner of his eye with her cleaning supplies, heading into a bedroom off the hallway, and he gave her a quick wink.

The guard knocked on the door and waited until a man's voice said, "Enter," and then he opened the door and then turned and took the tray from Dante, delivering it to her himself.

Dante didn't mind. He'd seen enough of the room. He hadn't been able to gain access to the son's room. This bungalow had a lot more daily traffic than the other, and Elizabeth—Yasmin—tended to stay to herself in the bungalow when she couldn't be escorted by her husband.

The curious thing was that Yasmin hadn't been alone in her room. She and Shiv had been standing face-to-face, and it wasn't difficult to tell by their body language that whatever they were discussing was very intense. Shiv hadn't looked well at all— he'd been pale and soaked with sweat. And whatever he'd been telling his wife must have been distressing because she didn't look much better.

Dante couldn't take the chance and stay around longer than a waiter was supposed to, so he gave Tess another wink. But when he got to the front door, it slammed opened, and he barely avoided taking it to the face. Raj Mittal wasn't a tall man, but intimidation didn't have a size. He'd kept himself in good shape for a man who was well into his sixties.

Dante moved out of the way quickly and let Raj pass, and then he slipped outside, ignoring the two guards Mittal had placed by the front door. His gut was screaming that something was about to go down, but he wasn't in a position to alert the others through the comm unit—not yet—there were too many potential ears close by, and he didn't want to blow cover until he had to.

Mittal was angry about something, and Dante made his way around the backside of the bungalow so he could hear what was being said. Yasmin had left the French doors open in the bedroom.

There was another of Raj's guards waiting at the side of the bungalow, and he was clearly interested in whatever was being said because he didn't even feel Dante's presence until it was too late. Dante had his hands on the man's head and was snapping his neck before the guard had the chance to gasp. He let him drop slowly to the ground, knowing that Raj's guards were all mercenaries and their only goal was to kill potential threats to their employer. It was a situation of kill or be killed.

He moved into position just outside the open French doors, and pulled the pistol from beneath his shirt at the small of his back. He then reached in his pocket and pulled out a silencer, quickly screwing on an attachment. It wasn't difficult to hear what was being said.

"Give me the launch codes," Raj spat. "I'll not

give you another warning. You are no longer a son of mine."

"That's the best news I've heard all day," Shiv said. "I'll not give them to you. Not when I know what will come of it. Those codes in the hands of a man like Joaquin Logan would be the end of us all."

But Dante could hear the fear in Shiv's voice, and he knew Raj could too. And he'd exploit it.

"Logan is smarter than that," Raj said. "I wish *he* were my son. We could do great things together. But all that matters is the money, and the very many causes I can fund with it."

"Which causes?" Shiv asked. "Terrorist organizations, or the rape and torture of more little girls?"

"Let me make this very easy for you," Raj said.

And then Dante heard a scuffle and a woman's scream of pain.

More guards appeared from around the side of the house, weapons at the ready, responding to the sounds of struggle. There was another guard pounding at the door, demanding to be let in. Dante took the two guards rounding the corner quickly—a double tap for each—one to the chest and another to the forehead. And then he moved around the corner of the French doors in time to see Elizabeth pull the trigger and kill her father-in-law.

The bedroom door slammed open and Dante

took care of the guards bursting through. Shock and panic had left Elizabeth frozen in place, the gun trembling in her hands. She watched the guards drop to the ground and then turned to stare at him, her eyes glazed and glassy, and she didn't even notice when he disarmed her.

Shiv was unconscious on the ground, so he leaned down and placed two fingers at the crook of his neck, feeling for a pulse.

"Oh, God," Elizabeth said, dropping to her knees beside her husband. "He hit his head when they started to fight. Raj . . . Raj struck me." She touched the red, swollen area of her cheek. "As soon as he struck me Shiv just went crazy. I've only ever seen him that way once before. When we were newly married and Raj thought he could still . . . could still . . ." Elizabeth shook her head, chasing the memories away and said, "it doesn't matter now."

"No, it doesn't matter now," Dante said, compassion for the woman who shared Liv's face rising up inside of him. He couldn't imagine what she'd been through. Couldn't imagine how he'd feel if it were Liv, knowing what had happened to her and wanting to do everything in his power to protect her.

"They fought terribly, but Shiv is not a fighter," she said, smoothing her hand over her husband's brow. "Raj tossed him like a rag doll, and he hit his head on the bedpost." Then she stopped and really took a look at Dante. "You're the man who was in my bedroom."

"I'm with Liv," he said, his mouthing quirking in a smile. "This place is about to be swarming with Raj's guards." He pointed to the briefcase sitting on the desk. "Take the case and find your sister. We've got to protect the contents. Don't let anyone but her have it."

"But my husband," she said, her face pale at the thought of leaving him.

Even as she said the words, Shiv began to wake, and rubbed the knot on the back of his head.

"Protect him," she said. "He's the only one who can make order out of all of this. Otherwise, we're all dead."

"With my life," he assured her. "Now go."

"WE'RE TAKING THE ferry to extraction point A," Elias said as more gunfire echoed through their comm units and all around the island. "Keep your comm unit on at all times."

"Got it," Liv said, already heading in the direction Dante and her sister were located. She chambered a bullet in her weapon, her finger off the trigger.

Elias and Miller took off in the opposite direction from the sirens and noise, headed toward where they'd left the ferry docked.

"What the hell is going on out there?" she said.

"No clue," Axel said, sounding out of breath. "Whatever it is, it's given these assholes permission to lose their damned minds. It's a free-for-all. From what I can tell, that alarm only goes off if the safe is broken into. Everyone thinks the launch codes have been stolen. So now we're in a guilty-until-proven-innocent scenario."

"Or as I like to call it," Deacon said, "shoot first and ask questions later. Tess, check in."

"I'm fine," Tess said calmly. "But I might need a little help. I'm inside Mittal's bungalow, hiding. There's a lot of gunfire."

"I'll get her," Dante said. "I'm right here. It's chaos around the compound. Raj Mittal's dead."

"Well, that certainly makes things interesting," Deacon said. "Get Tess out of there fast, Dante."

"Whatever I have to do, brother," Dante said.

"I'm on the south side of the island," Axel said. "There's a couple of men down. I'll do a sweep here and see if I can run those codes to ground."

"Good," Deacon said. "Levi, what's your position?"

"I'm east," Levi said.

"Work outside in," Deacon told him. "We'll all

meet in the middle and extract the girls. I'll work the north end. Liv, where are you?"

"I'm west, heading in from my bungalow," she answered. "I'm moving toward the girls now that we have the bunker location. Elias and Miller will have the ferry at extraction point A."

"Roger that," they said in unison.

Liv was almost to the grotto when palm fronds started shaking ahead and she could hear the slap of shoes against the ground. Her weapon was up and ready to fire when Elizabeth came bursting through the trees.

"Christ, Eliza—Yasmin," she corrected. "I could've killed you." And then she saw the briefcase in Elizabeth's hand.

"Holy shit, what have you done?" Liv looked at her sister, then grabbed her by the arm and pulled her behind a taller grouping of fronds and ferns.

"I killed him. Here," she said, shoving the briefcase at Liv. "You were right. He's a monster."

"Take a deep breath and tell me what happened," she said. "How many are following you?"

"Sit tight, Liv," Axel said in her ear. "We're heading in your direction."

"No," Liv said. "I'll meet you at the extraction point. Don't waste time. Just get the girls. I've got the codes."

"Copy that," Axel said. "We'll meet you at the extraction point."

"I started digging about the girls," Elizabeth said, her voice catching as tears filled her eyes. "They're here. Just like you said. Ten little girls. And he's keeping them in a hole in the ground like animals. I couldn't let him do that."

Liv couldn't help herself. She reached out and drew her sister into her arms, holding her tight. Something she thought she'd never be able to do again. They'd spent many an hour just like this, usually Liv comforting Elizabeth because of something Liv had done to get them into trouble.

As if reading her mind, Elizabeth said, "It looks like I got us into trouble this time."

Liv chuckled. "You're probably due. Did you confront him?"

"I went to Shiv," she said. "I told him what Raj was doing to the girls and about the launch codes. He confessed to everything and said he knew about the codes because his father had stolen them from him. He didn't know about the girls. But once we started talking about a plan, things spiraled from there."

"I didn't realize Shiv was going to get the codes so soon. We knew we needed to escape the island, but things weren't quite in place yet. I panicked, knowing he would kill us if he discovered they were gone before we could escape. And he tried," she said, choking back a sob.

"He was so angry. He struck me, and then Shiv went after his father like the devil himself. He hates his father, but Raj has so much power, so much control. It's why Shiv went off on his own with his computers. He didn't ever want to be dependent on his father, but it's a difficult life to escape. We have emergency money and plans in case we ever need to leave. But when Raj stormed in and confronted us, we weren't prepared. While he and Shiv fought I grabbed the gun from the nightstand. When Raj threw Shiv and he hit his head, I pulled the trigger. I killed him."

And then her shoulders straightened and a ferocity Liv recognized came into her sister's eyes. "And I'm not sorry either."

"It's okay," Liv told her. "You're both safe. That's what matters. And the girls will be safe too."

"I know," Elizabeth said. "You had that stubborn look in your eyes last night. I knew you'd find them with or without my help. But I wanted to help."

"Now that his father is dead, Shiv must move very quickly to consolidate his authority. Otherwise, someone else will try to move in and take over. He can do it," she said fiercely.

"We'll help him get things under control as fast as we can."

"We?" she asked.

"You don't think I'd come to this party alone, do you?"

"No, I met your friend," Elizabeth said, looking at Liv as if she were really seeing her for the first time. "He killed the guards and told me to bring you the case." She paused. "Do me a favor," she said.

"What's that?" Liv asked.

"Color your hair back as soon as possible. We're meant to be blondes."

Liv smiled and lowered her head to her sister's shoulder. She was older by twelve whole minutes, but she very much felt like the baby as she let the tears fall.

"I don't know what I'm supposed to do now," Liv said. "I've done nothing but search for you my whole life. I've carried the guilt of that day with me, and I felt the accusation in mother's eyes every time she looked at me.

"I think she hated me. Nothing I ever did, no matter what I accomplished, was enough in her eyes. But I always had father. And then he was gone and I had no one. I wasn't even surprised when I got the call about mother's death. It was *exactly* the kind of thing she'd do, killing herself so she could upstage father. But I still had to deal with the headache of the details of both funerals and the estate, while I was numb with grief over father. And the whole time, all I could think was that the horrible, soul-crushing grief wouldn't be quite so bad if you were with me. But you weren't."

"I'm sorry," Elizabeth said softly. "I never imagined that you'd be going through your own kind of hell. But it's time to close those chapters of your life. It's time for you to move on. I have."

The truth of her sister's words weighed heavy on her. This was it. She knew what had to be done now. She couldn't think about the future later.

"I have to go," Liv said. What if Shiv doesn't retain control?"

"He will," Elizabeth said confidently. "My place is with my husband. And he needs me to be at his side right now, not hiding in the jungle."

"Is this the last time I'll see you?" Liv asked.

Elizabeth looked sad as she shrugged. "I don't know. My place is with him."

Liv grabbed her sister in one last hug and whispered, "I've always loved you. I've never forgotten you." And then she released her, grabbed the briefcase, and headed toward the extraction point.

CHAPTER TWENTY-THREE

"**O**n my signal," Deacon said.

They'd cleared the brush away and stared down at a thick iron door, approximately three feet by three feet. It was going to be a tight fit, but it was the only way to get the girls from their prison below ground.

"Shape charge is in place," Elias said. "Hold onto your balls."

The shape charge was molded around the lock, a blasting cap placed inside, and Elias unwound the detonation cord from a spool until he stood a few feet away. Deacon, Axel, and Levi took a couple of steps back and Elias handed him the detonator.

"Fire in the hole," Deacon said, and everyone plugged their ears. He'd already put his own earplugs in.

"Fire in the hole . . ."

"Fire in the hole," he said a third time and pushed the button. There was a muffle *pfft* as the charge exploded, and they moved in quickly, he and Axel each placing a hand in the hole that was now in the door.

"On three," Deacon said. "One, two . . ."

They lifted the heavy door and tossed it to the side. Levi had the flashlight ready and shined it below. Five little girls huddled together, their hands over their eyes as light hit them for the first time in a long while.

Gunfire erupted from all over the island, and Deacon wasn't sure who was firing at who. Between the mercenaries, drug lords, and arms dealers, it was a toss up.

"Let's make this quick," Axel said. "Levi and I will cover."

"Damn," Elias said. "I wish I'd have called it. There's no way I'm fitting in that little hole."

Deacon rolled his eyes. "We're the same damned size." And then he got down on his belly and leaned into the hole, his shoulders just fitting in the space. The girls were terrified, but there wasn't time to try and calm them.

Deacon spoke to them in Russian, and then he began lifting them, one by one, handing them off to Elias. There were five in total, and Elias took the oldest, carrying her in a fireman's hold, and Levi took the two smallest, carrying each in an arm. Deacon and Axel took the other two, and then they ran for the extraction point.

"That's the sexiest damned woman I've ever seen," Elias said.

Miller stood on the deck of the ferry, a machine gun slung across her chest, while she waited for them to arrive. When she caught sight of them, she smiled in relief.

"There's a Zodiac waiting for us beneath the dock," Elias said.

Just before they stepped foot on the dock, Dante and Tess came running out of the trees like demons were hot on their tails.

"Tess," Deacon said, reaching for his wife and bringing her in close.

"Time for that later," Dante said. "The guys with guns are not going to be far behind us. Where's Liv?"

"We haven't seen her," Deacon said. "She said she'd meet us here."

"Shit," Dante said, looking back at the island. Then he checked his magazine in his weapon. "I need extras," he said, holding out a hand. Two magazines were immediately slapped into his hand.

"She knows the risks," Deacon told him. "But we won't sacrifice the team for one."

"Understood," Dante said. "But I recall a mission not too long ago where you stayed behind to make sure we all got out alive."

Deacon nodded. "Be fast. We'll hold them off as long as we can from the boat. Thank God Trident has a little extra unexpected firepower in everything they make."

Dante slapped Deacon on the shoulder and pocketed the extra magazines, running back into the line of fire to find Liv.

———

HE STAYED AWAY from the bungalows and buildings, knowing that everyone had taken their positions for ultimate cover. Those who hadn't made it or who were too unaware of the danger they were in lay dead among the vines and grottoes.

The humidity was thick, like walking through lukewarm soup, and moisture covered his body, making his clothes stick to his skin. His movements were fast and sure, and years of training kicked in as he saw even the smallest movements from the corners of his eyes and was alerted to sounds where there shouldn't have been sound at all.

He saw the flash of a wristwatch from behind a grouping of ferns, and then noticed the height of where the fern was shaking. Whoever was taking cover was too tall to be Liv. And then he saw the flashy watch glint again as he moved his arm. It was then he noticed the weapon raise and shots were fired in the direction opposite of where Dante was standing. Return fire was given, and Dante was able to see exactly where both of their positions were.

He took out the first shooter quickly and then moved quietly to a new position so he could get a better glimpse at the other shooter. He didn't want to kill Liv by mistake. And then the thought slipped into his mind before he could control it. *If* she was still alive.

He'd almost taken another step when something had him holding back. He didn't breathe, or take the chance of moving his head for a visual. All he could use were his eyes and the senses he'd been born with.

His heart thudded and sweat dripped from his eyelashes, stinging his eyes. And with every ounce of his ability as Simon Locke, he slowly squatted down so he was closer to the ground and in thicker cover. A split second later, tree bark exploded where his head had been.

He inhaled deeply, and then let out a slow exhale, taking in everything around him. What belonged. What didn't belong. And then he saw them, as if they were painted in Technicolor all of a sudden.

It was an ambush. There were four of them. Two

up in the trees and two more at his ten and three o'clock. And almost exactly parallel with him was Liv. He saw just the slightest flash of red hair from the corner of his eye. She'd gotten to the exact conclusion he had, and had stopped and taken cover before walking into the trap.

He slowly turned his head, and breathed out a sigh of relief when he found her gaze on his. She'd already seen him and was waiting. With just one of them it would've been almost impossible to take them on and win. But with two . . . with the two of them together they might have a fighting chance.

He made careful movements with his hands, alerting her that they should kill the two in the higher positions first, because once they fired they'd be easy to spot. Then he indicated that she should take the other guard on the left, and he'd take care of the right.

Dante had never had the occasion to see her shoot in a scenario such as this one, and if he hadn't studied her file so extensively he would've been worried about her capability of hitting two such difficult targets. But he knew she was an expert marksman, almost as good as Elias, and that was saying something.

He held up three fingers and then started the countdown, and when he only held up one finger he took aim and fired. He heard a second shot sound just slightly before his own, and then he smiled as two bodies fell from the trees they'd been hiding in.

His second target was taking aim in Dante's direction, but Dante was faster, hitting him center mass.

"Let's go," he said, noting Liv had taken care of her second target as well. "They can only hold the boat for so long."

She stared at him for a long second, her lips twitching in amusement. "Well, Lord Malcolm. I believe this is the first time I've ever seen you sweat."

And then she took his hand and they ran back to the extraction point, hoping to God the boat was still waiting for them.

"There she is," Liv said, as they broke through the cover of trees and their feet sunk into white sand.

"Thank God," Dante said. "I need a shower and an excellent glass of white."

"What if I offered to scrub your back?" she asked as they stepped onto the dock and ran toward the end.

"I'd say I can do without the wine for a few more hours."

Elias waited for them at the end of the dock in the Zodiac, the motor running and a machine gun in his lap.

"Good timing," Elias said as they lowered themselves inside.

Dante looked back to see the plume of black smoke rising from the south end of the island. *Fire*.

"Elizabeth," Liv said, moving to stand up, but Dante put his hand on her leg in warning.

"Shiv has things under control," he told her. "They've got an escape route. I talked to him before I came back to find you. Elizabeth is fine. I saw her."

Liv let out an audible breath and nodded, and then she purposefully looked away. "The past can't be changed," she said.

And he wondered if she was talking about her sister or him.

CHAPTER TWENTY-FOUR

The yacht, like everything, was owned by Trident. It wasn't the same yacht Elias and Miller had used on their little adventure—that one was smaller and possible to manage with only one person at the helm.

The yacht they were using to transport the girls and themselves back to the United States had enough bedrooms for everyone on board and took a crew of twenty to operate. It was big and white, a simple blue stripe painted across the hull, and a discreet gold trident on the side. In another twelve hours, they'd be back on land.

It was sunset, and they were sharing their last dinner before docking, celebrating a job well done. A long table sat on the deck, the white tablecloth blowing gently in the breeze. The dishes were elegant, the wine superb, and the eight people sitting around the table were enjoying cuisine that was as exquisite as the finest restaurants in the world.

"I don't know about you guys," Elias said. "But I could do without seeing another island for the rest of my life. We've decided to go to the mountains for our honeymoon."

"It's the only thing we can agree on," Miller said. "I just want to get married. I don't care when or how we do it."

"Fine," Elias said. "Let's do it now. The captain can marry us."

Miller's mouth hung open as the rest of the table cheered at the idea, waiting to see if she'd call his bluff.

"Fine," she nodded, tossing her napkin on the table. "Right here, right now."

Now it was Elias's turn for his mouth to hang open. "Are you serious?" he asked. "You'd really marry me right now?"

"Let's do it," she said, her smile growing. "All the people I care the most about are here, and I'm wearing a white dress. It's like a sign from God."

Dante laughed as he watched Axel bring a very surprised captain to the deck, but as things were explained to him, even the captain was on board with performing the ceremony.

"Things must never be dull around you guys,"

Liv said, leaning in close as everyone moved their chairs so they could see better.

"I welcome the dull days," he said. "It means I can sleep. Which is what I'd rather be doing right now."

Liv arched a brow. "Oh, really? Sleeping?"

Dante grinned rakishly. "Maybe just lying down for a bit. Naked. And with you."

"I'm glad you added that last bit," she said cheekily. "I was starting to worry."

It had taken no time at all for everyone to get in place and the captain to start the ceremony. And it had been a touching moment when the captain had asked for the rings and Axel had very stoically taken off his wedding band and handed it to Miller so she could place it on Elias's finger.

Dante felt satisfaction watching his friend—his brother—get married. It was just right. There was no other way to explain it. And he clapped and cheered with the others when Elias enthusiastically kissed the bride.

Only cold water was dumped on the whole thing when one of the large outdoor screens came on and Eve's face appeared. She arched a black brow at the group and waited for an explanation.

"Elias and Miller just got married," Deacon said.

Eve's gaze narrowed and she zeroed in on the happy couple, whose smiles had dimmed just a touch.

"Congratulations," she said, though the tone of her voice said anything but. "But if you don't mind, there is still work to be done. I'll meet you in the morning to collect the launch codes. Though I should be thanking Agent Rothschild for that, since the rest of you managed to let them slip through your fingers. Otherwise, all I'd have to show for this very expensive mission is a bunch of Russian girls and a newly married agent, which is useless to me. And don't expect to take time off for a honeymoon at the moment," she told Elias. "We've still got the Baltimore bombings to deal with. Though maybe I should get Agent Rothschild to handle that too since the lot of you have turned into a bunch of lovesick puppies. I'm not sure when my organization turned into the *Love Connection*."

Elias snorted out a laugh. "I think she just made a joke."

"Yet I'm not laughing," she said. "I'll meet you at zero eight hundred to collect the codes. And I want to see progress on Baltimore in twenty-four hours or I'll be paying you a visit in Last Stop."

The screen snapped off, and there was a heavy weight of silence after Eve's abrupt departure.

"I think you're right, Elias," Levi said. "I think that was a joke."

The tension was broken and the cheers started

up again for the happy couple, along with champagne and the flutes to go with it that the staff had hastily put together.

"To Miller and Elias," Dante said, holding up his glass. "May you be blessed with a lifetime of happiness and love. And may you never take the gift of what you've been given with each other for granted."

"Cheers," everyone said in unison. And Dante slipped his hand into Liv's and wished he could've taken his own advice two years before.

EVERYONE SCATTERED AFTER dinner and went to do their own things. Dante knew that Liv liked to sit on the top deck in the evening with a glass of wine as she watched the sun disappear behind the water. It was always isolated, and he'd taken to joining her the last couple of nights, where they'd just sit in silence and enjoy the quiet time together.

When he climbed up the ladder, she turned her head and smiled, patting the lounger next to hers.

He settled on the chaise and lay back, then took her hand in his as he normally did. He didn't think he'd be as nervous as he was. He was never nervous about anything. He looked down at his hands and saw they were trembling slightly. Love was making him a mess. Maybe retirement was the best thing for him if this is what was going to happen when things got interesting. He'd never known a thief with shaky hands. At least not one that wasn't in prison.

"I need to ask you something important," he said.

She pushed her sunglasses on top of her head and looked at him. "What's that?"

"Do you forgive me?" he asked. "For Simon Locke? For lying to you?"

She was quiet for what seemed like several minutes, though it was just seconds. "I do forgive you," she said solemnly. "It's in the past."

"And what about the future?" he asked.

"I don't know," she said. "Why don't you tell me? My life is in flux."

He blew out a big sigh of relief. "I was hoping you'd say that. It's frowned upon to be in a relationship during the Gravedigger contract term, but Elias and Deacon have both managed to make it work. You've met Eve," he said. "She can complicate life."

"I'd say so," Liv agreed.

"I need to tell you I love you," he said. "To your face this time and where you can hear my clearly. And I think we have an incredible future together. I'm sure I can convince Eve that you'd be an asset to the team. And you and Tess and Miller have become friends. We'd all help with your transition to Last

Stop. I've got a condo, but we could buy a house if you prefer, though I think you'll like the condo—"

"Hold on a second," Liv said, releasing his hand. "What's going on here? First you tell me you love me, and then you tell me what I'm going to do? You just assume that I'd be okay with becoming a Gravedigger, *if* Eve allows me to be one. Or that I'd be okay with living in Last Stop, Texas. Or that I'd be okay living in your condo, for that matter."

Dante had a sinking feeling that things weren't going to go the way he'd planned in his head. Things rarely ever did with Liv.

"Did it ever occur to you to tell Eve to take a hike and then you come to London with me? Or, hell, to Paris or Rome or Geneva?"

He shook his head, his brow furrowing in confusion.

"I can see you didn't think of it," she said. "And that's the problem. Everything always has to fit into your timeline, your wants and needs. You never have to work too hard at anything, so—"

"I'm willing to work hard at getting you to move to Last Stop," Dante interrupted.

"Because that's convenient for you," Liv said. "It's not so convenient for me. But you didn't even offer a compromise. You didn't even bother to tell me that I'm worth chasing across an ocean."

"I'm in a contract with The Gravediggers," he said. "I can't just move back to London. And there's also the little problem that I'm supposed to be dead."

"You were the best international art thief in the world. You're telling me you don't know how to get what you want, if you want it bad enough?"

He'd lost control of the situation somehow, and he could feel her spiraling out of his reach forever.

"Of course I want you," he said, panic consuming him.

She shook her head and stood from the lounger, walking toward the ladder. "You just don't want me bad enough. Have a nice life, Lord Malcolm." Then she climbed down the ladder and out of his sight.

When he woke in the morning, prepared to apologize once again and try to make things right, she was already gone.

EPILOGUE

London
Three Days Later

She'd made the right decision. She hoped.

Liv typed in her code and leaned against the back wall of the elevator. There was a soft whirring as it passed from floor to floor, and a ding as it stopped at the floor of her penthouse. The doors had been gaping wide for a few moments before she realized they'd opened, and she stared into the dimly lit foyer, trying to figure out why she was home in the middle of the afternoon.

Her brain was just on overload. Or maybe she was in shock. She'd completely turned her life upside down, and now she had to figure out what the hell she was supposed to do next.

Her time with Interpol had truly come to an end. When Beck had called and asked her to be reasonable and come back to work, she'd had every intention of accepting his offer. She was in the prime of her career, and she did good work. Important work.

But after her time with The Gravediggers on Imperial Island, her eyes had been opened to so much more. She was barely scratching the surface in what she was doing with Interpol. She'd put in a request with MI6 instead. The work was more dangerous—a life lived in the gray—but she wasn't married. She didn't have a family. It was a risk she could afford to take.

It was time to stop delaying and get her foundation off the ground. The Elizabeth Rothschild Foundation for Girls needed to become a reality. Liv owed it to her sister, and to all the girls over the years whom she'd stared in the face and told it would be okay. She'd need to hire someone full-time to oversee it and deal with the day-to-day minutiae, but it was time to use her money and experience for good and push forward with the project. Elizabeth was safe and happy, despite the trauma from her childhood, and other little girls deserved that as well.

Her footsteps sank into the plush carpet and the air-conditioning sent chills across her skin. She dropped her keys in the little bowl on the foyer table and went to adjust the thermostat.

She needed to call Donner and check up on him. And then what?

Watery light filtered in through the bank of windows, but she didn't bother to turn on any lights. The rain suited her mood, and she decided her best course of action was to put on a pair of lounge pants, pour herself a glass of wine, and spend the rest of the afternoon reading Miller Darling's latest release on the chaise in her bedroom.

Detouring into the kitchen, Liv took a bottle of white from the small wine fridge, going through the ritual of opening it. She poured herself a healthy glass, putting the remainder of the bottle on ice, and then carried it into her bedroom. The electronic shades were still down from when she'd closed them that morning, and she moved to the small round table next to the chaise, where she thought she'd left the remote for the shades. Not there.

She set down her wine and went to the bed, checking the nightstands. The housekeeper had been in and her bed was made. Maybe the woman had moved the remote somewhere.

The lounge pants and tank she preferred were folded at the end of the bed, and Liv quickly stripped out of her clothes and put them on. And then she searched through the bedcovers again for the remote.

"Damn it," she said. She'd had it that morning. She distinctly remembered closing the shades before she left to see Beck. She always closed them during the day in the summer because the sun made it impossible to cool the bedroom, even with the air conditioner on high. Maybe she'd taken it into the kitchen with her when she'd grabbed a bottle of water.

She flipped on the light on the bedside table, and she froze as the hairs on the nape of her neck stood on end. Hanging above the bed was a painting she hadn't seen in two years. It was the Degas that Dante had taken the night he'd died.

He was here.

Even as she had the thought, the remote landed on the bed just feet in front of her.

"Looking for that?" Dante asked.

He sat in a chair cast in the shadows behind the door, his legs crossed and his cheek resting on his fist.

She hadn't even felt his presence. As much training and experience as she'd had, he was just that good. If he'd been the enemy, she'd already be dead and not know what had hit her.

Her heart caught in her chest and she looked down at the bed, picking up the remote and giving herself a moment to breathe. She wasn't prepared to see him. Not when she'd said good-bye with such finality.

Liv cleared her throat. "I see you let yourself

in." She pressed the button on the remote, and the shades slowly started opening.

"Your security leaves something to be desired. You might as well not have any at all."

"I'm sure it keeps out ninety-nine percent of the riffraff," she said.

"But it's the one percent you have to watch out for. British Intelligence agents become targets."

She narrowed her eyes. "I don't suppose there's any point in asking how you know about that?"

"Not at all," he said, smiling. "But I would like to ask you to reconsider the offer MI6 intends to make to you. If you're interested, The Gravediggers have an opening for a qualified agent."

"You'd let a woman join the brotherhood?" Liv asked, saccharine sweet. "You're so progressive. But I believe I'm going to have to pass."

He uncrossed his legs and got up from the chair, putting his hands in his trouser pockets as he went to stand in front of the window.

"What are you doing here, Dante?" she asked. "I think I made myself clear back on the boat. This is exactly what I was hoping to avoid. I've been on an emotional roller coaster for almost two years. I can't do it anymore. Great sex isn't worth the heartache."

"What if I told you I love you?"

She stiffened and crossed her arms over her

chest. "I'd say you must need great sex pretty badly to pull out that card." Pain ricocheted through her body, and she hoped her strength to stand and face him held until he left. "If that's all you came for, you can leave. In fact, I insist on you leaving even if that's not what you came for."

"I've been told I have too much pride," he said, ignoring her. "Too much arrogance. And that's always been true. So I need you to look at me and see the truth."

He came toward her, and her knees gave out and she dropped down onto the bed. He took her hands and knelt down in front of her. She wanted to look away, but his gaze was captivating, and she saw something in the depths of his eyes she'd never seen before.

"This is just me," he said sincerely. "There's no Simon Locke and no Gravedigger. Only the real Dante Malcolm. A man who comes to you imperfect. A man who thought he had great worth, but was worthless. A man who was selfish, but finds himself wanting only to give to and serve one woman. A man who didn't become a real man until one woman showed him his true reflection."

His voice broke, and Liv realized she was holding her breath. A single tear fell from the corner of her eye and trickled down her cheek.

"You've made me a better man," he rasped. "A

man who loves you with everything he is, can be, and will be. You're worth all the risk. You're worth the fight. And if you'll have me, I'll do whatever it takes to prove it to you."

She didn't know what to say. Never in her wildest dreams had she expected Dante to humble himself before anyone, much less her. But here he was, on his knees, his pride in tatters and love in his eyes.

The guard she'd placed around her heart slowly came down and she touched the side of his face. "You really mean it."

"I love you, Liv. Always and forever."

The tears came faster and she launched herself at him, so they both fell to the floor. She wept against his neck, and he held her, whispering words of love and comfort.

"Is this a good kind of crying or a bad kind?" he asked.

"It's good," she said. "I love you too. You're worth the risk and worth fighting for."

"How do you feel about becoming Lady Malcolm?" he asked. "It's a defunct title, of course, now that I'm deceased, and you'd have no power or standing in society, but the benefits are good."

"What kinds of benefits?" she asked, arching a brow and feeling a lightness inside that had never been there before.

"These kinds of benefits," he said, rolling her to her back and kissing the side of her neck.

She arched against him and felt his hardness press against her.

"I think these are benefits that can be agreed upon," she said, her breathing coming faster. "Lady Malcolm has a nice ring to it."

"Speaking of rings," he said. "I've one in my pocket for you."

"And I thought you were just happy to see me," she said, her laugh choking off on a moan as he stripped off her tank and his lips found her nipple.

"A lady never laughs when she's about to be ravished," he said. "There are rules to being a lady."

"Says who?" she panted, his mouth driving her crazy.

"London society for hundreds of years."

He stripped off her lounge pants and his own clothes, and lay between her open thighs, the head of his cock pressing against her, stretching her.

Her mouth quirked in a sly smile, and then she hooked her leg around his thigh and deftly flipped him onto his back.

"This lady never follows the rules," she said, and then she sank down onto him and rode them both to oblivion.

ACKNOWLEDGMENTS

Thanks to my children—Ava, Ellie, Max, Jamie, and Graham. I'm pretty sure we hit the lottery with you guys for children. Thanks for your endless patience as I sit in front of the computer for hours. For learning how to cook and order take out. And for dragging me out of the chair to play foosball when I need a break, but am too stubborn to take one. You'll never know how much I love you.

Thanks to my husband, Scott. You've been my cheerleader, my sounding board, and my shoulder to cry on during some of the most difficult moments of my life. You work out scenes with me and stay up all night when I'm racing against the clock for deadline. You're a hero among heroes—my hero— and I love you.

Thanks to Lauren McKenna for pulling every- thing you could get out of these books. You're the rock star of editors, and I adore you. And thanks to Marla Daniels and the rest of the Pocket team for all their hard work (I know I made things interesting), but you guys make everything look easy, even when it's not.

Thanks to Kristin Nelson at Nelson Literary Agency for just being awesome in all things. From the emails to check on me to the business side of things, you're first class, lady!